WINK OF
AN EYE

WINK OF AN EYE

Lynn Chandler Willis

Minotaur Books

A Thomas Dunne Book

New York

A THOMAS DUNNE BOOK FOR MINOTAUR BOOKS.
An imprint of St. Martin's Publishing Group.

www.thomasdunnebooks.com
www.minotaurbooks.com

Design by Omar Chapa

The Library of Congress has cataloged the print edition as follows:

Chandler-Willis, Lynn, 1960-
    Wink of an eye : a mystery / Lynn Chandler Willis.
        pages cm
    ISBN 978-1-250-05319-0 (hardcover)
    ISBN 978-1-4668-5551-9 (e-book)
    1. Private investigators—Fiction. 2. Fathers—Death—Fiction. 3. Murder—Investigation—Fiction. 4. Women illegal aliens—Fiction. 5. Police—Fiction. 6. Texas—Fiction. I. Title.
    PS3603.H357258W56 2014
    813'.6—dc23

                                                          2014031501

Minotaur books may be purchased for educational, business, or promotional use. For information on bulk purchases, please contact Macmillan Corporate and Premium Sales Department at 1-800-221-7945, extension 5442, or write specialmarkets@macmillan.com.

First Edition: November 2014

10 9 8 7 6 5 4 3 2

To my nine grandkids, whom I affectionately call the "Grand Nine." Thanks for asking (every day) if I had finished with the book yet. I can honestly say, now, yes, it's finished. Thanks for keeping me humble. Love you all to the moon and back a thousand times over.

ACKNOWLEDGMENTS

More years ago than I care to admit, two people came into my life by way of a critique group and have stayed with me through thick and thin and relocations. Julie Parks and Doug Hewitt have helped shape my writing more than they will ever know. From the earliest, laughable, manuscripts to the finished product, they pushed me to write better, cleaner, and more focused. Thank you both for your continued support.

To Doug, Cindy Bullard, Demetria Gray, and Sandra Rathbone— thank you from the bottom of my heart for reading, rereading, and reading again in this journey to bring Michael "Gypsy" Moran to life.

To my editor, Toni Kirkpatrick, and editorial assistant, Jennifer Letwack—you're two of the best hand-holders ever! Thank you for loving Gypsy.

To Robert Randisi and the Private Eye Writers of America— thank you for making this possible.

To the people of Wink, Texas—thank you for welcoming me into your little town. I knew the moment I saw the name of the town, that was *it*. Gypsy's story could not have been told anywhere else.

To the neighborhood kids who grew up in Shannon Hills during the 60s and 70s—we were part of something good. We dreamed big. And sometimes those dreams came true.

And to Sam the cocker—thanks for sitting beside me on the couch while I plotted, researched, and wrote. You were the inspiration for Jasper. Except Jasper was a border collie and you're a cocker spaniel. Not that there's anything wrong with that. Cockers are pretty cool, too.

WINK OF AN EYE

CHAPTER 1

My father didn't kill himself." The kid's voice crackled with pubescent hormones. But other than the wavering voice, he had an unflinching determination. It was the third time he'd made the statement since showing up at my sister's house this morning.

The kid was twelve, and staring at me through a clump of blond hair that fell over his right eye. He was in dire need of a haircut. But I'm not the fashion police so it didn't matter to me if he got one or not.

"Look . . . Tatum, sometimes we don't always understand why people do the things they do." My own voice was scratchy from morning grogginess.

"He didn't kill himself." That was number four. Not that I was counting.

"Gypsy—can't you just hear him out?" My sister, Rhonda, asked. She joined me and the kid at her kitchen table.

It was 8:00 A.M. I was functioning on two hours' sleep after an eighteen-hour drive. Plus, I was still on my first cup of coffee.

"There's a lot more to it than just Ryce's death," Rhonda said.

"Who's Ryce?"

"My dad," the kid said. "Ryce McCallen. And he didn't kill himself."

Five.

"I meant to call you a couple weeks ago when Tatum told me about everything that had happened," Rhonda said. "And then when you showed up on my doorstep this morning at four-thirty, I thought, wow, divine intervention." She gnawed on her bottom lip, a habit she'd picked up during our messed-up childhood. It meant she wasn't sure. I'd think twice, too, before considering my presence divine intervention.

"Look, kid. I hate that your dad's dead. But I don't know what you want me to do about it."

"You're a private investigator. I want you to prove he was murdered."

Sure. And after that, I'd look into something simple like JFK's assassination. I scratched my chin, the morning stubble pricking my hand. Maybe I should have stayed in Vegas. There, people just wanted me dead. They didn't want me to actually work. "Homicide investigations are complicated. They're not easy to—"

"I have detailed notes."

Of course he did.

"Plus, I have the files of the cases he was working when he died."

I hated to ask but curiosity got the better of me. "What *cases*?"

"The eight missing girls."

I scratched my chin again. "Why didn't he just turn it over to the police?"

"He *was* the police." He rolled his eyes, an annoying rite of passage at his age.

Rhonda jumped in to defend the eye-rolling action. "He told you all this. It was before the coffee." She nodded quickly, like that made everything okay.

I was drawing a blank. "Refresh my memory so I'll feel better about saying no."

Tatum scooted his chair closer. "My dad was a deputy with the Winkler County Sheriff's Department. Back in the spring, my friend told me about her sister and how she'd gone missing. I told my dad about it and he started his own investigation, outside the department."

"Why didn't he go through the proper channels?"

He and Rhonda glanced at one another like they were sharing a secret. "He didn't trust them."

A paranoid cop who commits suicide. Unfortunately, it wasn't that unusual. "And you think this is related to your dad's death?"

"My dad didn't hang himself. He would never have left me like that."

I never thought my dad would leave of his own accord, either, but he did. Packed a bag and walked out. Just like that. In that respect, I could relate to this kid. "Look, Tatum, we don't always know what's going on in someone's head." I tapped my finger against my temple for illustration purposes.

"If he wanted to kill himself, why didn't he swallow a bullet like most cops would do? Why'd he hang himself?"

The kid had a point. I needed more coffee. I pulled myself up and slowly moved to the coffeepot on the counter. After pouring a fresh cup, I stood there a moment staring out the window of the house I grew up in. The house, and the care of our eighty-year-old grandmother, now belonged to Rhonda and her husband, Rodney. My mother lived a maintenance-free life in a condo in Kermit when she wasn't working at the hospital; my father was who knows where. We weren't so unusual. Still, I left Wink, Texas twenty years ago with no intention of ever coming back. And yesterday, or was it the day before—hell, I'd lost track of time—I left Vegas and probably *shouldn't* go back. Not if I enjoyed living.

"Gypsy?" Rhonda's voice reminded me I wasn't alone in the kitchen. At thirty-six, she was two years younger than me and as far as kid sisters go, she was a keeper. She avoided trouble like the plague, volunteered at the adult enrichment center, and taught math to hardheaded know-it-all sixth graders like Tatum at Wink Elementary as a career choice. And some called *me* stupid for going into the private investigation field.

I took my coffee to the table and resumed my position of avoidance. "Look, Tatum, I don't know how long I'm going to be here. I'm kind of on vacation," I lied.

"We'll pay you." He obviously didn't understand the concept of a *vacation*.

"Tatum lives with his grandfather. It's just the two of them now," Rhonda said, giving me that look that said there was more to this story and she'd explain later.

I didn't care if the kid lived with a tribe of pygmies. I had my own problems. I didn't know if I was even going to be alive tomorrow. I had issues with committing to anything other than lunch plans.

"They didn't even investigate it and grandpa says suicides are always investigated," Tatum said matter-of-factly.

"Who didn't investigate it?"

"The sheriff's department. They didn't even do an autopsy and grandpa says you always do an autopsy with a suicide."

I pushed my hand through my bed-tangled hair then took a long sip of coffee. "There's a lot of reasons they don't do an autopsy."

"But we requested one. They told us there wasn't any need and before we could insist on one, they had already made all the arrangements."

"*Who* made all the arrangements?"

"The sheriff's department."

I tried to hold in the surprised expression my face was fighting to show. I didn't want to give him the impression he had piqued my curiosity. With a stone face, I asked, "The sheriff's department made your dad's funeral arrangements?"

He nodded. "Sheriff Denny said it was too much for me or grandpa to have to handle. He said he didn't want us to have to worry about it—*with all that we'd been through,* he said." The corner of his lips pulled upward in a sneer. Despite my best effort not to, I was beginning to like this kid.

"Is there a reason Grandpa couldn't make the arrangements himself?"

He shook his head and the blond clump of bangs swept his forehead like a broom. "Me and Grandpa could have made them. Sheriff Denny wouldn't let us."

"Tatum's grandfather, Burke McCallen, is a retired deputy himself," Rhonda added.

"He got shot in the back and can't walk now. He uses a wheelchair to get around."

I held a swallow of coffee in my mouth before letting it go down as I tried to wrap my brain around this latest disclosure. After a moment, I swallowed. "He was shot in the line of duty?"

Tatum and Rhonda both nodded.

"He walked in on a break-in," Tatum said.

A deputy shot. In Wink, Texas. That certainly wasn't something that happened every day.

"They catch the guy who did it?"

He nodded.

So Grandpa's in a wheelchair and now Daddy's dead. Unless Mom was somewhere in the picture, the Department of Social

Services would probably be involved at some point in the near future. "Where's your mom?"

He shrugged his bony shoulders. "Last I heard, in San Antonio with some rodeo guy."

"Were your mom and dad divorced?"

He shrugged again. "I guess. I don't remember much about her. She left when I was three."

I was twelve and Rhonda was ten when our dad left. I remember Rhonda crying. I remember wrapping my arm around her shoulder, holding back my own tears. I was the big brother. Big brothers don't cry.

"No aunts or uncles, cousins?" I asked.

He shook his head. "Just me and Dad and Grandpa. Well, me and Grandpa now. But we do okay. I do most of the cooking and cleaning. He does the bills and stuff."

Ahh. Denial. It'll get you through for a while. Then one day your world comes crashing in on you and you wake up wondering why you didn't see it coming. Been there, done that, and no plans to go again.

"So will you take a look at my Dad's files? He was on to something. I know he was."

"I thought you wanted me to look into your Dad's suicide?"

"It's all connected. And he didn't kill himself."

That was number six. Not that I was counting.

CHAPTER 2

So, are you going to help him?" Rhonda asked. The kid had left a little while ago to check on his grandfather. Rhonda poured the last bit of coffee in my cup, then slid the pot in the sink of soapy water.

I slowly shook my head. "It's not something I really want to get involved with."

I could tell by her silence it wasn't the answer she was hoping for. "*Okay*," she finally said, dragging the simple word out into exaggerated syllables. "So how long are you planning on staying?"

"I don't know. A few days. I can get a room in Kermit if I'm in the way."

She popped me on the back of the head. "Don't be silly. Rodney will be back tomorrow and I know he'll want to see you."

"Where is Rodney?"

"He's at a training seminar in Dallas. The police department installed new software and no one knows how to use it."

Rhonda's two biggest faults were she couldn't cook worth crap and she married a cop. Rodney was an officer with the Kermit Police Department. He was a good guy. As far as brothers-in-law go, I couldn't complain.

"Why didn't Tatum ask Rodney to look into his dad's death?"

Rhonda took a deep breath and held it longer than was probably comfortable. Then she shrugged and gnawed on her lip, avoiding eye contact. "I don't know."

I smiled. "Either you're hiding something from him or he told you to stay out of it."

She wrapped a flaming red curl around her finger and continued gnawing on her bottom lip. She finally huffed then said, "Oh, come on, Gypsy. He's a good kid."

"Rodney?" I knew whom she was referring to but I liked to see her squirm. As an older brother I had earned that right.

She rolled her eyes. "Tatum."

"If he's such a good kid, why doesn't Rodney want to get involved?"

She huffed again and stared at the table, avoiding looking me in the eye. "I don't know. He just said there wasn't anything he could do. Maybe because it's two different departments. But the bottom line is Tatum's a good kid and he doesn't deserve the hand he's been dealt."

Not many people do but it had never been my ambition to save the world. "Maybe someone should look for his mother. Before social services gets involved."

Rhonda shook her head. "I don't know the whole story but apparently there were some drugs involved, and stuff like leaving Tatum alone in a hot car when he was two years old. Probably best to just leave her out of the picture." She raised her eyebrows for emphasis.

I'd done my share of tracking down people who didn't want to be found for one reason or another. I wasn't too fond of parents who disappeared. The adults left behind usually place blame on the person who takes off; kids are the opposite. They blame themselves. I should have cleaned my room more, should have eaten my vegetables, done better in school . . . they carry a list of *should haves* with them the rest of their lives. I know from experience. I'm still carrying my own list of *should haves*.

Regardless, my heart wasn't bleeding quite enough yet to get involved in Tatum McCallen's troubles.

"Look . . . Rhonda, Rodney's a good cop. He's a good man with a heart bigger than the state of Texas. If he said leave it alone, there must be a good reason."

"What would it hurt just to talk to Tatum? Gypsy, he has a four-inch file Ryce was keeping on the investigation he was doing off the clock. There's eight missing girls involved."

"Missing how? Runaways, kidnapped, what?"

"They were classified as runaways, but they were *good* girls. Happy. None of the parents believe they ran away."

We stared at one another for a long moment. I finally asked, "What do they think happened to them?"

Rhonda was quiet for a moment while she picked at a cuticle only she could see. "They were all illegals so there were no paper trails on any of them. Teenagers. Pretty girls."

"Ah, Jesus." I pushed my hand through my hair. "A trafficking ring."

She slowly nodded. "We think so. Will you just take a look at his files? Please?"

I laid my head on the table, gently thumping it against the warm wood. Was there anything in Wink that ever registered under 100 degrees?

"What would it hurt just to talk to him?" she asked.

I could think of a pretty good reason. "I could end up involved in something I don't want to be involved in."

She huffed. "You can be such an ass sometimes." She got up and went to her soaking dishes, catching me in the shoulder first with a solid punch.

She was average size but threw a punch like a sailor. I had taught her well. She had always been a scrappy kid with a fierce loyalty fired by an Irish temper. She'd inherited her red hair and unmanageable curls from our mother's side of the family. Many men find redheads extremely sexy. Having grown up in a house full of redheaded women, I avoided them like a disease. I knew the wrath they were capable of.

With Rhonda concentrating on the dishes, I felt safe to change the subject. "I need to tap into your Internet with my laptop." I was anxious to get my contacts and apps downloaded to my backup phone.

"Sure. It's wireless so you should be able to connect anywhere."

Wireless in Wink? Who'd have ever thought it? I went back to the spare bedroom and retrieved my laptop, then headed back to the kitchen. Might as well set up shop at the kitchen table. I powered up the iPhone and within minutes had access once again to my contact list and apps. I gave Rhonda my new number.

"What happened to your other phone?" She keyed my new number into her own phone.

"Long story."

Rhonda raised her brows. "One of those 'I could tell you but then I'd have to shoot you' things?"

If she only knew. After purposely smashing it with a hammer, then tossing it into the Pecos River, I felt safe that it was history. "Yeah. One of those." I smiled at her.

She stared at me suspiciously, then finished putting away the morning dishes. "I've got to go to the volunteer center for a little while. Why don't you come with me? It'll be fun."

I scowled and looked over my shoulder at her. She was kidding, right? I had no idea what she did at the volunteer center but hemorrhoids sounded like more fun. "I'll pass on that one. I think I'll grab a shower and head into town."

"Suit yourself. Towels are in the cabinet in the bathroom. You ready, Gram?" she yelled down the hallway for our grandmother.

"Coming," Gram answered. A moment later she shuffled into the kitchen, her old-lady purse hanging in the crook of her arm. "Can't wait to make my macaroni necklace." She looked at me and rolled her eyes.

Gram had always been a sassy one and I was glad it was Rhonda taking care of her and not me. Rhonda, Rodney, and Gram lived in the three-bedroom, one-bath house Rhonda and I grew up in. It was a brick ranch with a desert for a yard. The prickly pear cacti grew randomly, adding splashes of sporadic green to the ever-present brown. When we were kids, Mom tried planting grass one year so her kids would have a lush lawn to play on. She gave up, figuring the added expense of a mower and gas to run it wasn't worth the effort.

Mom worked sixty hours a week as a nurse at Kermit Regional Hospital, so after our dad left, Gram moved in and shared a bedroom with Rhonda. She was there to keep us out of trouble, fix us something to eat every now and then, and do the occasional load of laundry. So I learned to do my own laundry at an early age (starch preferred), cook a decent meal (something Rhonda never mastered), and keep a tidy house. Never did learn to stay out of trouble, though.

I waited until I was certain Rhonda and Gram had left for the volunteer center, then opened the public records search app on my laptop. I keyed in "Claire Kinley" but didn't hit enter. Instead, I sat there staring at the screen, debating whether I wanted to go down that road again. I had access to every aspect of her life at my fingertips, but couldn't do it. I couldn't count the times over the years I had typed her name but never actually opened a file.

Twenty years was a long time. Maybe some things are better left alone.

I shut down the laptop and headed to the shower.

After I showered, I escaped the suffocating humidity of the tiny bathroom and went into my old bedroom to dress. I dug around in my duffle bag and pulled out a clean pair of jeans, T-shirt, and a fresh pair of boxers. I had enough clothes for three days. Everything I owned of a personal nature was in cardboard boxes heading to Texas via UPS. My client files were in the back of the van; I didn't trust those to the little brown truck.

So when Frank Gilleni sent his henchmen, and I knew he would, the only thing they would find was an empty apartment, no forwarding address, and no cell phone. I had bought a little time, anyway.

I stared at the jeans on the bed and couldn't bear to put them on. Vegas was hot; Wink was unbearable. I went across the hall into Rhonda and Rodney's bedroom. Rodney and I were about the same size. I rummaged through their dresser drawers until I found where Rodney kept his shorts. The only thing I could find was a pair of pull-on net shorts, perfect for a game of hoops. It was either the shorts from another decade or the jeans. I found a matching tank top in another drawer.

After I dressed, I took a quick glance in the mirror. I wasn't used to looking like a geek. All I needed was a pair of tube socks and the ensemble would be complete. My hair, dry from the shower, was now slick with sweat. At least the encroaching gray around my temples blended with the dark brown waves and wasn't easily noticeable. My eyes were bloodshot from lack of sleep. I looked like I'd just waken from a drunken binge, trapped in an NBA player's uniform, circa 1983. There was no way in hell I could be seen in this outfit.

I stripped it off, put it back in the drawer, then went back to my bedroom and pulled on the jeans. I finished dressing, then headed outside. Wink, Texas, in early August and I was wearing jeans. I should probably see a shrink. About many things.

CHAPTER 3

The blistering heat grabbed my breath as soon as I stepped out the door, making me remember why I fled Wink not long after graduating high school. I unlocked the van and had the air conditioner on full blast before closing the door. I glanced in the back out of habit, just to make sure the thousands of dollars worth of equipment was where it was supposed to be. When I bought the van, I had a Captain's Chair installed in front of the bank of surveillance equipment. Smartest investment I ever made. It made long surveillance jobs a little more comfortable.

I pulled out of the driveway and headed into downtown Wink. Businesses were sparse; most had packed up and moved to Kermit or closed up shop altogether. Wink, at one time, had been a booming little town with a thriving population and enough business to contribute to a healthy tax base. But by the early seventies, despite a million-dollar urban renewal grant from the Feds, the town was barely clinging to life. By the twenty-first century, the population had dwindled to under a thousand and you could count the businesses on one hand. Most of the people that remained had been born here, like their parents and grandparents before them. Few people moved to Wink by choice. It wasn't a bad little town; hot as hell, but quaint.

One thing that did remain was Dunbar's, a greasy spoon that had been passed down from generation to generation of Dunbars. I figured I might as well stop in and grab a burger and support the local economy. The parking lot was filled with pickup trucks of every make and model, old and rusted to shiny and new. Inside, the place hadn't changed much. The tables were still covered with red-and-white plaid vinyl tablecloths, daily specials were still scrawled on a chalkboard propped on the counter. I'd been run out more than once by old man Dunbar for erasing the chicken fried steak dinner combo and adding a sixteen-ounce porterhouse for $1.99. Faded black-and-white photos of Wink's glory days shared wall space with color pictures of pump jacks silhouetted by glorious red-and-orange evening skies. I'd seen the sun set in Marina Del Rey, but it couldn't compare in beauty, or loneliness, to a Texas sunset.

I glanced around the diner and didn't see an empty table or a spot at the counter. The clientele was a mix of Wink's best. Ranchers with their Stetsons, farmers with their John Deere ball caps, oil workers in their dirty blue work shirts. Throw in a few teachers on summer break and that pretty much summed up the lunchtime customers and the general population. I didn't go out of my way to see if I recognized anyone, since keeping a low profile for a while was probably in my best interest. Just as I stepped up to the counter to order, I saw Tatum McCallen in a back booth waving me over. I gave him a tiny wave, acknowledging at least I'd seen him, then ordered a burger all the way, homemade chips, and a cola to go.

"Hey, Grandpa would like to meet you," Tatum said, suddenly at my side like a fungus no amount of penicillin was going to cure.

"I'd really like to, but I'm on my way over to the volunteer center. Rhonda wanted me to drop by."

"Oh, it'll only take a minute. It'll take 'em that long to cook your burger."

This kid was good. I glanced at the back booth. A folded wheelchair was leaning against the wall, out of the way. I sighed, then told the waitress who took my order where I'd be. I followed the kid through the maze of tables to his booth.

"Grandpa, this is Gypsy Moran, the private detective I was telling you about." The kid was grinning ear to ear.

"Pleasure to meet you. Burke McCallen." We shook hands. He had a firm grip and a strong hand attached to a muscular forearm, a result of the wheelchair I supposed. Tatum slid into the booth, sliding to the corner to make room for me to sit. Reluctantly, I sat down, sitting on the edge so I could make a quick getaway.

The old man was probably early sixties with weathered skin from too many days in the Texas sun. His gray hair was thinning but he wore it long, falling just below his collar. His lightweight plaid shirt complete with pearl snaps reminded me of a different era. I'd seen my own grandfather and his buddies wear the same shirt when I was a kid.

"Tatum tells me you pulled in from Vegas this morning." His voice was deep with authority. At one time, this man demanded respect.

I nodded. "Drove straight through."

"That's a long ride."

I nodded again.

"He tells me you're going to look into my son's death."

I threw a glance at Tatum, who quickly turned his attention to his chocolate milkshake. "Well, like I told your grandson, I'm really just passing through. I'm going to be here a week, maybe two. I don't know what I could do in that short amount of time. Besides, I'm not licensed in Texas. I wouldn't have access to records or—"

"I have the records. Well, Dad's files anyway," Tatum said, taking a breath from sucking down his milkshake.

"Ryce didn't kill himself, Mr. Moran," Burke said. "We just don't have any way of digging into it."

The waitress brought my order in a white paper bag and Styrofoam cup. Grease seeped through the bag, staining it in spots.

"Tatum told me you're a retired deputy. You've probably got better connections here than I'd ever have."

"Humph . . ." He stared out the dusty picture window, looking deep into a memory. "My connections ended the day I took one in the back."

Now I was curious. Law enforcement took care of their own, especially the wounded. But I didn't know these people. For all I knew Burke McCallen and his son, Ryce, could have been rogue deputies who got caught at whatever it was they were doing. Could explain Ryce's decision to hang himself.

"There's some bad things going on in the department, Mr. Moran. My son was on to something when he died."

"Yeah, Dad was getting ready to bust the whole thing wide open." Tatum took a hard pull on the straw, slurping up the last bit of his milkshake.

I couldn't stop the grin that spread across my face. The world is so simple to a twelve-year-old.

"Why don't you drop by the house tonight for dinner? Rhonda knows the address," Burke said.

The waitress brought their ticket and slid it across the table to Burke. He pulled a ten from a money clip tucked in his pocket and handed it and the ticket to Tatum. While Tatum headed to the register to pay, I opened the wheelchair that had been propped against the wall behind us. I rolled it to the edge of the booth.

"He's a good kid," Burke said, bobbing his head toward his

grandson at the register. "Ryce raised him right." He struggled out of the booth, then pulled himself into the chair. "Whatever your fee is, Mr. Moran, we'll pay it. We're not oil barons but we're not dirt poor, either."

I reached for the chair handles to help him but before I could get a grasp, he was ten feet ahead of me. I followed along behind, carrying my bagged lunch and soda. He maneuvered around the tables as if it was something he did everyday, obviously more secure with his limitations than I was. He did allow me to hold the door for him. Outside, he rolled himself along the concrete to a blue Ford pickup. Tatum hurried to his side and opened the passenger door. Burke hoisted himself up and into the seat, grimacing at the dead weight of his useless legs. Tatum rolled the chair around to the back, then heaved it up into the bed of the truck.

"Dinner'll be ready around six," he said, grinning. "Tell Ms. Walker and Grandma they can come too, if they want. There'll be plenty."

I followed the kid around to the driver's side and watched as he climbed in behind the wheel. I could remember times my dad would pull over and let me take the wheel, but it was always on some dirt road out in the middle of nowhere, not on a main road in the middle of town.

"You old enough to drive?" I asked, knowing the answer.

He shrugged, shifting his weight in the booster seat. "Somebody has to."

I watched them drive away, wondering if Ryce McCallen's death was something I wanted to get involved with. I hadn't actually committed to anything yet. I didn't even commit to dinner. I *was* interested in why Ryce had a case file in his possession. There were only two reasons I could think of and both involved a dirty cop.

I wasn't sure what to make of Burke's story, either. I'd have to do some checking into both father and son before I agreed to anything. I wasn't real keen on going up against an entire department, nor was I too keen on getting suckered by an ex-deputy with a score to settle.

As I started back to the van, a white Silverado Dually whipped into the parking lot and pulled into the empty space where the McCallens had been parked. A woman in jeans, boots, and a tight T-shirt climbed out. She threw a glance my way as she passed. Then we both stopped, frozen in time. We spun around and faced one another.

"Gypsy? Oh my God!"

Claire Kinley threw herself into my arms, nearly knocking me backward. My bagged lunch and soda hit the pavement. After I regained my footing, I lifted her and whirled her around like we were in some hokey movie.

"Oh my God . . . I can't believe it's you," she cried. "It's really *you*." She pulled away and cupped my face in her hands. Tears were streaming down her gorgeous face, streaking her mascara. "You're as beautiful today as you were the day you . . ."

Then she hauled off and slapped *the shit* out of me. "You deserved that, you bastard," she said, laughing, tears still rolling down her face.

She was probably right. No "Dear Claire" letter, no sweet last kiss. Just here one day and gone the next. Whether I deserved it or not, it didn't stop the welt from forming on my cheek. I rubbed my face and grinned. "Yeah, I guess I did deserve it."

Claire Kinley was as gorgeous today as she was twenty years ago. Her blond hair fell softly on her shoulders, shimmering like spun gold in the sunlight. Her eyes were still the color of cornflowers growing wild in the pastures; the teenage body where I had found heaven had filled out in all the right places.

She wiped away the tears, then gently patted my cheek where she had landed the good one moments earlier. "What are you doing in Wink? Last I heard you were in Vegas."

Should I tell her the truth? I half shrugged. "Just passing through. Got in last night."

She nodded. "You staying with Rhonda?"

"Until she throws me out." I laughed and took a step back to get a long look at the only woman I ever considered marrying. "Damn—you look good."

She laughed and shook her head. "It's requiring some work these days."

I teasingly pointed at the gray at my own temple and grinned. "Not using color yet but I've considered it." We both laughed and it was so easy, like it was so many years ago, before reality and heartbreak set in. "So . . . what are you doing with yourself these days?"

She pursed her lips and bobbed her head back and forth. "Managing the ranch. Daddy had a stroke four years ago so I took over the day-to-day operation." Sadness filled her eyes. I couldn't tell if it was from sympathy or regret. Had she wondered nearly every day, like I had, about what could have been? The K-Bar Ranch held her grounded to west Texas as much as the small-town living drove me away.

"Sorry to hear about your dad," I said softly.

She nodded. "He's still just as cantankerous as ever." She lightly touched the faded scar on my upper lip, a clear reminder of the deadly sword her father was capable of wielding.

A faint tune played from the cell phone attached to her belt. She glanced at the number, then rolled her eyes. "Daddy's wanting his lunch."

I glanced at my own lunch splattered on the ground, debating whether or not to get another. I guessed I could wait until dinner. "Yeah . . . I've got to get, too. Got some errands to run."

We both stood there for a moment, not wanting it to end, but no idea how to keep it going. "Look," she finally said. "Maybe we can get together for dinner tomorrow night?"

Before I could stop myself, I agreed. "Yeah. That sounds great."

She pulled a pen from her pocket, reached for my hand, and wrote her number on my palm. She smiled, then disappeared into the diner. I stared at the number scribbled in ink on the palm of my hand, thinking of a thousand reasons not to call. And a thousand and one why I should.

CHAPTER 4

Claire Kinley was as wild as the broncs her daddy used to sell. It was that spirit I fell in love with. The fact she was a knockout didn't hurt, either. She was named Prom Queen, Homecoming Queen, Miss Wildcat, Miss Winkler County 4-H, and adamantly declined every title. No one was going to box her into a perception of how she was supposed to look, act, or conduct herself in public. Not even me.

I programmed the number she'd scrawled on my hand into my phone, immediately considered deleting it, then saved it. The last thing I wanted was to drag her into this mess I was in. But it was just one dinner, right? What could it hurt?

I took 115 into Kermit and found the volunteer center where Rhonda was doing her daily good deed. Her SUV was parked out front of the one-story brick building. An old school bus from Garden Gate Assisted Living was parked crossways, taking up five parking spots. Not that there was a need. There were only four cars in the entire lot.

Although the air in the volunteer center was nice and cool, I drew in a breath and held it when I entered. The smell of ammonia was so strong I could taste it. A heavyset woman in flowered scrubs was leading a young woman with more challenges than anyone deserved to the restroom. The woman in scrubs eyed me suspiciously.

"I'm looking for Rhonda Walker. I'm her brother," I said, hoping to put the woman's mind at ease.

"Oh—so *you're* Gypsy!" She smiled broadly. "Rhonda never mentioned how handsome you were."

I winked at the woman. "You remind her for me."

She blushed, then pointed down the hall. "She's in the commons area, down the hall and to the left."

I found the commons area and stood in the doorway a moment watching Rhonda do her thing. I wondered where she got her compassion. Our mother was a great nurse but had no patience, especially with kids; our grandmother, for the most part, was indifferent. I remember our father was kind, funny, and proud, but I don't remember him being particularly compassionate. How could he have been? He walked out on his wife and two kids.

Rhonda was at a table with two women and a young man, all with various disabilities, leading them through some sort of reading exercise. She looked up at me and smiled. "Hey. Come on in. Guys, I want you to meet my brother, Gypsy." She said it with such pride, I felt guilty. I hoped she didn't think I was there to volunteer my time.

"Hey, Gypsy," one of the women said, her words terribly slurred. Her eyes were magnified through ultra-thick glasses. "I'm Marion."

"Nice to meet you, Marion."

"This is Jared, and this is Patricia," Rhonda said. Patricia waved with a palsy-stricken hand while Jared stared at me with untrusting eyes. Rhonda opened a children's book and handed it to him. "Jared, will you please read to Marion and Patricia while I talk to my brother for a moment?"

Jared continued to stare at me, not even trying to hide the

distrust. He finally turned his attention to the book and slowly began to read, struggling with each simple word. Rhonda praised him, then led me into the hallway.

"There's a couple forms we'll need to get you to fill out and we'll have to do a background check, but—"

"Whoa, Rhonda!" I held up my hands. "I'm not here to volunteer."

She pursed her lips, then folded her arms, looking at me with that disappointed-teacher look. "Oh. Well, then, what are you doing here?"

"I ran into Tatum and his grandfather at Dunbar's and I have a couple questions."

Joy replaced her disappointment. "So you're going to take the case?"

"I didn't say that. I said I had a couple of questions. They invited us over for dinner tonight and before I go, I want to know what I'm dealing with."

"They're good people, Gypsy."

"I'm sure they are. But something's not adding up."

Her expression softened. "Not adding up about Burke or Ryce?"

I realized I was treading in shallow water. Rhonda saw the good in everyone, especially when there was a kid involved. "There's some questions I have about both of them."

"Like what kind of questions? From what I've seen, they were a happy family."

I winked at her. "That's my point. You've only see what's been shown. What's the story with Burke's accident?"

Her eyes reflected deep concentration, then confusion. "I don't remember that much about it. Just what was in the paper and on the news."

"What about Rodney? Did he ever say anything about a fellow officer being injured in the line of duty?" In a town the size of Wink, a cop getting shot would have generated a loud buzz.

Now she was really confused. I could see the brain cells working overtime trying to recall everything she could about Burke McCallen's injury. "I honestly don't remember that much about it. What I do remember, was there was hardly any news coverage *about* it. Now that I think about it, that was pretty odd."

"Exactly. In a county this size, a deputy's ambushed and it barely makes the news? That in itself raises questions."

Her shoulders dropped with a mounting burden. "Gypsy, the whole idea was for you to help Tatum prove his father didn't hang himself. What's Burke's injury got to do with any of this?"

I shrugged. "I don't know. I hope it was just a run of bad luck and the two aren't connected. But I'm not going to agree to help Tatum until I know what I'm dealing with from all angles. Is the Kermit public library still open?"

She nodded. "They've moved over on Arlington Street, though."

"Think they would have back issues of the *Winkler Weekly* microfiched or maybe even online?"

"You'd probably have better luck with the microfiche than online. What time are we supposed to be at the McCallens'?"

"Six. I'll see you back at the house." I gave her a peck on the cheek. As I turned to leave, she grabbed my hand.

"Gypsy, I know you want to know what you're getting yourself into before you agree to anything. But if what you find out is going to hurt Tatum . . ."

I smiled warmly. "That's why we call it preliminary work."

The Kermit public library was a two-story brick building with a neatly manicured front lawn. A canopy of ancient cottonwoods draped over a few scattered benches, providing ample shade for quiet reading. I'd seen much larger and more modern libraries, but Kermit's was nice. Whether it had the information I needed remained to be seen.

The information desk was located in the back on the ground level. The attendant was an older Hispanic woman who maybe stood five feet in heels. Her black hair was streaked gray and pulled back into a short ponytail. According to her nametag, her name was Rosa. She was busy matching call slips to various magazines.

"Hi," I said, startling her from work. "I need some help with newspaper archives. I'm looking for back issues of the *Winkler Weekly.*"

She stared at me over the rims of her purple-framed glasses, then her mouth dropped open. "Gypsy Moran," she squealed. She hurried out from behind the desk and scurried to me, grabbing me around the waist in a bear hug. Her head barely reached my chest. Then it dawned on me who she was. My junior high librarian.

"My, my . . . look how you've grown. Such a handsome man." She pulled away and looked me up and down approvingly.

"It's good to see you again, too, Mrs. Garcia."

"I saw your sister at a retirement party last year and she told me you were living in Las Vegas. She said you were a *private investigator.*" She whispered the last part, even looking around at who might hear. At least Rhonda had told her the truth and didn't make up some grandiose story that I was an astronaut or in some other heroic field. "I always knew you'd end up on one side of the law. I just wasn't sure which side." She cackled and hugged me again then quickly jerked away and looked at me with a dead seriousness. "Is that why you need the newspapers? Are you looking into something that happened here in Kermit?"

"Oh, um . . . not really. I'm just curious about something."

She removed her glasses, sticking the end of one of the purple arms between her lips. Her dark eyes narrowed into tiny slits as she wagged a finger at me. "You're up to something, Gypsy Moran. You could fool others, but you never could fool me."

I couldn't help but grin. "I'm just gathering a little background information."

She bobbed her head up and down, then slipped her glasses back on. "How far back you want to go?"

"Three years."

"Those would be on microfiche. Do you know how to use the reader?"

"Oh, yeah. You taught me well." I followed her to the resource room where large cabinets with pull-out drawers lined the walls. Four desks with microfiche readers were in the center of the room.

"The *Winkler Weekly* is in this cabinet. If it was a particularly big story, it may be in this special edition cabinet on a separate file." She moved down to the next cabinet and removed one of the little boxes as an example. "Is it a big story you're looking for?" She looked at me with devious innocence.

I half shrugged and grinned. "That depends on what the *Winkler Weekly* considers a big story."

Her lips twisted into a tight smirk. "You're a devil, Gypsy Moran. Call me if you need me."

"Can I print from these machines?"

She turned her head and glanced out into the main room. "You're not supposed to but since it's you . . . you can print to the information desk printer. I'll grab them for you."

She showed me which button to push on the reader to queue a print job. As soon as she disappeared, I went to the special edition cabinet and scanned through the titles handwritten on the boxes. At least Burke's injury was big enough to warrant a special edition. I took the box over to one of the desks, loaded the film, then found

the article: DEPUTY CRITICALLY WOUNDED IN LINE OF DUTY. The date-
line was August 10; Kermit, Texas. The byline: Sophia Ortez.

> *A deputy with the Winkler County Sheriff's Department was*
> *critically wounded Tuesday night. Sergeant Thomas Burke*
> *McCallen was answering a call of suspicious activity at the*
> *Kermit Recreation Center on Ardmore Drive when he was*
> *shot from behind. McCallen was listed in critical condition at*
> *Winkler Regional Hospital.*
>   *Investigators have not yet been able to question the*
> *wounded officer due to his grave condition but authorities be-*
> *lieve McCallen may have interrupted a burglary in progress.*

I went back to the cabinet and scanned the other titles. Apparently his recovery or the investigation wasn't worthy of a special
edition, though. I opened the drawer for the regular editions and
pulled out the rest of August and all of September and October.

There were lots of 4-H articles, articles about Back to School,
Wildcats football scores, and Halloween safety tips but Sergeant
Burke McCallen wasn't mentioned again. A letter to the editor in
the October 30 election issue did catch my eye.

> *Dear Editor:*
>   *It's time for Sheriff Gaylord Denny to go. Winkler County*
> *deserves better. It's a shame Burke McCallen had to withdraw*
> *from the race.*
>
>   *Sincerely,*
>   *LeWellan Jacobs*

Burke's injury just got a lot more interesting. I dug out the November issues and read through the postelection articles. The

school board remained the same, the board of aldermen had two new members, and Gaylord Denny, who ran unopposed, won his fourth term in office. Politics in small towns were more vicious than anything on a national level but taking out your competition with a bullet? It would certainly explain Burke's resentment toward the acting sheriff, but could he honestly blame the entire department?

I printed the article and the Letter to the Editor, then put the films back in their proper place. Mrs. Garcia had the pages ready for me at the information desk.

"Not good, Gypsy Moran," she said as she handed me the copies. "You need to pick something else to look into." She made a *tsk-tsk* sound as she glared at me over the top of her glasses.

"This is between me and you, right?"

"Oh, I don't want to be involved with this and I don't think you want to, either. Bad stuff, Gypsy. Bad stuff." There was honest fear in her expression. I believed her when she said she didn't want to be involved with this one.

I shared her sentiment. But not quite enough to walk away just yet.

CHAPTER 5

So Burke had considered a run for sheriff. That made things a little more interesting. Why'd he consider running? What was his political platform? Had Denny done something, or not done something, during his administration to make Burke think he could do a better job? Certainly Gaylord Denny wasn't stupid enough to think he could have his political opponent shot and no one would notice. Some things you could chalk up to coincidence; some things you couldn't.

I sat down on one of the benches outside the library and brought up the Internet on my phone, easily finding Sophia Ortez in the first search. The most recent article she had penned that made it to the Internet was from the *Odessa Record*. I found the phone number and called it.

A tired voice answered on the third ring. *"Odessa Record,* please hold." After a moment of canned music, they came back on the line. "Thank you for calling the *Odessa Record.* How may I direct your call?"

"Hi, I'm trying to reach Sophia Ortez. Do you know if she's in the office today?"

"Hold one second and I'll find out for you. If she's not, would you like her voice mail?"

"Sure." Although I had no intention of speaking to her over the phone.

More canned music, then Sophia Ortez answered. "This is Sophia."

I hung up, climbed in the van, and headed for Odessa. I could make it in less than an hour, meet with Ms. Ortez, and be back in time for dinner at the McCallens.

I plugged the address in the GPS, then picked up Highway 302 and settled in for the ride. An oldies station filtered through the radio, bringing back way too many memories. "The Bluest Eyes in Texas" was playing. Yeah, those blue eyes had haunted me every night since the night I left. No amount of promises could budge her from that damn ranch. And no amount of promises on her end could make me stay. I glanced at the faded number written on my hand. It was almost unreadable now. I turned the radio off, deciding to take in the passing landscape rather than wonder about what could have been.

The good ol' van was up to eighty-five miles per hour and chugging along quite well, the nothingness of the road stretched out before me, whizzing by. Mile after mile of flat, sand-rock covered ground and asphalt met the horizon in a perfect line. Like an artist's canvas split in half, the green cacti and yucca plants ended where the cobalt-colored sky began. Claire had always tried to convince me to see the beauty in the loneliness of the land. *Beauty* and *loneliness* were two words I couldn't quite put together. I pressed the accelerator, watching the needle climb to ninety. The sooner I got off this highway, the better.

Odessa wasn't Vegas but it was a fair shade larger than Kermit. Although economic development had brought a variety of businesses and industry to the town, Odessa was still an oil town and always would be. I found the *Odessa Record* and parked in one of

the visitors' spaces. The building was a sprawling, multilevel facility with a tempered-glass entrance. Inside, framed editions of the
paper hung on the wall along with photos of Odessa's past and present and also several photos of former President George W. Bush. The
receptionist desk was in the shape of a horseshoe. The receptionist
looked like she'd rather be riding horses than taking another call.

"The classified forms are on that table over there, the obit forms
are—"

"I'm here to see Sophia Ortez," I said, stopping her before she
wasted any more breath.

"Oh. Can I tell her your name?"

"I'm the private investigator involved in one of the stories
she's working on."

Her brows raised with a look of surprise. "Oh. Okay. Just a
minute." She punched a number into the elaborate system, then
slightly turned away. She mumbled into her Bluetooth, then nodded
and ended the call. "She'll be right with you."

I had just sat down in one of the soft leather chairs when a
sharp-looking lady came into the lobby from the work area. The
receptionist nodded in my direction. Sophia Ortez gave me the
once-over before approaching. Finally, she walked over and stuck
out her hand. "I'm Sophia Ortez. And you are?"

I rose and shook her hand. "Michael Moran. And I am a private investigator."

"So that part's true."

I grinned sheepishly.

She was a damn fine looking woman. Early thirties, hair so black
it shimmered blue, cut pixie style, and warm bronze colored skin
framing strong cheekbones that highlighted her warm, brown eyes.
A pair of khaki capris exposed just enough leg to make a man
wonder if what wasn't exposed was just as fine.

"What can I do for you, Mr. Moran?" she asked, rudely inter-rupting my fantasy.

The nosy receptionist was all ears. I turned my back to her to make her work for whatever information she was going to gather. "Is there somewhere we can talk privately? I'd like to ask you a couple questions about an article you wrote for the *Winkler Weekly*."

Sophia's expression went from sheer confidence to concern.

"No one knows I'm here. No one even knows I'm looking into this," I said in a quiet voice.

She considered it for a long moment, then finally nodded. "Why don't we walk down to the park."

I held the door for her, then followed her along the walkway. We had walked an entire block and were stopped at the crosswalk before either of us spoke. "There's only one story from Winkler County I wrote worthy of an investigation," she said, looking ahead at the cross signal.

"There's only so much you can do with the 4-H," I said.

She looked up at me, cupping her hand over her eyes against the glare of the sun, and grinned slightly. The light turned green and she hurried across, leaving me a step or two behind. She was just as fine from the back as she was from the front. I figured it would be rude, though, to purposely lag behind. I strode to catch up with her.

The heat in Odessa was almost as suffocating as it was in Wink. Sweat beaded at my hairline and tickled the small of my back. If we didn't get to the park soon, any hope of impressing this Mexican goddess with my boyish good looks were going to end up in a puddle of stinking sweat.

Another block down, she stopped for traffic, then cut across the road and, thank God, into the Odessa Municipal Park. Luckily enough, she stopped at the first picnic table tucked underneath a large cottonwood. The much welcomed shade dropped the temperature a full ten degrees.

Sophia sat down on the table and stared at me. "So, Mr. Moran . . . what 4-H story are you investigating?"

"You wrote an article about a Winkler County deputy who was shot in the line of duty."

She grinned and nodded, then looked out into the park, watching a game of hoops on the basketball court. "Sergeant Burke Mc-Callen. He was shot in the back."

"What do you remember about it?"

She glanced at me, then returned her gaze back to the ballgame.

"I've been asked by the McCallen family to take a look at some different things and I want to know what I'm getting into before I agree to anything."

"What has Burke told you about it?"

"He doesn't know I'm here. We haven't really discussed it yet. I'm just doing a little background work."

She nodded, then finally turned her gaze back to me. "How is he?"

"Paralyzed."

She snapped a twig from a low-hanging branch and slowly picked at the leaves. "They were hoping the paralysis would be temporary."

"Did you ever do a follow-up story?"

She shook her head. "I tried to. Was told to leave it alone."

I sat down beside her on the table. "By whom?"

"The managing editor. Said we didn't want to embarrass the family."

I didn't understand. "Embarrass them how?"

She shrugged. "The editor hinted around that maybe McCallen was up to something he shouldn't have been up to, and there wasn't any need to embarrass the family anymore."

"They thought McCallen was a dirty cop?"

She looked at me and nodded. "Apparently."

"But you didn't believe them?"

She took a deep breath, then went back to picking at the leaves. "No. I believe there was a dirty cop involved but I don't think it was McCallen."

"Is that why there was very limited information in the article you wrote?"

She tossed her head back and laughed. "Oh my God, it was what—two paragraphs? I couldn't get information from the sheriff's department, I couldn't get information from the hospital. No one would talk."

"What about the family?"

She shrugged again. "I think the son wanted to talk, but, like everyone else, he was pretty tight-lipped. By the time McCallen was well enough to talk himself, the editor had told me to let it go."

"What about local television? Did any of the local news stations cover it?"

She shook her head. "No more than the paper. When it happened, it was a huge story, but within hours the information pipeline didn't just shut down, it was completely sealed off. In this business, when you can't get the information you need, you move on."

"But was there never any industry talk about the lack of information? The media usually thrives on conspiracy theories. Why didn't they run with this one?"

She sighed heavily. "I've often thought about that. Why didn't one of the more experienced reporters keep digging and digging? Why didn't they pull a Woodward and Bernstein and expose the corruption for what it was?"

"Why didn't you?"

She chuckled. "Sure, I had my eyes set on a Pulitzer, but I had rent to pay, too. I needed the job."

We sat there for a moment, neither of us saying anything. Finally, I asked, "Did they ever make an arrest?"

She shrugged. "I don't know. I moved on and never heard anything else about it. But I'd be interested to know if they did."

"What do you know about McCallen running for sheriff?" I asked.

Again, she shrugged. "I do know there was some talk before he filed, but it was mostly campaign talk. He couldn't really say too much bad about Gaylord Denny, considering he still worked for the man."

I made it back to Wink in time to grab a shower before heading over to the McCallens. I pulled on a clean pair of jeans and fresh T-shirt and was stepping into my sandals when Rhonda knocked on the open bedroom door. "You decent?"

"I've never been decent. But I am dressed."

She laughed, then stepped in and leaned against the door. She had the phone in her hand but it wasn't on. "There was a number on the caller ID. I think they might have been calling for you." Her jaw set as anger flared in her eyes. "Claire Kinley. Really, Gypsy?"

"I ran into her at Dunbar's," I explained. "She said something about maybe meeting for lunch one day. No big deal." I was seventeen all over again, lying to my mother about where I'd been, who I'd been with, reeking of sex and heartache. My heart was racing as fast as the van had been moving along Highway 302.

In my family's eyes, the Kinleys and Morans might as well have been called the Hatfields and McCoys. I never understood my mother's dislike for the Kinleys or anything to do with the K-Bar

Ranch. And I sure didn't understand why the disdain carried over to Rhonda.

Rhonda looked at the phone, then pressed a button. "Oh, oops. I'm sorry. I erased the number."

I didn't tell her I had it stored in my cell. I'd let her go on believing she was doing her part in keeping me and Claire Kinley apart. Again.

Outside, I helped Gram into the backseat of Rhonda's SUV. Rhonda was forcing her to go; she didn't trust her at home by herself. Something about the cable company's movies on demand and racking up an enormous cable bill.

Gram grumbled about the unfairness of getting old the entire ten minutes it took us to get to the McCallens'.

As Rhonda pulled into the driveway, she asked, "So what did you find out about Burke's accident?" Apparently she was over her little tiff about Claire.

"Not much more than we talked about. There was very little news on the subject."

"You know, I never really thought about it until you mentioned it. And you were right. For a story that big, it sure didn't get the news coverage you would have expected."

The McCallens' house was small, vinyl-sided, and set off the road, partially hidden behind overgrown mesquite trees. A wooden handicap ramp led to the front stoop. Rhonda parked behind the pickup truck Tatum had driven earlier. A black-and-white border collie bounded around from the back of the house, barking and snapping at the stationary wheels of Rhonda's SUV. She climbed out then tried to stroke the dog's head. "Jasper, calm down, boy."

The dog turned circles around her, lapping up the attention.

Tatum came to the front door and called the dog off. "I'm glad y'all came. Supper's almost ready." He offered me his hand. I'd never known a twelve-year-old to offer such a greeting without being prompted by a stern-faced adult.

I shook his hand, then Rhonda, Gram, and I followed him into the house. It was an older house with faded hardwood floors and years-old furniture strategically placed for wheelchair access. Burke wheeled himself from the kitchen to the living room, stopping at the doorway. Rhonda went to him and wrapped him in a tight hug, then playfully picked at his long hair. "Time for another haircut, old man."

"I think I'm going to let it grow. Pull it back in one of those ponytails."

They laughed together easily, then Burke turned to me. "It's good to see you again, Mr. Moran."

"Please, call me Gypsy."

"Well, Gypsy . . . I'm glad you decided to come."

Tatum excused himself, then scooted around the wheelchair and disappeared into the kitchen. The smell of ribs and roasted corn wafted through the house and I remembered I hadn't eaten all day. My bagged lunch had ended up splattered in the parking lot of Dunbar's. My ten-minute encounter with Claire had already caused problems, extreme hunger being only one of them.

"Would you like a beer?" Burke asked.

"Sure."

"I'll get it," Rhonda said. "I'll see if Tatum needs any help. Gram, why don't you come help us in the kitchen?"

Rhonda and Gram in the kitchen "helping." I wondered if I should warn Tatum neither could boil water.

Burke rolled himself into the living room and motioned me to the sofa. "Have a seat."

Rhonda came back in and handed both of us a beer. The bottle was cold, almost frosty, and I relished that first sip. As Rhonda disappeared back into the kitchen, I made myself comfortable on the sofa.

"Did you think anymore about my offer?" Burke asked.

So much for comfort and small talk. I leaned forward and spoke quietly, not sure how much Burke wanted Tatum to know. "Well, I do have a couple questions about your injury. You didn't seem real anxious to talk about it at the diner, and I do understand why. Tell me about Gaylord Denny and why you were going to run against him in the election."

He had started to take a sip of the beer but held the bottle at his mouth, surprise evident in his eyes. After a moment, he took a sip, swallowed hard, then nodded. "You've been doing a little home-work, haven't you?"

"Did you think I wouldn't?"

"Not if you're worth your fee." He winked, then settled his weight in the chair. I grinned and offered the bottle in a mock toast.

"So why were you running against him?"

He rubbed his chin thoughtfully. "Why does any candidate decide to run? I thought I could do a better job."

I wasn't buying it. I glanced toward the kitchen, then leaned closer to Burke. "Cut the bullshit, Burke. If you want me to help you, you've got to help me. How could you have done a better job? What was it with Denny's administration you didn't like? Corruption? Favoritism? Were you overlooked for a promotion? Candidates run for office because they want something changed. What was it you wanted changed?"

He shifted his weight, then glanced over his shoulder toward the kitchen. "Look, whatever happened to me, let it go. We're hir-ing you to look into Ryce's death, not *my* injury."

I shook my head. "I don't work that way. I want to know what I'm dealing with up front. If Denny's a dirty cop, I want to know it. If *you* were a dirty cop, I want to know it. Your grandson doesn't have to know it, but I do."

His eyes narrowed with disgust. "You're calling *me* a dirty cop? You're barking up the wrong tree, boy."

"Then tell me what happened."

He rubbed his chin hard, then chugged half his beer in one shot. After a long moment, he finally spoke in a quiet, controlled voice. "I served under Gaylord Denny for twelve years. In the beginning he was a good sheriff. But something happened in his last term . . . I don't know what . . . but there was a gradual change. People in the county started fearing deputies rather than looking at them as someone who could help them.

"Some of us questioned him on a couple of his decisions, some questionable calls. The ones that questioned him left for one reason or another, some of them quit, some were fired. I had too many years in to just walk away. Got bucked back down to patrol. Everywhere I went in the county, people were talking. They'd heard Denny was doing this or that and they wanted him out."

"Did anyone have any proof of wrongdoing?"

Burke smiled. It was a sad smile. "Proof? Nothing that would hold up in court. Nothing that could even bring an indictment. I mean, really, how are you going to indict the sheriff?"

"There's ways. It's been done before. It can be done again."

"Not without proof. And anyone who had proof either disappeared or they were too scared to talk."

"And you took one in the back."

He sighed heavily. "Yeah. I took one in the back."

"Did they ever make an arrest?"

He finished off his beer. "If you want to call it that. They told me a Hispanic kid, Hector Martinez, confessed. Said I walked in

on him while he was cleaning out the concession stand at the recreation center and he popped me."

"In the back . . ."

Burke smiled. "I spent twelve years in the criminal investigations department. I found the *confession* a little insulting."

"What happened to the kid?"

He shrugged. "Last I heard, he got shipped off down to Pecos."

"They sent a kid to Reeves?" I heard the surprise in my own
voice. Reeves County Detention Center wasn't for the faint of heart.
It wasn't a nice place to raise a kid.

He tilted his head, then shook it back and forth. "If I thought
for a minute that kid was the one that put me in this chair, I'd say
good riddance. But things being what they are, I almost feel sorry
for him."

"Have you ever talked to him?"

He shook his head. "I spent four weeks in intensive care, then
three months in rehab. By the time I came home, Hector Martinez
had already confessed, been sentenced, and shipped off. I never
really felt the need. What was done was done. Wasn't much I could
do about it."

"But you don't believe—"

"Of course I don't believe it. Whether it was some thug Denny
hired or one of his own, I don't know. But I'd bet my last breath
Hector Martinez didn't have anything to do with it."

"And what about your son? Was he with the department back
then?"

He nodded. "He took a family leave of absence when it happened, so he was out of the loop for a while."

"So he wasn't involved in the investigation at all? Not even
after hours?"

"You have to understand, Gypsy. Hector Martinez confessed the day after I was shot. Within a matter of days, he was on his way to Reeves."

"Did you ever discuss it with Ryce?"

He grinned. "Why do you think he transferred to the investigations department?"

I sat back on the sofa and finished off my beer. "Is it your case file he had a copy of?"

He stared at me long and hard, then slowly shook his head. "I was the tip of the iceberg."

CHAPTER 6

hankfully, Rhonda and Gram had helped only to set the table and hadn't actually helped with the cooking. When it was ready, we sat crowded around a small table in the center of their kitchen. It was obvious they seldom had company. They existed to take care of one another and had little time for anything else. I imagined Ryce had been about my age. I wondered if he ever dated? If he ever went with the guys to a bar to catch a ballgame and drink a few beers? Or if his entire life revolved around work, then caring for his kid and disabled father?

But if tonight's meal was an example of the kid's culinary skills, no one needed to worry about the McCallens eating well. My fingers were sticky from the ribs; butter from the corn clung to my lips like lip gloss on a whore. If I decided to take the case, I might just do it simply for the food.

"So, what do you think?" Tatum asked as he cleared the last dishes from the table. "Do you want to see the files I've got?"

The kid didn't beat around the bush. I liked that about him.

"Tatum, why don't you take Gypsy outside and show him where it happened before it gets too dark," Burke said. "I think you'll find that pretty interesting." He looked at me and slightly nodded. One investigator to another.

"Go ahead," Rhonda said. "I'll get the kitchen cleaned up."

The kid's face lit up with excitement. He looked at me for an okay so I stood up and motioned toward the door. I followed him out onto a deck overlooking the backyard. They actually had grass. In spots. The cacti were corralled to a landscaped area on the left side of the yard; on the right was a weathered wooden play set Tatum outgrew years ago. An aluminum shed was near the back, bordering a thin tree line, with an attached lean-to housing a push mower and other yard items. Three massive bur oaks in the center of the yard provided a nice shade source.

"It happened over here." Tatum went down the steps and stopped at the middle tree. Jasper blew by him in hot pursuit of a daring jackrabbit. "He was hanging from this branch." Tatum pointed upward, toward a thick branch at least ten feet off the ground. It was the lowest branch on the tree, though impossible to climb to without help.

I joined Tatum at the spot where his father had died, surprised at the kid's lack of emotion. He'd been around cops too long.

"What happened the day you found him?"

"I knew something was wrong as soon as I got home because his car was here. He never comes home during the day."

"So what happened?"

"I had just got home from school and I went inside, through the front door, and hollered for Dad. Grandpa had gone to the auction house with LeWellan Jacobs."

LeWellan Jacobs. The author of the Letter to the Editor.

"When I got off the bus, Jasper didn't come greet me, even when I called for him. I remember thinking something was up."

"So when you got in the house, what happened?"

"I hollered for Dad, then I hollered for Grandpa, thinking he might have got back early. I went into the kitchen and put my book bag on the table then went to the refrigerator to get a drink and that's when I saw him. I saw him through the kitchen window." For the first time, his voice cracked and it had nothing to do with puberty. "I called 911 and told them I needed an ambulance, then I ran outside. I know you're supposed to stay on the line with the operator but . . . I knew they'd come even if you didn't." He turned away from me, lifting his hand to his face and wiping away tears he didn't want me to see.

He sniffled, then squared his shoulders and turned back around. "I grabbed his legs and tried lifting him up, to take some of the pressure off, but . . . I wasn't strong enough."

I gently placed my hand on his shoulder. "I'm sure there wasn't anything you could do at that point."

He smiled softly, a sad smile that tore at my heart. "Didn't stop me from trying."

I walked around the tree, looking at the trunk and the branch that held Ryce's weight. It was a stout branch, capable of supporting a good-sized man. It still didn't explain how he got up there. "What else do you remember?"

"Jasper was lying underneath him, whining real bad. I ran and got the ladder and tried to loosen the rope, but . . . it was pulled too tight."

I wouldn't allow myself to envision the panic Tatum must have felt. That would be getting too involved and I wasn't sure I wanted to do that yet. "Where'd you get the ladder from?"

He pointed to the lean-to. "It was over there. But dad always kept it in the shed."

I looked at him. "You're sure about that? You're one hundred percent sure you got it from the lean-to?"

He nodded. "That was one of the things I wondered about afterward. Why it was there in the first place and how'd Dad get up to that branch without it."

"Did you tell the sheriff this?"

He rolled his eyes. "Yeah. He said Dad must have climbed the tree."

I walked around the tree again, paying closer attention to the trunk. I didn't see any scuff marks, no broken bark, no indication anyone had recently tried to climb the tree.

I scratched my head then asked him again. "You are *certain* the ladder was under the lean-to?"

He nodded.

"And there wasn't a box, or a step stool, maybe even the trash can, anywhere around the tree?"

He slowly shook his head.

I moved on, not wanting to dwell on the subject. The more I questioned Tatum about that one element, the more his memory would start inventing things that didn't happen. "What happened when the paramedics arrived?"

"They cut him down and laid him in the grass. They tried to find a pulse, all that stuff, and by that time a couple of the deputies were here. They kept trying to pull me away from him. . . ." His voice faded into a slight whisper.

"Do you remember the deputies?"

He sniffled then nodded. "Mark Peterson and Averitt McCoy. There were a couple others but I don't remember their names. Mark Peterson told me they'd call Grandpa for me."

"Did you tell them Burke wasn't at home?"

He shook his head.

"Then why would they assume he wasn't here?"

He stared at me with such intensity, I feared the trees behind me would ignite. After a long moment, he asked, "You want to see the case file now?"

I thought about it before saying anything. I felt for the kid, I really did, but I did not want to get involved in a homicide investigation. They were tiring, intense, much more detail-oriented than a cheating spouse. Not to mention dangerous.

I sucked in a long, deep breath, then pitched a slobbery toy Jasper had brought me to toss. "Tatum—if your dad didn't commit suicide, who do you think killed him?"

"Sheriff Denny. Maybe not himself, but some of his deputies."

I was afraid he was going to say that. Murder cases were tough enough. Even tougher when the suspects knew how to cover their tracks.

"You know no matter who did it, it's not going to bring your dad back."

He nodded slowly. "I know that. But at least the town will know he died with honor."

Crap. That one was going to be hard to walk away from.

Back in the house, I joined Burke and Rhonda at the kitchen table. Gram was in the living room watching some gossip show. Tatum went to his room to gather the case file Ryce had been working on. The air in the kitchen was a comfortable reprieve from the suffocating heat of the backyard. It was 8:00 P.M. and still registering 90 degrees. I wiped a line of sweat from my forehead with the back of my hand.

"Tell me what happened after Ryce died," I said.

Burke pushed away from the table and rolled himself to a cabinet under the sink. He pulled out a bottle of Jim Beam, then rolled back to the table. "Rhonda, would you be a sweetheart and grab a couple glasses?" He pointed to one of the upper cabinets.

"Sure." Rhonda got two glasses and set them on the table.

Burke poured the glasses about a quarter full, then slid one in my direction. "So, you want to know about the day Ryce died. What do you want to know?"

"Who knew you were going to the auction with LeWellan Jacobs?"

"Ryce, Tatum. It wasn't unusual for me to go. I go with him about twice a month."

If in fact Ryce was murdered, whoever did it had to know Burke wouldn't be home at that time. The old man may not have been able to chase after the perps but he could have loaded them full of lead.

"Now there were a couple calls on the caller ID that day that came up as unavailable," Burke said. "That's pretty unusual."

"How many times did they call?"

"Five, six maybe. About every thirty minutes up until around two o'clock."

"A little before Tatum got home."

He nodded.

"Why do you think Ryce came home early that day?"

Burke shrugged. "That one I can't figure out. There was a call on *his* cell phone about an hour before Tatum got home but we don't know whose number it was."

"Have you still got his phone?"

He shook his head. "Of course not. Denny took it as evidence."

"But I wrote the number down." Tatum pulled up a chair. He opened the brown file folder and showed me the number he had scribbled on the inside cover. I was growing more impressed with this kid by the minute.

I took a sip of the bourbon. It and Sophia Ortez, so far, were the nicest things about this trip. I didn't include my reunion with Claire. That had the potential to be as explosive as the situation in Vegas I was running from.

"Have you called the number?" I asked.

Tatum shook his head. "I didn't want to call from here. I have to be careful what phone I call from in case they have caller ID."

Burke and I glanced at one another. Burke looked away, fighting back a grin. I took the file from Tatum and laid it out on the table. It was at least three inches thick, dated, documented, and well organized. There were photos of different girls, all Hispanic, all in their teens. The photos were a collection of family snapshots and school photos, none from professional surveillance.

"That one on the top is Alvedia Esconderia," Rhonda said, pointing to the picture of a cute kid, no older than Tatum. "I taught her and Tatum last year."

"She's the one that started the whole thing," Tatum added. "I told my dad what was happening and he started looking into it."

"Eight young girls have disappeared in the last three years," Burke said. "All illegals, all between the ages of thirteen and fifteen."

"You think they were murdered?"

Burke shook his head.

I sighed. Weren't there any cheating spouses in Winkler county needing my services? I loathed cheating spouses but they paid the bills. Not nearly as complicated as this was turning out to be, either. I closed the file and pressed the balls of my hands deep into my eyes, feeling a massive headache coming on. I finished off the bourbon and poured myself another round. "This . . . Alvedia Esconderia, is she missing?"

"No. Dad wanted her picture, just in case," Tatum answered. "Her older sister, Alana, is missing." He flipped the page in the file and pointed to a picture of Alana. She was a beautiful girl with black curly hair pulled into a loose ponytail. Her teenage body was just beginning to round out. "She's sixteen now," Tatum said. "She disappeared when she was fourteen. Alvedia's scared the same thing will happen to her."

"And of course, with them being illegals, there's no record of 'em." I drank the bourbon in one shot, sucking the whiskey between my teeth before letting it slide down, then refilled again. "Okay, and this is related to your dad's death, how? You think this is the case he was working on when he died?"

"He wasn't officially working on it. He was doing all this after hours. The department wouldn't look into it because they said the girls were probably just runaways."

"And how do you know that's not the truth?"

Tatum opened the file and tapped his finger against the picture of Alvedia Esconderia. "She knows it's not true. She's a key witness."

Of course. Little Sherlock Holmes really needed to find a new hobby. "Shouldn't you be playing football or riding the rodeo or something?"

Burke smiled and poured himself another drink. "He's gonna make a damn good investigator one day."

"Take my advice, kid. Find another line of work."

"So what do you think?" Tatum asked, ignoring my comments and my mood.

"What is it you want me to investigate?" I asked, more snappy than I intended. "We've got three things going on here. Your dad's death, your grandpa's injury, and a human trafficking ring."

"And all three lead back to Sheriff Denny. That's what I want you to investigate."

I finished off the bottle.

Through one bloodshot eye, I watched tiny dust particles flutter from the bedroom blinds like micro-sized snowflakes. I squinted hard against the blinding sunlight filtering through the slats. Rhonda wasn't much of a cook *or* housekeeper. I rolled over on my back and watched the ceiling fan rotate until my stomach lurched. I squeezed my eyes closed to stop the spinning. My hair was soaked from sweat and it had nothing to do with the hangover.

"Mornin', sunshine," Rhonda said from the doorway. She came in and plopped down on the side of the bed. "Here, drink this."

I propped up on one elbow and downed the aspirin she offered, chugged the glass of tomato juice, then eased back on the bed. "Ohhhh . . . I guess I owe Burke a bottle."

Rhonda sighed. "At least you didn't wear a lampshade or do anything else stupid."

"Did I sing? I like to sing karaoke when I'm drunk."

Rhonda laughed. "No. You didn't sing. You didn't stop talking about Claire long enough." Her expression turned sour. "I almost deleted her number from your phone but thought that would be really mean."

We stared at one another for a long moment, neither of us saying anything. I went back to watching the ceiling fan, praying I wouldn't throw up. Finally, I sighed heavily, propped up on my elbow again, and glared at Rhonda. "What is your issue with Claire? You've never liked her."

She turned away. I stared at her back and continued with the interrogation. "I know Mama didn't like her because she was Carroll Kinley's daughter and I don't know what that history was about, and I don't want to know—but it doesn't explain why you don't like her."

"Because she made you cry," she said softly.

"What?" I pulled her around, forcing her to look at me.

"She made you cry. More than once. You're my big brother. You aren't supposed to cry."

I tried but couldn't help the giggle that escaped. "That's why you've hated her all these years? Because she made a lovesick teenage boy cry?"

"Not just any teenage boy—my big brother. Nobody ever made you cry. You didn't even cry when Daddy left."

"You were ten years old. What do you remember about it?"

"I remember you didn't cry. You said the hell with him. We'd be just fine."

Guess she didn't hear me cry myself to sleep that night. Or the night after that. Or the night after that. Finally, I forced my thoughts back to Claire. "Do me a favor and get over it already. I mean, she's not going to make me cry again, okay? I promise. I won't let her." All these years I thought Rhonda had just been jealous of the pampered princess.

"Good. Because I'd hate to have to kill her." She punched me on the arm. She then smiled and stood up. "You need to get up and get going."

"Going where?"

She jammed her hands on her hips. "Doing whatever private investigators do. You told Tatum you'd start today."

CHAPTER 7

Well, that would certainly teach me to never down another bottle of Jim Beam. I showered, then stumbled into the kitchen, where Rhonda had a fresh pot of coffee waiting. "So, when did I agree to this?" I fixed myself a cup of coffee, straight black, and carried it over to the table.

Rhonda was prepping mystery meat for the Crock-Pot. Bless her heart. "Somewhere near the end of the bottle."

"What exactly did I agree to? Did we talk fees or anything?" I did, after all, have to make a living.

Rhonda turned around and stared at me. Her hands were covered with a variety of spices. "You really don't remember, do you?"

I remembered mouthwatering ribs and said a quick prayer I hadn't agreed to take this case for food.

"You told them you'd do it pro bono; I mean, considering the insurance angle and all."

I stared at her. "What insurance angle?"

She sighed, turned back to the sink, and washed her hands, then sat down at the table with me. "As long as Ryce's death is declared a suicide, his life insurance won't pay a dime. Tatum will be able to collect survivors benefits, but . . . the house, Tatum's medical insurance, all of that still has to be paid."

"Ryce didn't have mortgage disability insurance?"

She shook her head. "Everything was tied into his life insurance. Tatum's his beneficiary, but it doesn't pay in the event of suicide. The mortgage was in Ryce's name and Burke, in his condition, can't qualify for a loan to assume it."

I took a long drink of coffee. "His condition shouldn't have anything to do with qualifying for a loan. That would be discriminatory."

"Not his physical condition . . . he can't afford it. For what the house and the land would appraise for now, he'd have to put nearly half down to get the payments low enough so they wouldn't have to struggle."

I scratched at my head, remembering the conversation Burke and I had at the diner. "Burke told me at Dunbar's whatever my fee was, he'd pay it. He said they weren't oil barons, but they weren't hurting, either."

"He's a proud man, Gypsy. He only told me because he asked me to help him find an affordable medical plan for Tatum."

"Does Tatum know all this?"

She shook her head. "To Tatum, it's all about restoring his dad's honor. Burke hasn't told him they may have to move. It's the only home Tatum's ever known. He was born there."

I finished my coffee, got up and poured another cup, then returned to the table. "Maybe moving wouldn't be such a bad idea. Every time he looks out that kitchen window, I can only imagine what he sees."

She stared at me a moment then sighed heavily. "Gypsy—I'm not telling you how to run your business, but can't you do it for me as a favor?"

I shook my head. Apparently she didn't understand my point. "If I said I'd do it pro bono, even if it was in a drunken stupor, I'll do it pro bono. What I meant was, maybe Burke should ask Tatum what he wants to do. He's a sharp kid. Burke, if anyone, should know that."

She didn't say anything. Which is what she does when she knows someone is right.

"Tell me about Alvedia Esconderia, and how you got involved in all this."

"She and Tatum are really good friends. She knew Tatum's dad was a cop so she confided in him and asked for help. Then, after Ryce died, Tatum came to me asking about you."

Something about the whole thing still didn't make sense. I took another long drink of coffee before I put my finger on it. "Does Rodney know about any of this?" Why did Tatum ask Rhonda about me when Rhonda was married to a cop?

She slowly pushed her hair away from her face and frowned. "He said to leave it alone," she finally said in a quiet voice.

"He told who to leave it alone? You or Tatum?"

She got up and walked over to the sink, pretending to busy herself with the few dirty dishes.

"He told *you* to leave it alone, didn't he?"

She slammed a dish towel on the counter, then spun around and glared at me. "Teenage girls are being stolen from their families and forced into God knows what. I can't leave that alone, Gypsy."

"Hey—I'm not the one who told you to leave it alone. Don't take your disappointment with your husband out on me."

"You sonofabitch." She hurled a dish towel in my direction, then let loose with a string of profanities. "You have no right to judge Rodney," she snarled.

"I'm not judging him. I'm just pointing out the obvious." If I had been within striking distance, she would have gone upside my head. I let it settle a moment, then said, "Either Rodney's scared of Gaylord Denny or he knows more than he's telling."

She conceded and sat back down at the table, defeated, burying her face in her hands. After a long moment, she straightened up and looked at me. "I don't think he knows what's going on. He's scared of Denny. Everyone's scared of Denny. I mean . . . look what happened to Ryce."

"But Rodney doesn't work for Denny. He works for an entirely different department."

"Don't you understand, Gypsy? Denny's influence stretches way beyond his own department."

I thought of Sophia Ortez and what she said about the managing editor telling her to drop the story of Burke's injury. I couldn't really fault Rodney. Only a fool would get involved with something that appeared to have this many poisonous tentacles. A bigger fool would do it for free.

"Where does Alvedia live?" I asked, figuring that was as good a place to start as any.

"I'm not sure of the house number. Tatum would know."

Tatum. My pubescent sidekick.

"Call him and tell him I'll pick him up in twenty minutes. And tell him to let Alvedia know we're coming over."

"Seriously, shouldn't you be riding junior rodeo or something?" I asked. Tatum was in the passenger seat of the van ogling one of my pricey cameras.

"I don't like horses."

I cut a glance at him, then smiled. "Isn't that against some ancient law in Texas?"

He laughed. It was the first time I'd heard him laugh. "Probably."

"I never cared for them, either. I don't care too much for animals that can kill me."

"Me either. Turn left at the next light."

"So, tell me about Alvedia. She your girlfriend?"

He snickered as his cheeks flushed. "Noooo. We're just friends."

I nodded, grinning. Friends, my ass.

I pulled up to one of the three stoplights in Wink, waited for a truck to pass, then turned left as my sidekick had instructed.

"It's the fourth house on the right. It's a trailer with a dirt driveway."

I counted off the houses, then pulled into the fourth driveway. Dust rose around the van like thick plumes of smoke. The trailer was a single wide with aluminum underpinning. An overworked air conditioner poked through a front window, balanced precariously on twin two-by-fours. The dirt underneath was wet with moisture from a constant drip. A dark-haired young girl peeked around the drapes, then opened the front door. She stepped out onto the small wooden stoop, smiling a toothy smile. "Hey, Tatum."

"Hey, Alvedia." He was blushing again. My sidekick had turned shy. "This is Gypsy. The guy I was telling you about."

"Come on in. My mother's here. I thought you might want to talk to her, too."

We followed Alvedia into the house and I thought I was going to die. The stifling heat wrapped itself around me like an unwelcome blanket. The poor air conditioner was doing all it could but it wouldn't put a dent in this inferno.

Alvedia's mother was sitting on a yard-sale sofa, the tiredness seeping from her pores like the sweat poring from mine. She gazed at me with empty eyes.

Alvedia sat down beside her. *"Mamá, éste es el investigador privado que Tatum nos habló. El está aquí hacernos algunas pregun-tas sobre Alana."*

"She told her you were here to ask some questions about Alana," Tatum whispered.

I nodded, fully understanding what had been said. I did hope, however, we could do this in English. My Spanish wasn't 100 percent and I always worried I was losing something in translation.

"Usted habla inglés?" I asked.

She nodded, then turned to Alvedia. "Get them a cola, something cold to drink. Please, have a seat." Her accent was heavy and thick, but understandable.

I sat on the other end of the sofa, leaving a rough-looking recliner for Tatum. "My name is Gypsy. It's a pleasure to meet you," I said, offering my hand.

She accepted the offer. "I'm Malita Esconderia. Tatum has told you about Alana?"

I nodded. "He's told me what he knows. I was hoping you could tell me more."

Alvedia returned to the cramped living room and handed me a canned soft drink, then one to Tatum. She then sat on the worn carpet at her mother's feet.

"She disappeared two years ago. She had just turned fourteen," Malita said.

"How did she disappear?"

"She had stayed late at school and was walking home by herself. The last time anyone saw her was at school."

"Why'd she stay late?"

"She was helping one of her teachers grade some papers. I believe it was Mrs. Carter, her science teacher. Alana loved science. She wanted to be a veterinarian."

"Did anyone talk to the teacher?"

Malita slightly shrugged. "I assumed they did. But now, I don't know."

"When did you report her disappearance to the authorities?"

She glanced at Alvedia. "Alvedia called me when Alana didn't come home. I said maybe she's just running late and told Alvedia not to worry. I told her to keep the doors locked until one of us got home."

"Alvedia was here by herself?"

She nodded. "The elementary school lets out about forty minutes before the junior high. She was usually here by herself only about an hour."

"And you were at work?"

"Yes. I'm a housekeeper at the hotel in Kermit. I get off at four so the girls weren't ever here by themselves very long." Her voice took an apologetic tone. I wondered how many times she had blamed herself for Alana's disappearance.

"And when you got home and Alana still wasn't home, what did you do?"

"I wasn't too worried right then. I thought it was probably taking longer than expected but Alvedia had a soccer game at six o'clock and when she wasn't home by then, I called the police. Alana wouldn't have missed her sister's game. I knew something was wrong."

"Did you call the Wink police or the sheriff's department?"

She shrugged. "I just called 911—a sheriff's deputy came to the house."

"And what did they say?"

She rolled her eyes. "They said she had probably run away and not to worry. Said she'd probably be back in a day or two."

Whether a crime had been committed or not, it was sloppy police work. Sloppy as hell. "And you don't think, even for the slightest minute, that could have been possible?"

She set her jaw firm. "No. Alana was a good girl. She was happy. She made good grades, she had friends."

I looked to Alvedia for a more honest answer. Sisters know everything. "Was there anything going on she might have been troubled about?"

Wide-eyed, Alvedia shook her head. "No. She never got into trouble."

"What about a boyfriend? Or maybe a girlfriend she had an argument with?"

Again, Alvedia shook her head. "She didn't have a boyfriend. And all of her friends were really upset when she disappeared."

"Are her friends mostly Hispanic or white?"

"Both," Alvedia and Malita answered at the same time.

"Did any of them drive? Would she have gotten in a car with one of them?"

Malita shook her head. "No. Her friends were all in junior high. None of them had their license yet."

"Would she have gotten into a car with a stranger?"

Wink wasn't the kind of town where a kid was snatched off the main road in broad daylight, or even in the cloak of darkness for that matter.

Again, Malita shook her head. "The school's only four blocks away. She wouldn't have needed a ride."

I asked Tatum if he would get my notepad from the van, suggesting Alvedia help him. As soon as they were outside, I turned to Malita. "Is your family here legally?"

Her eyes blazed with fear as she seemed to literally sink into herself.

I moved a little closer and spoke in a quiet voice in case curious preteen ears were within range. "Malita, I'm not with INS or any other agency. No one's going to report you. Did Alana know y'all were here illegally?"

She looked away from me and stared at her trembling hands. She slowly nodded.

"Would she have gotten into a patrol car?"

She gnawed on her bottom lip as tears welled in her eyes. "She was scared of the police."

"Would she have gotten into a car with one?"

She nodded. "She would have been scared *not* to."

"When she didn't come home, did you go back to the police?"

She brushed away the tears with the backs of her hands. "Yes. They told us they would list her with that center for missing children. They told us to go home and wait."

"Did you ever follow up with them?"

After a long moment, she shook her head. "My husband . . . he was scared."

Tatum and Alvedia came back in. Tatum handed me the spiral notepad I kept stashed above the visor. I thanked him, then asked Malita what her husband's name was.

"Rogelio."

"Does he work?"

She nodded proudly. "Yes. He's a wrangler at the K-Bar Ranch."

I choked on the swallow of cola I had just taken. "He works for Carroll Kinley?"

She rolled her eyes again. "Used to. He works for the daughter now. Ai yai yai."

So the K-Bar was in the practice of hiring undocumented workers. It wasn't like it was a foreign concept in the area. Still, it bothered me knowing Claire was involved. I pushed the thoughts to the far corners of my mind. My plate was full enough without the added concern of Claire's hiring practices.

I thanked Malita and Alvedia for their time.

"Can I show Alvedia your cameras before we go?" Tatum asked.

"You drop one and you're going to pay. And that's a lot of allowances for a kid your age."

Tatum grinned, then grabbed Alvedia's hand and the two hurried out to the van. Malita stood up and walked me to the door.

"Thank you for taking an interest," she said. "She wasn't a runaway. I know that in my heart."

I smiled softly. I didn't want to tell her that the chances of finding her daughter were slim to nothing. And bringing the people responsible for her disappearance to justice probably wasn't as high on her priority list as having Alana back home where she belonged, safe and sound.

She gazed out the door at Tatum and Alvedia. "She's so scared now. I have to take her to work with me because she's scared to stay by herself."

"Does she have any friends she can stay with?"

She smiled. "The days I can't take her with me, I take her over to Tatum's. Mr. McCallen doesn't seem to mind, and Tatum . . . I think he enjoys it."

I'd say that was a safe bet.

I took little Romeo back home and followed him into the house. Burke was in the kitchen fixing a sandwich for lunch.

"You don't look as bad as I thought you would." He glanced at me and grinned. "Care for a sandwich?"

"No thanks," I said, my appetite not yet what it should be for this time of day. "I wanted to go over Ryce's files again. See how far he got so I'm not duplicating efforts."

Burke nodded, then balanced a tray in his lap as he rolled over to the table. He seemed perfectly capable, so I didn't offer to help. Tatum bounded into the kitchen with the file folder in hand. The kid must sleep with it under his pillow. He handed it to me, then fixed himself a sandwich and joined us.

"When was the last disappearance?" I asked.

"We think about two months ago," Burke answered. "But it's hard to pinpoint it. They're all listed as runaways, and they're all illegals, so there's no paper trail."

"But even if they're listed as runaways, they should be documented as a missing person. Right?"

Burke guffawed. "In a perfect world. But this is Gaylord Denny's world."

I looked through the file, staring at the different pictures, reading the notes Ryce had collected. He'd already interviewed parents, teachers, and friends. There was one girl who caught my attention. Victoria Martinez, kid sister of Hector Martinez—Burke's so-called shooter. She disappeared July 20, three years ago, three weeks before Burke was shot.

I turned the file around and slid it toward Burke. "Did Ryce interview Hector Martinez?"

Burke slowly shook his head. "He was planning to the week he was killed. Visitation at the prison is Thursdays and Sundays. Ryce had Thursday off."

"And Denny would know that," I said.

Burke stared at me hard.

"Who's Hector Martinez?" Tatum asked between a mouthful of bologna and bread.

"Someone you don't need to worry about," Burke said sharply.

"But if he's in the file—"

"Did you feed Jasper this morning?"

Tatum and his grandfather stared at one another for a long moment, then Tatum quickly finished his sandwich, hopped up, and headed outside. Whether the kid had fed the dog didn't seem to be the point. Burke didn't want to talk about Hector Martinez in front of Tatum and the kid understood that.

When we were alone, Burke propped his elbows on the table, clasped his hands together, and looked at me. "There are some things about the case I'd rather him not be involved in." There was an apologetic tone to his voice.

"I understand. But it's all related, Burke. Ryce's death seems to be the culmination and Hector Martinez is a common thread."

Burke slowly nodded. "And if I knew Ryce's death was the culmination, I'd say bust it wide open. But I've got a twelve-year-old boy out there to think of. I can't risk anything happening to him, or to me."

I understood where he was coming from as far as Tatum's safety was concerned, but I didn't understand what he asking of me. "I can't prove Ryce was murdered without proving who did it. You of all people should understand that."

"I don't want that kid to come home one day and find me hanging from a tree, too."

I sighed and pushed my hands through my hair. "You're scared of Denny, I can understand that."

He slammed his hand on the table. "I'm not scared of Denny. What else can he do to me? What I'm scared of is what would happen to Tatum if something *did* happen to me. I'm all that kid's got, Gypsy."

I thought of Malita Esconderia and the sadness in her eyes when she spoke of her missing daughter; I thought of Alvedia and the fear she lived with every day. And I thought of Tatum and the childhood that was stolen from him, the fire raging in him to prove his father didn't take his own life.

"Tatum's not going to let it go, Burke. Even if I walk away from it, he's going to keep digging. Would you rather have him go at it alone or have a little help?"

Burke sighed heavily, pressing his fingertips to his forehead. After a long moment, he pointed a stern finger at me. "If anything happens to that boy, it's on your head. And if anything happens to me . . . you inherited yourself a kid."

CHAPTER 8

Rhonda called my cell as I was climbing into the van, heading back to her house. "Yeah," I said as I buckled up.

"Why is there a UPS truck in my driveway?"

"Oh! My clothes are finally here. Sign for it. I'll be there in a minute." I ended the call and backed out of Tatum's driveway with Jasper furiously nipping at the wheels. Dumb dog. He finally gave up once I hit the pavement, standing at the edge of the yard, barking his fool head off.

A few minutes later, I pulled into Rhonda's driveway. The UPS truck was gone, leaving behind several large boxes and an irritated Rhonda.

I barely got out of the van before she started. "Gypsy—what is all this?"

"It's my shorts. I couldn't fit everything into the van."

"How many pairs do you have?"

I rolled my eyes at her. "It's my shorts and other worldly possessions."

She glared at the boxes. "I thought you were just here on vacation?"

"Really, Rhonda, who goes to west Texas in August for vacation? Can you give me a hand?"

I hoisted up a box and carried it inside, carrying it back to the guest bedroom, my room, so she couldn't blame me for cluttering the living room. She was standing in the same spot when I went back outside, still staring at the boxes. "Gypsy—why is everything you own packed in boxes? And why are those boxes in my front yard?"

"Are you just goin' to stand there or are you goin' to help?" I picked up another box and handed it to her. She struggled under the weight, so I took it from her and carried it inside myself.

Seven boxes total were scattered around the bedroom. Rhonda had moved inside and now stood in the doorway staring at the boxes. She peeled back the top of one and peered inside. Of course of all the boxes there for her to look through, she had to open the one with a framed picture of Claire lying on top. She took the picture out, stared at it a moment, then tossed it back inside the box. "Mind telling me what's going on?"

"Yes!" I found my shorts and other clothes tucked underneath a Navajo blanket.

"Gypsy?"

I spun around and looked at her. God love her. She did look confused. I sighed, then took a deep breath. "Look, Rhonda, it'll just be a little while. I promise. Maybe a few weeks."

She folded her arms across her chest and huffed. "Gypsy, it's not that I mind you being here, but why are you here? What is all this?" She swept her arm over the boxes. "This looks like you've left Vegas for good."

I sat down on the edge of the bed wondering how I was going to explain this. The less she knew, the better. For her own sake. "I needed to get out of town for a little while."

Her shoulders dropped and she blew a deep breath. "Oh God, Gypsy. What did you do?" She plopped down beside me on the bed.

"Nothing illegal. You're not harboring a fugitive or anything so you don't have to worry about that."

"About *that*? What *do* I need to worry about?"

I looked at her for a moment, then stared at the boxes that held my life. "I'd never put you in the line of fire. You should know that. I'm the big brother, remember?"

"So, in other words, you can't tell me why you're here, who you're obviously running from, or why they won't track you down to my house. Great, just freaking great." She leapt up and started out of the room.

"Rhonda—just trust me on this, okay? I'll tell you the whole sordid story when the time's right."

She stood in the doorway with her back to me and slowly nodded. "You keep way too many secrets, Gypsy."

She was probably right. But odd as it was, it was the secret I *didn't* keep that got me into this mess.

I traded my jeans for a pair of plaid shorts, then threw on a fresh T-shirt and my leather sandals. The new ensemble was so energizing, I felt like I'd just downed one of the high-energy drinks I lived on during a long surveillance. I bounded out to the van to retrieve Ryce's file, then set up the laptop at the kitchen table.

Gram shuffled into the kitchen, then carried the cookie jar from the counter over to the table. She offered me a cookie as she settled in to watch me work. Within a few minutes, I had access to everything a person would ever want to know about another person. I went for phone numbers and addresses first, did a reverse lookup on the phone number scribbled on the inside of the folder, then sat staring at the name. It didn't surprise me. Mark Peterson. One of the deputies on the scene when Ryce died. So Peterson had called Ryce about an hour before he died. To tell him what? Details about a case they were working? About a hot girl at the diner? Or to lure him home?

I went to a different program and did a quick background check on Mr. Peterson. He was born in El Paso, thirty-eight years old, married to Susan Peterson, no kids. He'd been with the Winkler County Sheriff's Department ten years. Prior to that, he spent five years with the Border Patrol. No demerits, not even a speeding ticket.

I switched programs and did a more advanced search, digging deep into his financials. His tax records indicated his net income was $42,000; Susan pulled in $27,000 as an administrative clerk at Kermit Regional Hospital. Not a bad joint income. Their credit history was clean, nothing out of the ordinary. They paid their few bills on time; their credit-to-debt ratio was minimal. There were no bank notes, no car payments, no mortgage payment. Utilities, insurance, home owners' association dues, and an American Express with a small balance appeared to be their only bills.

The Petersons' joint income was good, but not that good. Since when did cops live in a neighborhood with dues? The tax value on their home was $335,000. Impressive home on a cop and a secretary's salaries. Although they had no kids to support, it didn't explain their high standard of living.

I hooked up the portable printer and printed the Petersons' financial information, wondering if he could really be that stupid. Cops on the take get busted everyday for living above their taxable means.

Gram looked over the printout. "Isn't this illegal?"

"What?"

"What you're doing. That there's personal information."

"That's what I get paid to do, Gram. Find out stuff like this."

"But they ain't paying you for this job, are they?"

She had a point. I snatched the paper from her hand, then stuffed it in Ryce's file. I then did a search on Averitt McCoy, the second deputy on the scene. He was a fifteen-year veteran with Winkler County, and had spent ten years before that—also with the Border Patrol. I went back and compared McCoy's stint with the patrol to Peterson's. There was a one-year overlap, so Peterson and McCoy did work for the patrol at the same time. They had left the patrol at different times and migrated to Winkler County.

McCoy's finances had been pitiful. Poor guy had been in debt up to his eyeballs. An ex-wife collecting alimony and child support for three little McCoys, a mortgage for a house he no longer lived in, and a car payment for a car he no longer drove. Up until two years ago, he ran thirty to sixty days late on rent and credit cards and paid his utilities by cutoff notices. Over the last year, Mc-Coy had cleaned up his act—or come into more money. I checked his tax returns for a noticeable increase, but there was none. Standard cost of living, maybe a merit increase, a little overtime could easily explain the difference. But there was nothing out of the ordinary.

Could this whole thing really be that simple? Two cops on the take. Two stupid cops. I needed to give these two a serious lesson in covering their asses. I hated to waste the paper for blatant stupidity but printed all the information I had found on Peterson and McCoy and added it to Ryce's file.

I then logged on to the National Center for Missing and Exploited Children Web site, keyed in my password, and did a search of each of the girls in Ryce's file. Not a single girl was registered. It disappointed me but it didn't surprise me. Peterson and McCoy had a nice little racket going and I wondered how much Gaylord Denny knew? Did he know and look the other way? Or was he the ringleader? The parents of these girls were terrified to press the issue, to demand an investigation, or to raise hell until they received proof someone was looking for their daughters.

Had Ryce tapped into something others knew about but ignored? If so, it made them just as dirty as Peterson and McCoy, and Gaylord Denny.

Denny had to know. If he didn't, Peterson and McCoy were a lot smarter than I had originally thought.

Rhonda padded into the kitchen. "Gram—what are you eating? You know your sugar's going to get out of whack." She grabbed up the cookie jar and returned it to the counter. Gram looked at me and rolled her eyes, then pretended to pout.

"Do y'all want a sandwich?" Rhonda asked.

"An old woman's got to eat and since you took my cookies away, I guess I better eat a sandwich."

I grinned, then drove the balls of my hands deep into my eyes to combat the fatigue. I either needed glasses or a laptop with a larger screen. "I'm good, but thanks anyway."

Rhonda lifted the lid on the Crock-Pot and stabbed the mystery meat with a fork, then frowned. "Hmm. This thing's still tough as nails."

I closed my eyes, wondering if I really wanted to get involved. Then I realized if I wanted something other than the special down at Dunbar's, I probably needed to investigate. I walked over to the counter, then bit my lip to curtail the laughter. "You've got to cook it before you can simmer it."

"The instructions said to cook it slow," she said pitifully.

I turned the dial up. "Slow is normally six to eight hours, not three days."

I reconsidered the sandwich. Whatever was in that pot wouldn't be done before midnight.

"Maybe we should just order a pizza for dinner tonight," she said, obviously understanding the situation. "We can save this for tomorrow night."

I nodded, in full agreement.

I drug out the bread, mayo, and a pack of sliced turkey and was fixing the three of us a sandwich when the phone rang. Rhonda picked the phone up off the charger and stared at the caller ID, frowned, then set her jaw and tossed the phone at me. "I believe it's for you," she snipped, then pushed me out of the way to finish the sandwiches.

"Yeah," I answered on the fifth ring.

"I was beginning to wonder if you were really here," Claire said, her voice as sweet as a lullaby.

I glanced at Rhonda, then quickly turned away, feeling the heat rise in my face.

"I thought it might have been a dream," Claire cooed.

"Or a nightmare," I quipped.

She laughed and I could see her tossing her head back, her eyes sparkling with amusement. After a moment, she asked, "Still want to get together tonight for dinner?"

My head was telling me every reason why I shouldn't; my heart was telling me every reason why I should. "Uh, sure." I glanced at Rhonda, then slowly migrated toward the living room. "Where and when?"

"There's a roadhouse called Grigg's near Monahans. Around seven good with you?"

"Sure."

"Good. I can't wait to see you again."

I stared up at the living room ceiling wondering what in the hell I was doing. "Me too."

"I'll see you at seven."

"Yeah . . . I'll see you then." I clicked the phone off and stood there a minute before going back into the kitchen. I returned the phone to the charger without saying anything to Rhonda.

She slammed my and Gram's sandwiches on the table, then stuffed the bread back in the bin, shoved the mayo and turkey back in the fridge, and slammed the refrigerator door. "I guess you're seeing her tonight?"

"Oh hell," Gram mumbled.

"We're having dinner. I won't come home crying, I promise. No tears, see?" I moved in front of her, grinning, pointing at my eyes.

Rhonda wasn't amused. She turned away and pulled three glasses from the cabinet and slammed them on the counter.

"Rhonda—it's just dinner, for crying out loud." I was a grown man—I could handle whatever Claire Kinley dished out.

With her back to me, Rhonda said, "You do know she's married?"

That I couldn't handle.

"Oh hell," Gram said again.

Rhonda spun around and glared at me. "She did tell you that she's married, didn't she?"

"Of course she did," I lied. "As a matter of fact, he's joining us for dinner."

She stared at me with a growing fury, then laughed sarcastically. "He's joining you for dinner. Really? He's coming all the way from Austin just for dinner?"

I thought it best not to invent anything else at the moment since it was obvious I had no idea what I was talking about. "Rhonda—it's just dinner."

She laughed a laugh that was birthed from Satan. "Yeah. *Just dinner.* Tell me that again in the morning."

CHAPTER 9

Okay, so she didn't tell me she was married. I was sure there was a logical explanation to that little omission. For one, we didn't talk that long. It was hi, how are you, whap on the cheek, we ought to get together for dinner. Total conversation, ten minutes. Twelve tops. It wasn't like she purposely forgot to tell me. I hoped.

I'd done enough cheating-spouse investigations to know the hurt cheating caused. Infidelity was one fault a significant other would never be able to pin on me. There was only one case I was involved in where I felt sympathy for the cheater. And sympathy cost Gina Gilleni her life and tossed my life into cardboard boxes stacked in my sister's spare bedroom.

I supposed I could consider dinner with Claire a business appointment. After all, I did need to talk with her about Alvedia's dad, Rogelio Esconderia. I wondered how many other illegals worked at the K-Bar Ranch?

I had a couple hours before dinner so I headed into Kermit and over to the *Winkler Weekly* to stir up a little trouble. The paper was published every Thursday so I figured with it being Tuesday, the staff would be at the office giving their computers a workout.

The *Winkler Weekly* was housed in an old clapboard building with dirty windows and a gravel parking lot. Inside wasn't faring much better. It reeked of cigarette smoke and stale coffee. It was a throwback to the old newspaper days of deadline-induced chain-smoking reporters frantically searching for a new, creative way to describe the latest 4-H competition. I had a hard time imagining the delightful Sophia Ortez hunkered down over one of the ancient computers. The *Odessa Record* suited her much better.

The office, on one side, was crudely divided into cubicles with dingy cloth-covered walls. On the other side was an old light table with a mock-up of the paper about to go to print. A man in his late fifties in polyester pants and a white short-sleeved button-down shirt was pasting ad slicks into designated holes in the grid-lined flats. At the front desk, an older woman with a beaklike nose greeted me with a scowl. "Can I help you?" she asked, obviously annoyed at my presence.

"I'd like to see the editor in chief." I smiled just to annoy her more.

"And you are?"

"Michael Clark. I'm here to talk to him about the missing teenagers."

She raised her painted on brows, staring at me hard. "The what?"

"The missing teenagers."

The man at the light board stopped pasting and turned to size me up. He hiked his pants up over a protruding belly, then sauntered over to Miss Congeniality's desk.

"I'm the editor in chief. Can I help you?"

I smiled and offered my hand. "Michael Clark. I'd like to ask you a couple questions about a teenager who recently went missing."

Reluctantly, he shook my hand. "Ed Rankin. You say a kid went missing? From Winkler County?"

I couldn't gauge his reaction. I couldn't tell if he was playing stupid or honestly didn't know anything about it. "Could we possibly talk in your office?"

Miss Congeniality huffed, then went back to doing whatever she was doing before I interrupted.

Rankin made a poor attempt to shrug off my request. "Look, I'd like to help you but we haven't heard anything on it, so I really don't think we'd be much help."

"Ed—mind if I call you Ed? You haven't heard anything on it because it, like several others, was swept under the rug. We can either discuss why your paper doesn't see it as newsworthy right here or in your office."

He cleared his throat with a loud grumble, hiked up his pants again, and motioned for me to follow him. He led me by the makeshift cubicles, down a short hallway, and into a cluttered office. Old flats were stacked haphazardly in a corner of the office. His desk was a salvage-store, metal-topped monster strewn with files, papers, and cigarette butts that had spilled out of an ashtray. The only decoration was a Dallas Cowboys wall clock with dead batteries. Either that, or it was still noon.

Rankin cleared a stack of papers from a guest chair. "Have a seat, Mr. Clark. I can give you about ten minutes. We are under a deadline and I've got one out with a stomach bug and another one that didn't even bother to call in."

"I understand."

Rankin sat behind his desk, shoved a stack of files aside, and propped his arms in the cleared space. "First off . . . if you don't mind me asking, who are you and what interest is it of yours what stories I choose to run?" He frowned.

"I'm a private investigator hired by the family of one of the missing teenagers."

He nodded curtly. "Great. A private dick," he mumbled.

I smiled at him.

He clasped his hands together, lacing his fingers. "Like I said, I haven't heard anything about any missing persons."

"You do get police reports, I assume?"

"Sure. But like I said, there haven't been any reports of anyone missing."

"Eight teenagers have gone missing in the last three years. You don't think that's the least bit odd?"

He shrugged, unwound his fingers, and spread his hands in apology. "Probably runaways. I try not to publish domestic issues, out of respect for the families. I figure they've got enough to deal with. The last thing they need is to see their troubles splashed across the front page."

An admirable position, I supposed. If we were dealing with runaways. "But even if they were runaways, there should be a police report about it. The parents reported it to the authorities, those officers in turn should have filed a report. Those reports have to be somewhere."

"Then maybe you should check with the sheriff's department. They can probably help you a lot more than I can." He shifted his weight.

"Well, see, that's where the problem starts. The sheriff's department doesn't have any records of these disappearances, either."

Rankin cracked his knuckles then twisted his mouth. "Look, *Mr. Clark*—if the sheriff's department doesn't have it in their records, then we're certainly not going to have it, either. The parents of these missing girls aren't going to come to us before they go to the authorities. Now if you don't mind, I really need to get back to the paper." He stood, reached across the desk, and offered his sweaty hand. "Sorry I couldn't be any help."

I smiled and shook his hand. He'd been more help than he realized. "Thanks for your time, Ed."

"Let me know if you find out anything," he said as he walked me to the front door.

"Oh, I will." I smiled at Miss Congeniality and treated her to a devilish wink. She blushed and hurriedly turned away.

I climbed in the van and turned the air on full blast. So Ed Rankin knew more than he was telling. I purposely never said anything about the missing teens being girls. And if I were a betting man, I'd bet a paycheck, if I were being paid, Rankin was already on the phone with the sheriff. I grinned, satisfied I'd played that one pretty well.

Gaylord Denny would soon know someone was snooping around, digging up information on the eight missing girls from his county. Denny and his two idiot deputies didn't appear to be the brightest bulbs in the lamp and stupid people have a tendency to make sloppy mistakes when they're under a little pressure.

Tomorrow, I'd head back over to Odessa and see if Sophia Ortez was up to scooping her old boss.

I drove back to the house, grabbed a shower, then slipped into a clean pair of shorts and a clean shirt. After that, I headed out to Grigg's Roadhouse. Rhonda mumbled something and shook her head when I told her good-bye.

Monahans was about thirty miles south and more in the middle of nowhere than Wink. As a town, it wasn't Dallas, but it was larger and more populated than Wink. The lingering question of why Monahans kept tickling the gray matter in my head but I kept pushing it toward the brain cells Johnnie Walker had already killed. There were plenty of restaurants in Kermit. I could think of several reasons why she probably chose Monahans, and I didn't like any of them.

Grigg's Roadhouse was about two miles outside the city limit on TX-18 across the street from a strip shopping center and next door to a truck stop that shared a massive parking lot with a motel that charged by the hour.

The roadhouse was a large, wood-sided building with barn-door shutters and hitching posts out front. The parking lot was dominated by pickups of every make and model. I spotted the Silverado right off and parked beside it. A George Strait tune greeted me at the door.

My breath caught somewhere between my lungs and my throat as Claire two-stepped her way over to me. Part of me wanted to turn around, climb back in the van, and head back to Wink where it was safe; the other part wanted to do things to her right there that I'd probably get arrested for.

She smiled softly, then took my hand and led me out to the nearly empty dance floor. A few couples glided their way around the floor, two-stepping in time to George Strait. Some were decked out in tight jeans, western shirts, and boots; others, like me, were in shorts, sandals, and T-shirts and were probably more comfortable in a ball cap than a Stetson. Claire, of course, didn't fit into either category. She made her own rules, wearing a simple white sundress with a halter top and open back that showed off her bronze-colored tan. We stumbled over one another for the first few chords, silently fighting over who was going to lead. After a moment, she gave in, and we once again found our old rhythm. Whether on the dance floor, or in a bed, our bodies had always moved together like a well-oiled machine.

"Well, this is certainly nicer than our last meeting," I whispered in her ear, and smiled.

She laughed and gently stroked my cheek where she had landed the blistering slap. "Sorry about that."

The jukebox slowed down with one of George's ballads. I hesitated before pulling her closer. She wrapped her arms around my neck and laid her head on my shoulder. I breathed her in, my hands finding joy in the curve of her back. I was walking headfirst into dangerous territory and no matter how much that little voice inside my head was telling me to walk away, I couldn't do it. I pulled her even closer, feeling her heart beat in rhythm with my own.

After the song ended, we continued to stand there a moment gently swaying to a melody only we could hear, lost in our own little world of memories and what-could-have-beens.

Finally, Claire lifted her head from my shoulder and smiled. "I guess I need to feed you since I did invite you to dinner."

I grinned and shrugged slightly. Food was the last thing on my mind at the moment.

She pulled away, took my hand, and led me to a booth in the far corner of the restaurant area. "This okay? It's a little bit quieter back here." She slid into the booth and I sat down across from her. There were a few couples scattered around the dining area, far enough apart to ensure privacy.

A waitress in jeans and a T-shirt and with more hair than some wildlife came over and handed us two menus. We ordered two Lone Star beers and a plate of smothered cheese fries to get started.

"So, how long are you staying?" Claire asked after the waitress had left.

"Until I piss Rhonda off or Gram drives me crazy."

She burst out laughing, her blue eyes dancing like tiny sparkling stars. "So you're leaving tomorrow."

After tonight, that might be a possibility. I laughed with her then shook my head slightly. "I don't know. Maybe a couple weeks."

She raised her perfect brows. "Really? Is this like an extended vacation?"

"Who vacations in Wink?"

She twisted her mouth into a tight knot. "Good point."

Before she could delve further, I seized the moment. "So, tell me what you've been up to."

She bobbed her head back and forth. "Just minding the ranch. The Herefords and Longhorns keeps me pretty busy."

"Longhorns? I thought they were almost extinct." I *was*, after all, from Texas.

"They've made a pretty good comeback in recent years. Nothing like a Longhorn." The mere thought brought a twinkle to her eyes.

"No horses?"

She laughed again. "Gypsy . . . you know me better than that. We're still breeding and training quarters, mostly for show and rodeos."

I thought of Rogelio Esconderia. Malita had said he was a wrangler. Just as I was about to broach the subject, the waitress came back with our beers and fries.

"Ready to order dinner?" she asked as she placed the fries between us. Then she set out two small plates.

"Oh . . . we haven't even looked at the menu," Claire said, giggling like a schoolgirl. "Do you know what you want?"

I knew what I wanted but everything about it was wrong. A pale, tan line encircled her finger where a wedding band had obviously been. "I'm fine for now." I smiled at the waitress.

Claire looked at me then shrugged. "Me too."

The waitress sighed. "I'll check back in a little bit."

I took a long swig of the beer and damned if it wasn't good. So there were two things in Texas I missed. And I had the pleasure of both their company tonight.

"Tell me about Vegas."

I took another long drink, thinking of what to say. Less was probably better. "It's . . . interesting."

"How can you stand all the . . . people? I get claustrophobic in Dallas."

I laughed. That was my Claire. More comfortable around a herd of cows than in a crowd of people. "It's different than anything around here, that's for sure."

"Have you ever won big in the casinos?"

"Depends on what you call big. I won ten grand once in a poker tournament."

She squealed to stroke my ego. "Ten thousand dollars? I'm impressed." Ten thousand dollars to Claire Kinley was a week's pay. "God . . . remember the games of poker we used to play? I used to lose on purpose—just so you could undress me."

"You never lost on purpose. You just never could beat me."

"Bull! I can't count the times I let you win."

We laughed until we were both nearly in tears. We spent the next two hours like that, laughing until we cried, reliving memories with such clarity they could have happened only moments ago. We were once again picnicking by the Rio Grande, hiking the Big Bend, sneaking down to Juárez, where teenagers could buy beer.

We never did eat a meal, just sat there picking at the fries and downing beer after beer until we were both buzzed. I never did ask about her husband. Maybe I didn't really want to know.

Garth Brooks's "More than a Memory" hit the jukebox, and this time I led her to the dance floor. I pulled her so close we could feel each other breathe. It had taken me years to get her out of my head; I could honestly say I had never really gotten her out of my heart. "Claire," I whispered, "what are we doing?"

She hesitated, then, with the gentleness of a fairy, brushed her lips across mine. "I don't know," she whispered. "But I don't want it to stop."

Sometime after midnight, I dozed off, lulled to sleep by the constant hum of the rickety air conditioner propped in the dust-covered window. Each wobbly rotation of the ancient ceiling fan hanging above the bed brought a faint but welcome push of air. The red neon sign outside the window flashed VACANCY.

Claire stirred beside me, then settled back into a sound sleep. The air conditioner cycled off; the sudden quietness interrupted my dozing, slapping me fully awake. I lay there for I don't know how long, watching the silhouette of the ceiling fan circle above the bed, wondering what in the hell I'd done.

We had moved together so effortlessly, so naturally, it *couldn't* be wrong. Although nearly twenty years had passed since we had last made love, we were still so in tune with one another, we were driven by instinct. We knew where to touch each other, where to kiss one another, when tenderness was needed and when a heated frenzy was more to the liking. I wondered if her still unnamed husband could take her to the body-spasm heights I could? I wondered if he teetered on the verge of a blackout when she took him in her velvet mouth?

I eased out of the bed, careful not to wake her, slipped my shorts on, then stepped outside. The air was still stifling hot, forcing my lungs to work overtime just to catch a breath. The crowd at the roadhouse had long gone, drawing unwanted attention to the lone van and Dually still parked where they had been hours ago, the occupants' whereabouts obvious given the close proximity to the pay-by-the-hour motel next door. I walked down to the vending machine near the motel's office and dropped a dollar for a bottled water, then walked back to the room. I sat in the cheap motel room chair across from the bed and watched her sleep.

My head and my heart weren't in agreement. Damn Claire Kinley. Or whatever her married name was. Did he hate her as much as I did? Did he love her as much as I did? Did she love him, like she used to love me? There had been many women in my life, but only one Claire. Once, when we were teenagers, she came damn close to killing her own father to protect me. There were times after that I often wondered if pure love and hate really could spark the fire of insanity. Rhonda had been right. Claire Kinley was the only woman who had ever taken me to my knees.

"What are you doing?" Claire asked in a sleepy voice. She sat up, covering herself with the damp sheet. She brushed tangled hair from her eyes.

I didn't answer her. There were so many things I wanted to say, but kept coming back to the one thing I wasn't sure I wanted to know.

"Gypsy?"

"Tell me about your husband."

She stared at me for what seemed like an eternity. Even in the shadowy darkness, I could see the fury in her eyes. Finally, she sighed heavily, then fell back on the bed. "His name's Steven," she said matter-of-factly.

"How long have you been married?"

"Twelve years. Twelve long years."

Cue the excuses. I was sure there were dozens of reasons she was in a fleabag motel with a man other than her husband, and I had heard them all. He doesn't pay any attention to me . . . he works all the time . . . he's a lousy lover . . . I'm lonely . . . I'm horny . . . I like the excitement, and, my personal favorite, he's screwing around, too. Nothing like a good revenge fuck to screw with everybody's heart.

"Does Steven work on the ranch, too?"

She sighed heavily again, then propped herself on her elbow and stared at me. "He's a state senator. He spends ten months out of the year in Austin."

Ahh . . . so it was going to be the combo special: "he works all the time, I'm so lonely" excuse. And judging by the way she was in bed a few hours ago, you could probably safely add the "I'm horny" excuse, too.

"Gypsy," she said softly.

I pulled myself up from the chair, then slowly walked over to the window and stared out at the blinking sign, a flashing reminder of my indiscretion. "I'm not in the habit of sleeping with married women, Claire. I've seen too often the trouble it brings."

I felt a pillow whap me on the back. "You pompous ass!"

I spun around and came face-to-face with her fury.

"How dare you judge *me*! Unless you made some earth-shattering discovery within the last few hours, you knew I was married when you met me here." She leapt out of the bed, dragging the sheet with her. She wrapped it around herself then flung another pillow at me. I batted it down, which infuriated her even more. She headed toward me, trapping me in the corner. "Don't get righteous with me, Gypsy Moran. You were pretty quick to drop your pants, too."

"Why didn't you tell me when I ran into you at the diner?"

"We spoke . . . what? Maybe five minutes?"

"You had plenty of time tonight at the restaurant to tell me."

Her eyes cut right through to my soul. "Would you have left?"

Neither of us said anything for a long while. We just stood there staring at each other, hating each other more than humanly possible. Loving each other more than either of us ever imagined. No matter the years and distance, some things will never change.

"I used to wish I could stop loving you," she said in a tiny voice. "I wished *every night* you'd come back and love me the way I loved you. But you never came back. You never came back, Gypsy."

I took a step toward her. "I begged you to come with me."

"And I begged you to *stay*."

I reached out, grabbed her, and pulled her to me. Her warm tears rolled down my bare chest. I lifted her chin and gently kissed away each tear, wishing to God I could stop loving her.

CHAPTER 10

It was approaching 5:00 A.M. when I pulled into Rhonda's driveway. All I wanted to do was crawl into a decent bed and catch a couple hours' sleep. Claire and I had made love the rest of the night, never mentioning what's his name or how wrong it was for us to be there, or how right it was.

I climbed out of the van and stumbled up the walk, then quietly opened the door. Or tried to. I tried it again as quietly as I could, not wanting to wake Rhonda or Gram. I finally jiggled the knob—it was locked. She had locked me out!

I thought of going around to her bedroom and banging on the window but I wasn't in the mood for a lecture so I stumbled back to the van, laid the seat back as far as it would go, and tried to get an hour in before the dawn broke. Damn her. Damn Claire. And damn Gina Gilleni. Damn women in general. If Gina hadn't gone and gotten herself killed I wouldn't have had to leave Vegas, I wouldn't have run into Claire and slept with a married woman, and I wouldn't be sleeping in a van in my sister's driveway because she was pissed and locked the door.

It was miserable hot even with the windows down and I was hungry to boot. We never did eat dinner and my stomach was protesting. I didn't want to crank the engine and run the air out of fear of some freak leak somewhere that would pump the van full of carbon monoxide.

I was totally drained physically, mentally, and emotionally. Either I dozed off or passed out from hunger and heat exhaustion because the last thing I remembered before my eyes closed was cussing Rhonda for everything she was worth. And now here she was in a tank top and pajama shorts standing beside the van, arms folded across her chest, jaw set firm. I batted my eyes against the painful sunshine and struggled to sit up, reminding myself of an old man trying to get out of a recliner.

"What time is it?" I asked, my throat as parched as the Texas landscape.

"Seven-thirty. I've got the coffee on." She turned on her heel and stomped back to the house.

I didn't want coffee. I wanted a real bed with a real pillow in a cold room. I forced my legs to carry me inside. Rhonda was stationed at the arch between the kitchen and living room, sipping a cup of coffee through the scowl on her face.

"I'll grab a cup later," I mumbled. "Right now I'm goin' grab a few hours of sleep. How about waking me up around ten?" I did need to drive back up to Odessa and visit with Sophia Ortez again.

She pursed her lips and nodded, then asked coldly, "How was your *dinner*?"

I took a deep breath and steeled myself for the coming lecture. "It was nice."

She nodded again. "I bet. Next time check yourself in the mirror before heading out. Your shirt's on inside out."

I was so busted.

At 10:15, Rhonda flipped open the blinds and smacked my bare feet. "Up and at 'em."

I squeezed my eyes closed against the light.

"Tatum called and wanted to know if you needed him today." She sat a fresh cup of steaming coffee on the nightstand, then sat down on the edge of the bed.

Tatum. My sidekick. I grumbled, then sat up and swung my legs over the side of the bed. I pushed my fingers through my mussed-up hair. It was damp with sweat and sticky with fluids I was too much of a gentleman to identify. "Tell Tatum he has the day off. Tell him I said to take Alvedia swimming, cool off those pubescent hormones."

Rhonda laughed. "He'd probably like that except he can't swim."

I glanced at her then took a long drink of coffee. "Seriously?"

She shrugged. "Seriously. He's terrified of water. One of the kids had an end-of-school pool party and I thought the poor kid was goin' to have a heart attack."

I thought all kids these days could swim. What'd I know?

"Rodney'll be home this afternoon," Rhonda said. She was gnawing on her bottom lip, a sure indication there was more to the statement than what was said.

I sighed. "You want me to get a motel room?"

Her eyes flew wide and she quickly shook her head. "No— that's not what I meant."

Thank God. I didn't know if I could stand another night on a motel bed.

She tugged on her right ear, a habit she'd had since she was a kid when something was weighing on her mind.

"Okay . . . so Rodney will be home this afternoon. And that means . . . ?"

"Remember I told you he didn't want me to get involved with Ryce's death," she said in a small voice, still gnawing on her lip.

I recalled the conversation and nodded. "He told you to leave it alone."

She gazed at me with pitiful eyes. I took another long drink of coffee, considering our options. Did I help her keep a secret from her husband? Between her, Claire, and the recently deceased Gina Gilleni, I wondered if I was wearing a sign on my back saying TRUST ME, I WON'T TELL YOUR HUSBAND.

I let out a long breath. "He told *you* to leave it alone. He didn't tell me to."

Her eyes lit up and matched her tentative smile. "You'll cover for me?"

I draped my arm around her shoulder and gave it a gentle squeeze. "I won't tell your husband your little secret if you won't lecture me about Claire."

"Uh—Gypsy! That's not fair." She punched my shoulder. "Someone has to talk some sense into that head of yours about that woman."

It wasn't my head that needing talking to. "That's the deal, baby. Take it or I spill my guts as soon as he walks through the door."

She sprung up from the bed and stomped out of the room, mumbling something about me being evil.

I grabbed a quick shower, then powered up the laptop at the kitchen table. Gram was at the table eating some graham crackers with peanut butter. She looked like a dog trying to lick peanut butter from the roof of its mouth. Must be a bitch getting old.

I Googled the phone number for the *Odessa Record,* then punched the number in my cell. I listened to the dial-by-name directory, then pressed Sophia Ortez's extension.

"This is Sophia Ortez," she said on the second ring.

"Miss Ortez—Gypsy Moran. We met earlier in the week."

"Ah, Mr. Moran. The private investigator. What can I do for you?"

"Have lunch with me. I have a story you might be interested in."

She hesitated before saying anything. "Does it involve Sergeant McCallen?"

"Not directly. Remember that Pulitzer you were chasing? This story might get you noticed."

"You're goin' to have to tell me more than that."

"Trust me—it'll go national."

"Trust you? I don't even know you. You're goin' to have to give me a reason to cancel my lunchtime hair appointment."

I grinned. Miss Ortez was pretty sharp. "Eight missing girls and a human trafficking ring. That enough to pique your interest?"

"Missing from this area? Why haven't we heard anything about it before now?"

"My point exactly."

She didn't say anything for a moment, then said, "The Rojo Grande, one o'clock."

"I'll see you there."

We hung up and I map-searched the address, then keyed it into my phone's GPS. I then searched for Reeves County Detention Center and clicked on the Web site. I did an inmate search for Hector Martinez. There were twelve inmates named Hector Martinez so I narrowed the search by age. There were five between the ages of seventeen and twenty-three, but only one pulling time for attempted murder and assault on a law-enforcement officer. Hector Martinez was in gen-pop with no altercations so paying him a visit tomorrow shouldn't be an issue.

I gathered up Ryce's files and the copies I had made of Peterson's and McCoy's finances and personal information, and gave Rhonda a peck on the cheek. "I'm off to Odessa. I'll check in later."

She glared at me with narrowed eyes. "Are you going to be here for dinner . . . or do you have *other plans*? I'm not lecturing. Just asking."

"Lecturing about what?" Gram asked. "Did he get laid?"

"I'll be here." I grinned. Although, truthfully, I wasn't looking forward to the Crock-Pot mystery meat that never made it past simmer. Besides, I needed a night to recover. Last night proved I wasn't seventeen anymore.

The Rojo Grande was, as expected, a barn-shaped building the color of ripe tomatoes. The sign out front guaranteed the BEST TEX-MEX IN TOWN! Sophia was seated on the leather bench beside the hostess stand and smiled slightly when I entered. She was wearing white capris and a sleeveless black top, the top button strategically unbuttoned. I liked Sophia Ortez. She knew how to play the game. Any other time, I would have considered playing along, but at the moment, I didn't have the energy to even flirt.

The hostess seated us at a back booth, handed us the menus, and said the waitress Tammy would be with us in a minute.

"So, tell me about these eight missing girls," she said, direct and to the point. No fooling around with this gal. Maybe that top button was unbuttoned because it was 112 freaking degrees outside.

"All between the ages of thirteen and fifteen. All illegals."

She nodded. "So there's no paper trail or way to identify them."

"Exactly."

"And you have proof of this?"

Tammy the waitress hustled over to take our order. Sophia ordered a chicken and black bean special; I ordered the *pollo adobado* and an extra glass of water.

"Do I have proof?" I said after Tammy had left. "Yes and no."

She glared at me with the eyes of a trained skeptic. "I'm not going to win that Pulitzer with a story I can't prove."

"It's a complicated situation, Sophia."

She nodded, unimpressed. "Life in general's complicated." She glanced at the thin gold watch on her wrist. "You have thirty minutes to un-complicate it."

I leaned into the booth, speaking quietly. "Remember when you were in Wink and were told to forget about the Burke McCallen story?"

She stared at me, unflinching.

"Why do you think you were told to ignore one of the biggest news stories in the area?"

"My editor wanted to present happy news. The shooting of a cop didn't fit his editorial philosophy."

"Bullshit. You know the reason he wouldn't run it."

She huffed and sat back in the booth, pressing her back against the soft leather. "It's like I told you the other day—the information wasn't exactly forthcoming."

"Exactly. And why do you think that is?"

She looked away and stared at the two teenage girls in the booth across from us. "So you're chasing a conspiracy theory."

I patted Ryce's files. "It's not a theory. I just need a little help proving it."

Tammy brought our lunch, laid the ticket at the corner of my plate, then went to refill the two teenagers' drinks.

"Are there claims of UFOs in that folder, too?" She dug into her lunch.

I laughed and shook my head. "No UFOs. Just a crap load of police corruption at its worst."

I told her everything I had learned so far about Peterson and

McCoy, Sheriff Gaylord Denny's long-reaching arms, and Ryce's death. I told her about Hector Martinez and Alvedia, and about the eight missing girls.

She studied the files with interest, then asked, "What is it you want me to do?"

"Do what you've been trained to do—start digging for the truth."

She grinned, then pushed her empty plate aside. "No offense, but aren't you a private investigator?"

I returned the smile and laughed softly. "At least that's what it says on my business cards." I finished off the hot-as-hell chicken concoction and drained my third glass of water. Once my tongue had cooled, I leaned into the booth to explain the situation. "Look, I need help because I'm not licensed in Texas. I haven't checked into the state's reciprocity laws yet, but I need help from someone in an investigative field."

"And what about any evidence you gather? It won't be admissible in court and could cause charges to be brought against you."

I scratched my head. "I'm working on all that."

She nodded slowly, apparently not believing me. She was smart as well as gorgeous. "Why don't you just go to the Rangers' office? Investigating corruption is one of the things they do best."

"I will. When I've got a nice, neat little package all wrapped up for them." I motioned for Tammy to refill my water. "Look, whether or not you ever write a story about this is totally up to you. But I want the sheriff and his two henchmen to think someone's digging around for a story. People get sloppy when they get a little nervous. Sooner or later, they mess up. It's human nature."

"And you want to be there when they mess up."

I grinned. "Camped out in the van with the cameras rolling."

CHAPTER 11

By the time I got back to Rhonda's, Rodney's police cruiser was parked in the driveway. Although I had promised Rhonda I wouldn't let on that she had played a part in initiating the investigation into Ryce's death, I was anxious to hear what Rodney knew about it. Her secret was safe, but it wasn't going to stop me from picking his brain.

Rodney was a good guy. He was friendly, didn't drink excessively, and adored Rhonda. If he was anything, he was boring. Rhonda had settled for safe.

"Gypsy!" he said, springing up from the sofa as I walked in. He wrapped me in a bear hug. "Good to see you again, man."

"It's good to see you, too. How was the training?"

"Good. Very informative." He sat back down on the sofa and continued pulling on a pair of sneakers. "I'm heading over to the gym for a game of hoops. Want to come?"

He had put on some weight since I saw him last and was the proud owner of a bulging belly. He still had a buzz cut, a style leftover from his army days. He was wearing those wretched net shorts and a T-shirt with the Nike logo.

Rhonda bounded into the living room, smiling at me nervously. "Look, Gypsy, Rodney's home."

I smiled back at her. "Yeah, I see."

"I invited him to come shoot some hoops with me." Rodney stared at me, looking me up and down. "You want to change into something more comfortable?"

"Ah . . . sure. I'll grab my other shoes." I had about as much interest in a game of basketball as I had in riding a horse. But it would give me a chance to see what he knew about Ryce's death.

Rhonda followed me back to the spare bedroom, staying close to my heels. I dug around in the cardboard boxes until I found my black ankle socks, then sat down on the side of the bed.

"You're not going to say anything, are you?" she whispered.

I slipped the socks on, then pulled on my shoes. "I told you your little secret was safe."

"Shh!" She glanced over her shoulder. "I just wanted to make sure you remembered. You hadn't had a full cup of coffee when you promised."

I stood up and kissed her on the check. "As long as you hold up your end of the bargain, I'll hold up mine. Ahh . . . *Claire*. Like the smell of jasmine in the air," I teased.

"Whatever," she grumbled. She grabbed my elbow as I moved past her. "Gypsy—he's a little out of shape. Don't wipe the court with him."

"You ready?" Rodney yelled from the living room.

Thirty minutes later, we were pulling into the parking lot of the Kermit Recreation Center, the same center where Burke was shot. I did a quick count of the number of unmarked cars in the parking lot and decided the game just got a lot more interesting.

The rec center was an older one-story building with a weight room, full-sized basketball court, and small meeting rooms where different civic groups did whatever they do. Behind the center were three ball fields and two concession stands. I wondered which one Hector Martinez was allegedly breaking into when he supposedly shot Burke.

I tagged along behind Rodney into the gym where a group of stout-looking guys were lacing sneakers, stretching their muscles, or punching one another in mock fights. They greeted Rodney in a fraternal way with lots of fist tapping and high fives.

"This is Rhonda's brother. He's in from Vegas for a while so y'all go easy on the city boy."

They laughed like a bunch of drunk sailors, some offering their hands to shake along with their first names. My interest perked up when a tall guy with shoulders broader than a doorway introduced himself as Mark. Could I really be that lucky?

Big Mark palmed a ball and headed out onto the court for some practice shots. The name across the back of his jersey said Peterson. I smiled, grabbed a ball, and joined him at the foul line.

I sank a couple, missed a few, and stood back when big Mark dunked one, hanging onto the rim a few seconds for dramatic purposes. All of a sudden I was hearing my Little League coach reminding me baseball games were won by base hits, not by trying to put it over the fence at each bat. Besides, he used to say, you ain't all that big, *boy*.

Big Mark divided us into teams, putting me and Rodney on the same team, which, of course, wasn't his. Ten minutes later, I was wishing I had stayed at Rhonda's and taken a nap.

These guys played like scouts from the Lakers were in the stands. They played full court, which left me sucking for breath, and I was in pretty decent shape. Poor Rodney plugged along, his belly flopping with each heart attack–inducing sprint. Somehow, the man-on-man defense pitted me, at a full inch shy of six feet and 180 pounds, against Monster Mark, who I was sure topped out at six five and weighed in well over 220.

To everyone's surprise, and the monster's embarrassment, I managed to weasel in and steal the ball right out from under him in mid-dribble, then sink a three-pointer. The constant squeak of the rubber soles against the wooden floor came to an abrupt halt as everyone froze in place. Seconds later, they erupted in hooting and hollering and juvenile cheers, rewarding me with slaps on the back. Monster Mark sported a fake grin, unimpressed.

The elbows started flying soon after. The first one was to the ribs and I let it go. The second time was to the kidneys and it took me a moment to catch my breath. The third time was to the mouth and drew blood. I used the tail of my shirt to wipe my busted lip, the coppery-tasting blood pooling between my lip and bottom teeth.

"You okay?" Rodney asked in a winded voice. He was beside me, bent over, trying to catch a much-needed breath.

"Yeah." I spit blood then wiped my mouth again. "I'm fine."

"He . . . takes it a little too seriously."

"So do I." I wiped my hand across my bloodied lip. I stared at the blood on the back of my hand. I don't tolerate bullies very well. I hurried to rejoin the game.

Peterson was near the foul line preparing for an unguarded jump shot. I leapt just as he let go, slamming the ball back in his face. Blood gushed from his nose from the impact. Rodney grabbed the ball and actually ran it to the other end of the court and scored. He and one of our teammates did the obligatory chest bump, then finished with high fives while Peterson remained at his own foul line, hands on his hips, blood running from his nose, his eyes slicing through me like a sword.

During our next possession, Rodney passed the ball to me. I drove in for a layup, shoving my shoulder square into Peterson's chest, driving him backward. He lost his balance and went down on his ass. With that shot, we were up by a basket.

The next couple of plays were a back-and-forth of missed shots and smack downs but no goals. Since I seemed to be the go-to man of our team, one of my teammates passed me the ball for an easy jumper. I was clear; Peterson was nowhere around. I steadied for the shot and just as I hit midair, Peterson was suddenly there, connecting with a massive knee straight to the crotch.

I dropped with a thud to my knees, then all fours. I fought the urge to curl up in the fetal position and shout to Monster Mark that he had won.

Rodney protectively had his hand on my back. "You okay, man?"

Hell no, I wasn't okay. I would probably feel a hell of a lot better if he'd put a bullet through my head.

"Oh, come on Mark, that was a low blow," someone said.

"Dude . . . that was pretty rough, don't you think?" another one said.

My head was spinning and the voices were melding together as tiny stars danced in front of my eyes.

"So Pretty Boy does have balls," Peterson said. I etched his voice to memory.

One of the guys from the other team brought me a bottled water. Rodney hooked his arm under mine and helped me sit up. I took tiny sips of the water, afraid it would get hung on the testicles lodged in my throat.

Rodney stood beside me like a faithful pup while I sat there on my knees. Finally, with the pain just a little less than unbearable, I managed with Rodney's help to stand up.

"Same time next week," Peterson said to his cop buddies, slinging a gym bag over his shoulder. There were collective mumbles of confirmation.

"Let's go," I told Rodney, pushing through the pain just to walk.

He was behind me with his hand on my back, probably afraid

I'd go down again any minute. "Come on, Gypsy. Don't start anything," he said, his voice racked with concern.

"I'm not starting anything." But I was sure goin' to finish it. I
was going to make sure Peterson would have time to play with all
the balls he wanted. There were guys in prison just waiting to
make someone like Mark Peterson their bitch.

Outside, in the parking lot, I watched him climb into his
department-issued burgundy Crown Vic and drive away. It was
going to be a pleasure to take him down.

"I think Rhonda's got some frozen peas at home you could use
as an ice pack," Rodney said.

I was not going to put a pack of frozen peas on my crotch. I
took a deep breath and held it as I climbed into Rodney's pickup.
"I'll be all right." As long as I didn't move or breathe.

Rodney cranked the engine, then pulled out onto the road, following the procession. "I don't know what got into him today. He's
always cocky and likes to throw his weight around, but man, you
pushed a button or something."

"What do you know about this guy?"

"Mark?" He shrugged. "He can be a jerk sometimes."

"My testicles are proof of that. What else?"

He shrugged again. "I don't really know him personally. I
worked a case with him last year and he was all right. I guess."

There was hesitation between statements, which meant everything might not have been as *all right* as Rodney thought. "What
do you mean, you guess?"

"He's pretty stubborn. It's his way or the highway."

I stared out the passenger window at the barren landscape.
Peterson definitely fit the profile of a cop on the take. Living well
above his means, he pissed attitude, and he had the grand illusion
of being irreproachable.

We passed the sinkholes, Wink's two claims to fame. The second one to form was much larger than the first and now had a dilapidated fence around the massive perimeter. The red DANGER signs were visible from the road. As long as Mark Peterson was wearing a badge, the giant, sucking sinkholes weren't the county's only danger.

"What do you know about Ryce McCallen's death?" I asked.

Rodney threw me a sideways glance, his brows knitted with question. "Ryce McCallen?"

"Yeah—the cop that supposedly killed himself a few weeks ago."

His face turned cherry red as he slammed his palm against the steering wheel. "Damn her. I told her to stay out of that."

"Told who to stay out of what?"

"Your sister. I told her to leave it alone."

"Rhonda's not involved. Burke McCallen hired me to look into his son's death."

He slammed the wheel again, pursing his lips into a tight line. He shook his head slowly. "Leave it alone, Gypsy. You don't know what you're getting yourself into."

"How much do you know about it?" I prayed to God, for Rhonda's sake, that Rodney wasn't turning his head the other way.

"I know Burke McCallen may not want to know the truth. Sometimes things are better left unsaid."

"Ryce wasn't on the up-and-up?"

He cut his eyes at me. "More like on the down-low."

I wasn't expecting that one. "Ryce was gay?"

He pulled into the driveway and parked beside the cruiser. He didn't seem to be in any hurry to head inside. "From what I understand, he had a fondness for teenage boys. He supposedly got caught up in a sting over in Odessa and . . . I guess the shame of

being arrested and exposed, drove him to do what he did. Everybody kind of kept it hush-hush out of respect for the family."

It would be a believable story if not for the file I had in the
spare bedroom.

"I ain't telling you what to do, Gypsy . . . but if I were you,
I'd think twice about digging too deep. That poor kid's been
through enough as it is."

His concern was genuine. At least I knew now Rhonda's
husband wasn't turning his head. He was just looking down the
wrong road. "I've got something to show you when we get inside,"
I said.

He sat there without saying anything, staring at me hard.
After a moment of stern silence, we got out and I hobbled up the
walkway.

Inside, Rhonda had the table set for dinner. The mystery meat
was proudly displayed on a platter beside a bowl of shiny green
peas. My ice pack, ready to eat.

"Good Lord," Rhonda gasped. "What happened?" She flew
over to inspect my busted lip.

Gram was at the table, staring at me through her thick glasses.
I moved slowly to the table and eased into the chair.

"Rodney?" Rhonda spun around and glared at him. "What
happened?"

He slowly shrugged. "Things got a little rough."

"A little rough? He looks like he's been in a bar fight." She
grabbed a rag and wet it, then attempted to scrub the dried blood
from around my mouth, doing more damage than good.

I squealed like a girl, pushing her hand away. It was a good
thing she was a great teacher because she would have made a lousy
nurse.

"Dinner ready? It sure smells good." Rodney was either trying to change the subject or my injuries had taken a backseat to his hunger.

"It's ready," Rhonda said. "Gypsy, take your shirt off and let me get that blood out before it stains."

"I'm . . . fine," I said, but she was already headed back to the spare bedroom to get me another shirt.

"Brad Whitlock used to beat the shit out of you everyday on your way home from school," Gram said.

I stared at her, wondering why she wasn't in a nursing home.

When Rhonda came back, she helped me pull the T-shirt up over my head then let out another gasp. "Good God—Rodney! What did y'all do to him?"

"I didn't do anything! Holy shit—did he ever nail you."

I glanced down and on the right side of my rib cage, spreading around to my back, was a dark purple bruise the size of a small island. And I thought having my nuts driven up into my lungs was the reason I couldn't breathe.

Gram poked two arthritic fingers at my ribs. "Hurt?"

"Hell yeah it hurts!"

Rhonda pushed Gram's hand away, then poked at the bruise herself. "You're going to need ice, or something on that. You might have broke ribs."

"Can we eat now?" Rodney asked.

My ice pack was sitting in a bowl on the table with Rodney and Gram eyeing it. Damn, it hurt to laugh, but I couldn't help it. "Rhonda, I'm fine. Let's eat before Rodney has a stroke."

Rodney took his cue that he had my blessing to eat and filled his plate. Rhonda frowned. "You sure you don't want me to make up an ice pack?"

"I'll be fine. Now sit. Eat."

She frowned again then sat down beside Rodney. "Did you

actually get in a fight, or did you trip, or what?" she asked as she sawed into the meat on her plate.

"Oh, that's not the worst of it," Rodney said between mouthfuls. "But I don't think he wants to show you *that* bruise."

Rhonda stared at me a moment then her eyes widened. "Oh. *There*, too?"

"That sucks," Gram said.

"Let's just say I had to help him to the truck." Rodney speared another chunk of meat and plopped it on this plate.

Rhonda grimaced. "So who were these guys? Are they the same guys you play with all the time?" She looked at Rodney.

He shrugged. "The normal guys. I don't know what it was, but something about Gypsy tripped Mark Peterson's trigger."

Rhonda cut her eyes at me.

"Mark Peterson?" Gram asked. "Isn't he one of the—"

"Gram, could you pass the corn, please," Rhonda snapped.

Gram looked around the table. "What corn?"

Rodney stared from one to the other like they had both lost their minds. He shrugged it off then went back to eating.

I took a small bite of the mystery meat and to my surprise, it wasn't that bad. Amazing what thirty-six hours in a Crock-Pot can do.

CHAPTER 12

After dinner, Gram retired to her room to watch television. I went to the bedroom and got Ryce's file, then carried it back to the kitchen. I set it on the table in front of Rodney. "Take a look at it and then tell me if you still think Ryce McCallen killed himself."

Rhonda was at the sink rinsing the dishes and spun around, her face etched with fear.

"I told Rodney about Burke McCallen hiring me to look into Ryce's death," I said. She swallowed hard, then hurriedly turned back to the dishes.

Rodney stared at the file, hesitating to open it. "What is it?" His voice had taken a deeper, serious tone.

"It's a case Ryce was working before he died. It probably raises more questions than it answers, but they're questions that deserve an answer."

He sighed heavily, then flipped open the file. His brows raised a notch as he stared at Mark Peterson's financials. "He was keeping a file on Mark Peterson?" He looked up at me, his eyes shadowed with uncertainty.

"That's actually my file. I don't know that Ryce had started putting two and two together yet, but the mere fact that he's dead tells me he was on the right track. And apparently Mark Peterson knew he was on the right track, even if Ryce didn't."

He read on, stopping every now and then to ask a question. Rhonda had finished the dishes and joined us at the table. "Do you think Mark Peterson knew who you were?" she asked me.

I shook my head. I'd considered it after the knee to the crotch but quickly discarded the thought. "I'm sure he knows by now that someone's snooping around but I don't think he can trace it back to me. Not yet, anyway."

Rodney closed the file, then furiously rubbed his hands over his face. He let out a heavy breath and propped his chin on his hands. His face was cherry red again, like it was in the truck. He looked like an overheated bulldog.

"How much do you know about this?" he asked sharply, turning to Rhonda.

"Just what I've told her," I said. "We were about to get busted and there wasn't anything I could do about it."

"Where'd you get this file from?"

"Burke," I lied. "Ryce kept it at home."

He quickly nodded. "And how did you meet Burke?"

"Tatum asked me for his phone number," Rhonda quietly offered.

"And that's why you're here? To work this case?"

"Look, Rodney—it doesn't matter how he got hired, what matters is there's some serious wrongdoing going on and the McCallens are just the tip of it."

Rodney leaned back in the chair and locked his hands behind his head. "What matters is I don't want you involved in it."

"There's eight missing girls—"

"And Mark Peterson nearly castrated your brother today during a basketball game! A basketball game, Rhonda . . . can you imagine what he'd do if he really thought he was being threatened?"

I couldn't go to bat for her on that one. The farther she stayed away from all this, the better I'd feel. "So you think there's something to it?" I pointed at the file.

He scrubbed his face again with his hands, then sighed heavily. "It could be. But you know as well as I do, Gypsy, there's not enough evidence there linking Peterson to those girls to even get an indictment."

"Are you crazy?" Rhonda grabbed the file. "There's plenty of—"

"Coincidences," I said. "Rhonda, he's right. The most anyone could nail him with right now would be sloppy police work for not filing a missing persons report on the girls. Even if there was enough to bring charges, any half-ass defense attorney would laugh all the way to the bank."

Her disappointment turned to anger. "So he's just going to get away with it?"

"He didn't say that," Rodney said. "What he said was we need more proof."

I liked that "we" part.

"So you're going to help him?" Rhonda asked.

He scratched at his head. "I need to do some thinking on it. Would you be a sweetheart and run down to the store and grab a six-pack?"

She looked a little confused but agreed. Obviously it wasn't something Rodney requested everyday.

"Y'all want anything else?" she asked, her car keys in hand.

"Get Lone Star." I'm a picky drinker.

She was barely out the door when Rodney leaned in, folded his arms on the table, and looked at me hard. "Last summer, Rhonda and I got hit for about a month with one thing after the other. Her car blew a head gasket and that cost about two grand to repair, the central air went out and that had to be replaced, the motor on the washer went out and it was going to cost more to have that replaced than to buy a new set. We just had a real string of bad luck."

"Rodney, if you and Rhonda ever need anything, all you have to do is call. I'm not Wells Fargo, but I've got a little put back."

He was quick to shake his head. "You're missing the point. Every week I'd go to the gym bitching and moaning about some new disaster we couldn't afford. After about a month of listening to my sob stories, Peterson said he had a job I could do, make a little extra money."

He had my full attention. "Did you ask him what kind of job?"

He shook his head. "He said we'd talk about it later. I messed up my knee and missed a couple games and he never said anything else about it."

"You think he was trying to recruit you?"

He shrugged. "I don't know. Hell, he could have been talking about mowing yards for all I know."

He was right, so I tried to keep a level head. "But what if he wasn't? What if he was trying to recruit you? Rodney, you could be our way in."

He threw both hands in the air. "Whoa! As much I want to help, man, I'm not so sure about that. Apparently, Peterson has no qualms about killing a fellow officer or trying to take the balls off a guy for something as little as showing him up on the court."

I could understand where he was coming from, and I couldn't say I blamed him. But there were eight teenage girls out there somewhere having to do things no one should be forced to do. I wanted to make sure there wouldn't be a ninth. "Rodney, the girls that are missing . . . realistically, I don't know if we'd ever be able to find them. But they deserve to at least have someone look for them. A twenty-four-hour surveillance on Peterson is a waste of time if I don't have a general idea of when he's going to make a move. If I had you on the inside—"

"Just hold up a minute." He rubbed his face again with his hands then blew a long, deep breath. "I'm a patrol officer, Gypsy. I write traffic tickets, do welfare checks, and break up the occasional bar fight. I know everybody comes on the force with grand illusions of being a top-notch investigator. They dream of breaking their first homicide case. They get an adrenaline rush with a high-speed chase." He looked at me with truthful eyes. "I'm not one of those guys. I'm sorry, Gypsy—I'm just not the Superman kind."

Rhonda came in carrying two six-packs and a pound bag of coffee. "Man, it's still a hundred degrees out there."

Rodney leapt up and helped her, relieving her of the heavy bottles. I wondered how many of those top-notch investigators would have jumped up to help their wives carry such a small load?

He tossed me a beer, took one for himself, then put the cardboard carriers in the refrigerator.

"So, did y'all discuss what you needed to when you sent me on a bogus errand?" Rhonda said and smiled.

I laughed as I popped the top. "A beer run is never a bogus errand."

"You could have just told me to go watch TV." She kissed Rodney on the cheek.

He grinned sheepishly. "Uh-huh. And your ear would have been plastered to the wall." He took a long drink, then sat back down at the table. He turned to me. "I'll help you with surveillance, or running reports, or doing your legwork."

"I appreciate it." And I did. But it would make it so much easier if he, just once, wanted to be Superman. "Is there an investigator you've worked with in the past who might let me work under their license?"

He glared at me over the top of the bottle. "Shit. You're not licensed in Texas."

Rhonda sat down between us. The technicalities of an investigation were over her head so she looked back and forth between us as if she were watching the French Open. "So, what does not being licensed in Texas mean?"

Rodney sighed. "It means whatever evidence your brother manages to get wouldn't be allowed in court. And could end up getting him in trouble."

She looked confused. "But evidence is evidence. I mean, if the proof is there, how can they not allow it?"

"If the evidence is obtained illegally, then it can't be used," Rodney said.

"Illegally? But y'all aren't doing anything illegal, are you?"

Rodney rubbed his forehead with his fingertips. "Your brother doesn't have a license to gather evidence in Texas—"

"That's never stopped him before."

"Whoa!" I threw my hands up in defense. "I'm legit. Most of the time."

Rodney slowly shook his head. "Maybe we should just call the Rangers' office."

"We will," I said. "As soon as I have something to give them."

The next morning, I showered and shaved, carefully navigating the razor around my busted lip. I dug around in the cardboard boxes until I found what I needed: a pair of khakis and a black, short-sleeved button-down shirt. Although I had folded everything very neatly before shoving it in the box, the road trip had been hard.

I carried the pants and shirt into the kitchen, where Rhonda
was putting away last night's dinner dishes. Gram was at the table
slurping her oatmeal. "Do you have an iron?" I asked.

Rhonda stared at me like she wasn't sure what I had asked.

"An iron . . . to get the wrinkles out?"

"Oh, an iron. Of course I have one." She grinned, embarrassed.
She went to the laundry closet and drug out the brand-new ironing
board and never-used iron. "We just usually throw whatever we
want to wear back in the dryer for a few minutes."

I set up the board, plugged in the iron, and adjusted the setting, then got a cup of water from the tap and carefully poured it
into the reservoir.

"You have to add water?" She picked up the iron and examined it closely.

I smiled. God love her. "I don't suppose you have any spray
starch?"

Gram laughed. Rhonda pursed her lips, then shook her head.

No starch. It wasn't the end of the word. At least I could walk
and my testicles were back where they belonged. Life was good.

"Black shirt and long pants . . . you do know it's supposed to
be a scorcher today?" Rhonda asked.

"Why should today be any different? I'm going to Reeves County
Detention Center today to pay Hector Martinez a visit. I need to look
the part." I finished the pants and laid them gently across the back of
a chair, then ironed the shirt.

"The part?"

I smiled. "You'll see."

Back in the bedroom, I pulled on the khakis and the shirt, complete with belt, then slipped on a pair of loafers. I then scrounged
around in the boxes until I found the rest of the outfit. In a separate
box, I found my accordion-style file folder holding various IDs. I

found the one I needed and slipped it into an empty manila folder, then started out.

I met Rhonda in the hallway. She stared at me with a dumbfounded expression. "A priest? Oh, good Lord."

"He is good, isn't he?" I smiled and adjusted the white snap-on collar poking out of my shirt.

"Do I even want to know what you're doing?"

"Probably not."

She slowly shook her head. "Sometimes I wonder about you, Gypsy."

I kissed the top of her head. "That's Father Mike to you, missy. Can I borrow Rodney's truck for a little while?"

She had a puzzled look on her face. "Sure. I guess."

"I don't know if they do a vehicle search at Reeves and if they do, they might wonder why a priest has surveillance equipment and a hundred thousand dollars worth of cameras in his van. The Catholic Church doesn't need any more scandal."

Outside, I paid for the sin of impersonating a priest. The black shirt was a magnet for the heat. It was barely 9:00 and the thermometer in the truck was already hitting 94 degrees. The weatherman on the local news said the high today would hit 105. His fake smile gave the impression it was something we were supposed to look forward to.

I grabbed my favorite Nikon from the van and carefully tucked it away in the truck's glove compartment. I planned to head back over to Burke's later and take another look at the backyard where Ryce had died. When I had been there before, I still wasn't sure I was even going to take the case. Taking pictures hadn't been a priority.

I programmed the address for Reeves County Detention Center in my phone's GPS, then headed for Pecos. It was about a forty-minute drive south along yet another road dividing brown dirt and pale green cacti. I settled in for the ride, then called Sophia Ortez.

"Good morning. Can you do me a favor?"

"I'm already doing you one and one's the limit."

"Well, this one's related to the other. It should only count as one big one."

"Yeah, one big one. You've got that right. What is it this time?"

"Need you to check with your sources in the Odessa PD and see if there was any kind of prostitution sting that went down recently. Word 'round here is Ryce McCallen got busted with an underage boy."

"Oooh. That couldn't be good."

"Supposedly that's the reason he hung himself and it's been kept hush-hush out of respect for the family."

"Makes sense."

"Yeah, but I ain't buying it."

"And you think *journalists* thrive on conspiracy theories." She snickered. "I'll check it out. You are going to share that whopping check you're getting at the end of all this, aren't you?"

It was my turn to laugh. If she only knew. "Yeah, I'll share the check if you share the Pulitzer."

"Good-bye, Gypsy."

"Bye, Sophia." I clicked the phone off. Even if the rumor came back as the truth, it didn't explain the eight missing girls. Ryce was on to something and I didn't think it had anything to do with a fondness for underage boys.

The Reeves County Detention Center was divided into three facilities; Hector Martinez was in Reeves III, a medium-security compound. Although it was a federal prison, it, like many others across Texas, was managed by a private corporation. It was the single largest employer in Pecos. Over the years, Reeves had made a name for itself for its riots and for its large population of illegals shipped in from across the southwest. The inmates who were allowed visitors each had an approved-visitors list and to make the list, one had to submit to a complete background check. It could take as much as thirty days to be approved to visit. I didn't have thirty days. Attorneys and clergy were cleared to visit at any time, providing the facility wasn't in the middle of a lockdown or mass riot. No matter how desperate I was, I couldn't in good faith pretend to be an attorney. I did have some standards.

The facility was surrounded by two rows of eight-foot chain-link fencing topped with razor wire. Guards' towers were stationed about every hundred yards. I dug out my fake clergy ID from the manila folder and showed it to the gate guard. He waved me through without a second glance. I parked in the visitors' lot, then carried the folder with my fake background information to the visitors' entrance.

I fell in line behind a Hispanic family waiting as the female correctional officer confirmed they were on the approved visiting list. She checked each bag as another officer did a wand search. The family had obviously been here before and knew the routine.

I moved up in line and handed the officer my fake identification papers. "I'm here to see Hector Martinez," I said, and smiled softly. I gave her Hector's inmate number so there wouldn't be any surprises. "Family emergency," I added quietly.

She looked over my papers, then waved me through to the next officer. He did a quick wand scan, then spoke into the radio attached to his shoulder. He rattled off Hector's inmate number, then instructed whoever was on the other end to bring Hector to private visiting room 3.

"Hey, Randy," he called to another officer standing nearby, "Can you take the Father to visiting room three?"

Randy seemed a little too eager for his job. Like maybe he wasn't fully trusted yet to carry a weapon. "Sure. Right this way."

He ushered me into a small windowless room. The only thing in the room was a card table and two chairs. A phone was mounted on the wall near the door. "A guard will be waiting outside the door, if you need him for anything. When you're finished, just knock on the door and someone will escort you back to check-in," Randy said. "If it's an emergency, that phone rings directly to the guard station."

"I'll be fine," I assured him.

"You sure? Looks like you've already been a couple rounds with one of our residents." He pointed to his lip and grinned.

I laughed. "A rough game of hoops."

"Ought to be a law against beating up a priest."

"Fortunately, there's laws against beating up anyone."

I let out a long breath when chatty Randy finally left. I feared he was going to ask me to pray with him. I couldn't remember the last time I'd been to confession and the last time I'd lit a candle was in St. Timothy's outside of Vegas when Rhonda called and said Uncle Angus had died. I couldn't remember if you were supposed to light the candle before someone died or light it after they passed, but it seemed right at the time. We weren't very good Catholics.

About ten minutes had passed when the door opened again and a guard escorted Hector Martinez into the room. The guard gave me a quick nod, then closed the door behind him as he left.

Hector was about my height and more ripped than I'd ever dreamed of being. His biceps stretched the fabric of his T-shirt. It wasn't hard to guess how he spent most of his days. The kid could probably bench press a whale.

"*Usted habla inglés?*" I asked.

"What happened to Father Thomas?" His eyes were as black as night and just as cold.

"Why don't we sit down?"

He didn't budge. "They said there was a family emergency. Is it Victoria?"

The sister who went missing three weeks before Burke was shot.

"Yes and no. I don't have any new information on her but I am looking into her disappearance."

He folded his arms across his massive chest and stared hard at me. "Why would a priest be looking into my sister's disappearance?"

I didn't have much time to gain this kid's trust and what time I did have was ticking by. "Sit down, Hector. We've got a lot to talk about in a short time."

"Man, I don't even know you." He started toward the door.

"My name's Gypsy Moran. I'm a private investigator hired by Burke McCallen."

He stopped, turned around, and glared at me. "That old deputy?"

"Yeah. The one you allegedly shot."

He guffawed. "So why'd he hire *you*?"

"To find out what really happened."

"Good luck with that. When you find out, let me know."

"Why'd you confess if you didn't do it?"

He smiled a cocky smile. "Who says I didn't do it?"

"Sit down, Hector."

He slowly moved toward one of the chairs but still didn't sit. "What's this got to do with Victoria?"

I pulled out one of the chairs and sat down, leaning into the table. "Victoria disappeared three weeks before Burke McCallen was shot. Seven other girls have gone missing since."

That took him by surprise. I wished I could see the thoughts spinning through his mind at the moment. He finally sat down across from me. "You think they're connected?"

"I don't know. I was hoping you could tell me what happened the day she disappeared."

He picked at a hangnail. "She just didn't come home one day. It was the summer and she was working at the grocery store. She got off at four and just never came home."

"And you don't think there was any possibility she ran away?"

He shook his head. "No . . . she was a good girl. She was never in any trouble."

"When she disappeared, did your family report it to the cops?"

He hesitantly shrugged. "For what good it did. My mother and father . . . they tried to keep a low profile if you know what I mean."

"And what about you? Did the cops know you?"

"About a month before Victoria disappeared, I got busted with a bag of weed. That was the only trouble I'd ever been in. Then Victoria disappeared, and that cop got shot, and I'm getting dragged down to the station for an *interview*."

"Where were you the night Burke McCallen was shot?"

"Hanging with some friends at the lake." He stared at me with truthful eyes and I believed him.

"They wouldn't alibi for you?"

He laughed. "A bunch of weed-smoking illegals? They were all scared to come forward."

"And the cops nabbed you because they knew your name."

He nodded. "I guess."

"Do you remember who made the arrest?"

"A big guy, blond hair. Something Peters, I think."

"Peterson?" I asked.

He nodded. "Yeah, that was it. Peterson."

"What happened with the drug bust? Were you ever charged?"

"Not at the time. When they brought me in for questioning about the deputy, that Peterson guy *reminded* me about it. He said they'd make it go away. And I guess they did." He grinned sarcastically.

"So you confessed to shooting a law-enforcement officer to get out of a drug bust?" That didn't make sense. He could have walked from the drug bust.

Hector slowly shook his head. "No. Peterson told me they knew where Victoria was and if I wanted them to bring her home, I'd do what they told me to do."

"Did you see Victoria?"

He glared at me. "What do you think?"

I didn't answer. "Have you ever thought of recanting your confession?"

"I don't want the same thing to happen to Maria."

"Who's Maria?"

"My younger sister. They told me she might disappear, too, if I ever talked."

"How old is Maria?"

"Fourteen. I don't want her to disappear, *Mr. Moran.*" I felt the chill of his black eyes deep in my bones.

"Does she stay at home by herself during the day?"

He shook his head. "She goes to work with my mother and father."

"They work at the same place?"

He nodded. "My father works the horses at a ranch. My mother is a housekeeper for the rich bitch owner."

I took a small breath. "Which ranch?"

"The K-Bar. Ever hear of it?"

Yeah, I'd heard of it. And I was growing more concerned each time I heard its name.

CHAPTER 13

Why would the wife of a state senator make a practice of hiring illegals? Maybe Claire wasn't the one doing the hiring. Whether or not she was doing the hiring, it didn't look good for illegals to be anywhere near a payroll a state senator might be connected to. Political careers had ended because of much less. Hiring is usually the job of the ranch foreman. I wondered if Sam Amos was still the foreman. Sam defined the word *cowboy* in my book. He was loyal to a fault and smartly honest—he knew when to keep his mouth shut and when to offer his opinion. He'd walked in on me and Claire in the barn with our pants down more than once. He never said a word. But there was a new pack of condoms waiting on us in the upstairs loft each time we snuck away.

I was halfway back to Rhonda's when my cell beeped. It was Sophia.

"Have you had lunch?" she asked.

It didn't matter if I had just eaten; the delightful Miss Ortez was going to hear that I was starving. "Sure haven't. You?"

"Can you meet me in Kermit? There's a little sandwich shop in a strip center on Austin Drive called Coney Island Subs. There's a big chain drugstore on the corner."

"Everything okay?"

"Yeah. I just need to go over some things with you. When will you be here?"

"I'm about twenty minutes out."

She hesitated, then said, "I'll wait."

I mashed the accelerator. It was rude to keep a lady waiting.

Coney Island Subs was sandwiched between an easy-installment insurance agency and a Great Bargains dollar store. A row of booths lined one wall of the sub shop. Sophia was in the back booth looking dangerously radiant in a red tank top and tiny sweater.

"Isn't Coney Island known for its hot dogs?" I said, sliding in across from her.

She arched her brows and stared at me without saying anything. Finally, a cynical grin spread across her gorgeous lips. "Forgive me, Father, for I have sinned."

I felt my face redden to the color of her top and immediately jerked the white collar from around my neck. I don't embarrass easily, more like never, but my face felt as hot as that damned chicken dish I'd had at our last lunch. Sophia Ortez made me blush! I wasn't used to blushing; I didn't know how to recover. I didn't like not being in control.

"You're apparently a man of many talents, but priest? I have a hard time buying that one."

I grinned sheepishly. "I needed a way to get in to see Hector Martinez."

She smiled and slowly shook her head, then lightly touched her lip. "And I guess you got into a prison fight while you were there?"

I ran my thumb over my busted lip. "A rough game of hoops."

"It looks like it. Well, I hope your trip to the prison paid off."

"It did. I'm convinced the kid didn't shoot Burke McCallen."

A barrel-chested guy with enough hair on his arms to make a toupee came over to take our order. Sophia ordered a turkey club on toasted wheat, hold the cheese. I ordered the Italian sub, all the way.

"So, if Hector Martinez didn't shoot McCallen, who did?" she asked after Hairy Arms left to get our drinks.

"That's a whole 'nother conspiracy theory. But—Hector Martinez is connected to the missing girls, and apparently, the missing girls are connected to Ryce's death. Or did you find out something different?" I prayed for Tatum's sake there wasn't any truth to the rumor about Ryce doing the nasty with an underage boy.

"That was one thing I wanted to meet with you about. No— Odessa PD hasn't done a prostitution sting in over a year and they've never nabbed a fellow officer in any sting. And they'd never heard of Ryce McCallen."

I wasn't surprised, but I was relieved.

Hairy Arms brought our drinks, then wobbled on a bum knee back over to the deli counter.

"What else did you find?"

"You told me that everyone in the county seemed scared of Sheriff Gaylord Denny." She popped a straw in her glass of water. "I don't think it's the sheriff they have to be scared of."

"Why do you say that?"

"I just came from Sheriff Denny's office. I spent over an hour interviewing him."

I nearly choked on a drink of water. "Interviewing him about what?"

"The missing girls."

Hairy Arms brought our sandwiches and slid me the ticket. Sophia reached for it but wasn't fast enough. I folded it and slipped it in my pocket. "What'd he say about the missing girls?"

She shrugged. "He said he didn't know anything about it, but he would look into it." She took a hungry bite of her sandwich.

I stared at her, waiting for the punch line. "And that's it? He's just going to *look into it*? Darlin'—he may be the one *behind* it."

She shook her head, took another bite of sandwich, then wiped her mouth with a paper napkin. "Have you ever met him?"

I cocked my head, not sure where she was going. "No. I haven't had the pleasure."

"He's a doddering old man. That's why it took an hour to interview him. His mind kept . . . wandering, like he has dementia or something."

I took a bite of my sandwich and chewed slowly, wondering how long it had been since Burke had seen his former boss. "You think maybe he was playing you?"

She was quick to shake her head. "I have an aunt with dementia. I've seen it firsthand. If Denny was playing me, the man deserves an Oscar for his performance."

I still wasn't convinced. "If he is losing his faculties, you don't think people would notice? The sheriff of any county's a public figure. There's meetings they have to attend with county management, there's conferences, there's—"

"I get it. But that's what the undersheriff's for. I've got an intern pulling the minutes of the past year's board of alderman meetings to see if the sheriff actually attended, or if he sent a representative."

I took a couple bites of the sub while considering Sophia's theory. "If he's that bad off, who's running the department's day-to-day operations?"

She looked at me and shrugged. I wasn't comfortable just *accepting* the sheriff was a feeble old man who couldn't remember the last thing he'd said. Or that he had no idea eight teenage girls were mysteriously missing from his county.

"You don't like it. I'm sure he has some lucid moments." She finished her sandwich and pushed the plate aside.

"He's got to have more than some lucid moments. He's still doing interviews—if he was that bad off, those in his inner circle would close in. Reporters, or even the general public, wouldn't have access to him."

She propped her chin in her hand and looked at me. She was on the verge of speaking but carefully considering what she was going to say. Finally, she slightly grinned, reached in her bag, then slid a business card across the table.

I read the card then burst out laughing. Baskets to Go—Sophia's Custom Creations. "Gift baskets?"

"At least I didn't impersonate a priest."

We laughed until we were both breathless and I was amazed at how easy it was. There were no fleeting moments of wanting to choke the lifeblood from one another followed by the burning desire to rip one another's clothes off. Not that I hadn't already imagined what that gorgeous bronzed-colored body would look like covered only in a shadow.

"Okay, so what's next?" she asked.

I quickly pushed the previous thoughts out of my mind in case she was a mind reader on top of her other talents. "I'm heading over to the McCallen's to take another look at the backyard where Ryce died. What's next on your agenda?"

"Interview the parents of the missing girls."

"You don't trust Ryce's notes?"

She shook her head. "It's not that. He was very thorough. But, professionally, I can't just accept them as the unadulterated truth. I need to speak with these parents myself."

I stared at my half-empty water glass wondering if I should be an optimist and say it was half-full and it was just a coincidence that two of the missing girls' fathers worked at the K-Bar Ranch. That left six whose fathers didn't. Or at least that I didn't know about. "When you're interviewing the parents, pay close attention to where they work."

"You think there's a connection?"

I slowly shrugged. "I just don't want to overlook anything."

Jasper the border collie met me in Tatum's driveway, turning circles and yapping his head off. I dug the camera out of the glove compartment and got out, telling Jasper to hush. He darted off behind the house, moving ten times faster than I could on a good day. He was back with a slobbery tennis ball clamped between his teeth before I made it to the front door. He dropped it at my feet and barked my instructions. Toss it, you human idiot. . . . I tossed it once, then escaped into the house before he brought it back for round two.

"Burke, it's Gypsy," I yelled from the living room.

"In the kitchen."

He was at the table writing out a grocery list. I pulled up a chair and sat the camera on the table. He glared at me over the rims of his reading glasses. "Wedding or funeral?"

"Pardon?"

He looked me up and down. "Only time people get dressed up 'round here is for a wedding or a funeral."

I laughed. "How 'bout visitation day at Reeves. Does that count?"

"You dressed up for Hector Martinez?"

I grinned and nodded. "Yeah." I didn't feel like going into the priest story again.

He pushed the grocery list aside, removed his glasses, and gave me a look over. "I hope whoever beat the hell out of you looks worse than you do."

"I had a run-in with Mark Peterson's elbow."

He raised his brows. "Peterson? What happened?"

"Seems my brother-in-law has a once-a-week game of hoops with a bunch of fellow officers. He invited me to tag along. Peterson doesn't play nice when he's losing."

Burke studied me hard for a moment. "And did Mr. Peterson meet *your* elbow, too?"

I laughed and the pain in my ribs nearly took my breath. "He met a ball in the face, bloodied his nose a little," I said, slightly wheezing. I wondered if Mom was on duty at the hospital.

"I guess that put an end to it when he saw you weren't goin' to roll over and play dead." He smiled.

"Not really. He ended it on a high note. Let's just say I seriously thought I'd be singing soprano the rest of my life."

He raised his brows again. "That hurts."

I slowly nodded. And experts say you can't really remember pain. I say they've never had their balls shoved into their throats.

"So what happened with Martinez?"

I filled him in on the visit. He hung on every word.

"So he won't recant his confession because he's scared his kid sister will disappear, too."

"Legit reason, I guess."

"You know, with no real evidence against him, no serious previous record . . . a jury might have found him not guilty. But he didn't want to take his chances with a jury." Burke rubbed his chin, running his fingers slowly over the stubble.

"He said Peterson told him he knew where his sister was and if he ever wanted to see her again, he'd cooperate."

"So to get him to confess, they told him they knew where the older sister was, and to keep him from recanting, they told him the same thing would happen to his kid sister."

I nodded. "That's pretty much it."

Burke slowly nodded. "But why tell you this? If he's not goin' to recant his confession, what difference does it make who told him what?"

I slowly shrugged. I hadn't figured that out yet. There was a lot to this case I hadn't figured out yet. "Where's Tatum?" I asked.

Burke bobbed his head toward the bedrooms. "In his room playing a video game. Too stinking hot to do too much outside."

That was God's truth. But there was work to be done. "Well, I'm goin' drag him outside for a few minutes. I want to go over what happened when he found Ryce."

Burke slowly nodded.

"What do *you* remember about it?"

He rubbed his hands over his face and sighed heavily. "They'd already removed the body by the time I got here. They took him straight to the morgue. Told me not to worry about anything. They'd handle it." His lips twisted with disgust.

"Who is they?"

"Peterson and Averitt McCoy. Sheriff Denny showed up about twenty minutes after I got here. For all the help he was."

I thought about my conversation with Sophia and wondered, giving Burke's feelings toward the sheriff, if his perspective could have been skewed. "How did Denny act?"

Burke shrugged. "He offered his condolences. Said if there was anything the department could do, to call." He looked at me through squinted eyes. "Why?"

I told him about Sophia's meeting with the sheriff. He thought about it, then rolled over to the cabinet and pulled out a new bottle of Jim Beam. He got two glasses from the dish drainer, then rolled back over to the table. I do wish he drank Johnnie Walker. He poured me a shot, then one for himself.

"So this gal thinks Denny's not running the department," he said.

"I'm not really buying it, but it's something to consider, I suppose." I took a careful sip of the whiskey. Last time Burke brought out a bottle, I finished it and agreed to work pro bono. I was prone to mistakes but seldom made the same one twice.

"Peterson's not high enough up the command chain to run things behind the scene," Burke said.

"So that means either someone higher up is involved or Peterson has something on Denny. And if that's the case, Denny knows what's going on but he's looking the other way."

Burke swallowed his whiskey in one shot, then poured another round. I waved him off as he tilted the bottle in my direction.

"Maybe your shooting wasn't related to the election at all. Maybe it's related to the missing girls."

"Or . . . if Denny was looking the other way and if I had won, that would have put a damper on their little trafficking ring."

"Did they recover the bullet?"

He nodded. "But I never saw it. Surgeon told Ryce he handed it over to someone in the department as evidence."

"But there's no evidence file."

"Not to my knowledge anyway. I think Ryce had asked to see it and, of course, no one could find it."

I wondered if the surgeon would know the difference between calibers. "What's the department's standard issue?"

"Glock .357 sig."

"Interchangeable with a .45." It didn't matter what type of gun Burke was shot with if we couldn't find the bullet. And I'd bet finding it wasn't ever going to happen.

Burke poured himself another shot, then capped the bottle. "I appreciate your interest in what happened to me, but, like I said earlier . . . my main concern is what happened to Ryce."

I slowly nodded. "But if I'm right, it's all connected."

"And if you're wrong?"

I smiled. "I'm not. Just have to prove it, old man." I pushed away from the table, grabbed the camera, then walked down the hallway to Tatum's bedroom.

He was sitting cross-legged on the floor at the foot of his bed, a video game controller gripped tightly in his hands. His bedroom was small and compact. A twin bed, a corner desk, and four-drawer dresser were the only furniture. The room was tidier than my apartment had ever been. No clothes on the floor, no empty drink glasses sitting around waiting to be washed. The bed was even made. "Hey," he said, never taking his eyes off the small television perched on the dresser. "How's the investigation coming?"

I sat on the edge of the bed and watched him take out several bad guys in his pretend game of shoot-'em-up. If the kid could handle a real gun like he handled a video controller, he could cover my back anytime.

"I met Mark Peterson."

He jerked around and looked at me, focusing on my busted lip. "Geez . . . did he beat you up?"

My pride wouldn't let me confirm that. "He got a busted nose out of it."

He turned back to his war game and laughed. "You went for his nose? I would have gone for his jugular."

I chuckled. "He's only about six inches taller than me."

"All the more reason to go for the jugular. It was closer."

I popped him on the back of the head. "Where's your girl-friend?"

He cut his eyes up at me, fighting a boyish grin. "She's not my girlfriend. She went to work with her mom today."

"Oh well. Maybe you'll get to see her tomorrow."

He shook his head and laughed. "She's not my girlfriend."

"Yeah, whatever. I need you outside. I want to walk over the scene again."

He slowly nodded and sighed lightly. I guessed revisiting the scene wasn't one of the things he wanted to do today.

I gently mussed the top of his hair. "You miss him, don't you?"

He nodded quickly but didn't say anything.

I exhaled deeply, understanding the longing. I wished I could tell him it would get easier but I wasn't going to lie to him. You never accepted it, you just learned to live with it. Sooner or later the anger burns down, but never completely out. It's always there. Smoldering, waiting for the chance to lash out because he wasn't there anymore. And he never would be again.

I finally spoke. "Tatum, you know whatever did happen to your dad wasn't your fault."

I caught a glimpse of tears rolling down his cheek before he hurriedly wiped them away with the tail of his shirt. "I'm the one who told him about Alvedia's sister," he sniffled.

That was going to be hard to get over. It tugged at my heart thinking the kid was going to be carrying that guilt for years to come. "But you know you did the right thing. And I'm sure your dad is very, very proud of you. It'd be nice, though, if he were still here to tell you that himself, wouldn't it?"

He nodded again, then rubbed his face with his shirt. He turned the game off, then got up and stood staring at me with reddened eyes. "You ready?"

I followed him outside to the backyard. Jasper ran circles around us, the sloppy tennis ball clutched in his mouth.

"Your dog needs something to herd." I took the ball from Jasper and tossed it as far as I could, hoping it would buy some time between yaps.

Tatum laughed between sniffles. "He likes to herd the rabbits. Be careful where you walk—he likes to dig trenches, too. Dad sprained his ankle last year and threatened to shoot him." A tenderness crept into his voice.

I knew exactly where he was coming from. Memories of something my dad had said or done, or something silly that made him laugh, or something Rhonda or I had done to make him angry would pop up in my brain every now and then like random snapshots. I often tried to pull them all together and piece them side by side like a patchwork quilt to make some sense of why he left. But I never could find the pattern. At least Tatum knew Ryce didn't leave him by choice. Not that it made any real difference.

We were standing underneath the tree where Ryce died, both of us looking up at the branch as if it held the answers.

"Tell me again what happened when the paramedics got here."

"They got him down and laid him over there." He pointed to a grassy spot about twenty feet away.

"How'd they get him down?"

"They cut the rope."

"But how'd they get up to him?"

"They used the ladder. I had already gotten it from the lean-to and was trying to hold him up."

"Do you remember what kind of rope it was?"

He nodded, the image firmly implanted into his memory. "It was yellow nylon. The kind you see on boats."

I walked back to the shed and lean-to and took a quick look around. "Did your dad keep rope like that around the shed?"

He shook his head. "I'd never known him to use a rope for anything."

"Not even to take a tree down or maybe pull up a shrub?"

Again, he shook his head. "Dad didn't do a lot around the house. He could do the basic stuff but for big stuff he usually hired someone who knew what they were doing."

Ryce McCallen was a smart man.

So the rope was something Tatum couldn't remember seeing around the house. Which meant either Ryce bought it that day for the sole purpose of ending his life, or someone brought their own rope when they came to kill him. I made a mental note to see if Peterson or McCoy owned a boat.

I studied the ladder under the lean-to for a moment and spotted several smudges that were probably fingerprints. Although I knew the prints wouldn't do me any good, I still took a couple pictures.

"Nice camera. I bet that thing cost a pretty penny," Tatum said.

"Yes, it did." And I didn't buy it by working pro bono, either. But that wasn't the kid's fault so I didn't mention it.

The various shoe prints around the shed and lean-to wouldn't do me any good either, but I took shots of those as well. I then headed back over to the tree, carefully dodging Jasper's trenches, and studied the massive oak from every angle.

"Can you handle the ladder?" I asked Tatum.

He gave me a twelve-year-old's smirk, then dragged the ladder over to the tree. I helped him position it, then climbed up to the top rung where I could get a look at the top-side of the branch. There was a slight wear pattern that looked like the rope had sawed through the top layer of bark. I took a couple shots, adjusting the flash to accommodate for the shade from the overhead branches. From that vantage point looking down on the ground, I spotted it.

The lay of the grass coming from the driveway was different. My gaze followed along a perfect trail of crushed grass, barely noticeable, but it was there. It dipped in places, thanks to Jasper, exposing the sandy dirt underneath. But it wasn't just one trail—it was two, running side by side, the width of a truck. I came down the ladder and crept alongside the trail.

"Tatum, have you driven the truck back here?"

"No." He was so close behind me, he would have bumped into me if I had stopped.

"Did the paramedics drive the ambulance back here?" I knelt down and gently pushed a layer of grass aside and studied the tire tracks beneath it.

Tatum shook his head. "They parked in the driveway and carried him out on a stretcher."

The tracks wobbled and spread out in the middle of the trail heading toward the driveway, indicating whoever was driving had turned the wheel at some point, forcing the front tires to veer off the trail by a few inches. Judging by the double tracks near the driveway, the truck was backed into the yard and came to a stop underneath the tree branch.

"Can you bring me the keys to the truck?" I asked.

He ran inside then returned a moment later with the keys. Burke rolled out onto the back deck and parked his chair beside the railing. I climbed into their old pickup, then drove slowly into the yard, carefully maneuvering around the trail. I drove toward the back of the yard then backed up to the tree, coming in from the opposite direction of the first set of tire tracks. I yelled out the window to Tatum to tell me when the tailgate was underneath the branch.

"A little bit more," he said, then yelled, "Whoa."

I cut the truck off, hopped out, then went around to the back and let down the tailgate. "How tall was your dad?"

Tatum looked up on the deck to Burke for the answer.

"About your height," Burke said.

I climbed up on the tailgate and stood directly under the branch.

"About a two foot difference," Burke said.

So that was how they did it. They didn't use the ladder to hoist him up, they used the back of a truck. And when the noose was tied, they pulled the truck away.

I looked across the yard at Burke. "There's tire tracks leading away from the tree."

"Averitt McCoy has a truck," Tatum reminded me.

Burke nodded but didn't say anything. He turned away and slowly rolled back into the house.

CHAPTER 14

After I left Tatum and Burke's, I drove to the hospital in Kermit, hoping Mom was on duty. Each breath was becoming more painful; I was hoping she wouldn't mind wrapping my ribs without all the paperwork. The less paper with my name on it, the more trouble Frank Gilleni would have trailing me from Vegas.

The hospital was a six-story building that had been added to so much over the years, part of the building was white brick and part was glass and chrome. The emergency department where my mother had worked for thirty years straddled the past and the present, connecting the old with the new.

I parked and went in, stopping at the check-in desk. "Is Angie Moran working today?" I asked the nurse behind the desk.

"Angie? Sure. She's here. Can I tell her who's here to see her?"

"Her son."

She smiled, showing ultra-bleached teeth. "So you're Gypsy."

I slowly nodded, wondering what stories my mother had divulged.

She paged my mother to the front desk and a minute or two later, Mom came bounding down the hall leading from the trauma rooms. She was wearing blue scrubs and white sneakers—the only thing I could ever remember seeing her wear.

"Hey," she said as she approached. "What's up? Other than you've been in a fight." She poked at my lip. She wasn't quite as rough as Rhonda, which, given her profession, I supposed was a good thing.

I jerked my head away and grinned. "Can we talk a moment?"

Her eyes immediately filled with questions. "Sure." She told the nurse at the desk she'd be on break for a few minutes then led me down the hallway. "Want to grab a cup of coffee in the cafeteria?"

"Are one of these trauma rooms empty?"

She stopped, then turned around and glared at me. "Yeah, but they don't serve coffee in a trauma room. What have you done, Gypsy?"

I pulled my shirt tail from my pants and gently lifted the right side.

Mom stared at the bruise, then twisted her lips and rolled her eyes. *"Nice."* She pushed the door open to one of the rooms, then closed and locked it behind us. "Take your shirt off and get up on the table."

She pushed her fingers around the bruise, causing me to gasp. "You've got some broken ribs. You'll live unless of course it punctures a lung."

"Thanks, *Mom*."

I remembered when I was a kid other mothers kissed boo-boos and spoke in soothing voices when their kids were hurt. Our mom ripped off Band-Aids, taking the first layer of skin with it.

"Take a deep breath," she said, standing back to watch the movement of my chest. She then grabbed a paper towel and handed it to me. "Cough."

"I haven't coughed up anything."

"I need to see if there's blood in it. Cough."

"But I haven't coughed—"

"Cough," she snapped, so I forced myself to cough. She stared at the nonexistent mucus in the paper towel, then tossed it in the trash. She then cut several pieces of adhesive and wrapped them from my sternum around to my back, pulling them like she was yanking out a tooth.

I gasped in pain. "Are you trying to kill me?"

"Oh, if I was trying to kill you, you'd have been dead long before now. You goin' to tell me how you did this?"

"A basketball game," I said between grimaces.

She glared at me with one eyebrow raised. "I hope you won."

I didn't feel up to recounting the story again so I forced a grin. Mom finished wrapping my ribs, then tapped at my lip. "You need a stitch or two in that. It's probably going to scar worse than it was. Want me to open it back up and—"

"No!"

She cocked a brow, then leaned against the counter, arms folded across her chest. There was no doubt Rhonda was her daughter.

"How's your grandmother?" she asked.

"She needs to be in a home."

"For what? Grouchiness? She's in perfect health, Gypsy."

I sighed. I wasn't used to living with anyone and Gram's irritable disposition was enough to make me appreciate my solo lifestyle.

"Be nice to her. She's old."

"I don't see her living with *you*."

"I ain't stupid. Do you need something for pain?"

My mother—my angel of mercy.

"I can't give you the strong stuff because you're already having trouble breathing, but I can get you some prescription-strength ibuprofen."

As teenagers, Rhonda and I were too terrified to ever experiment with drugs. Mom had us convinced anything stronger than aspirin would kill us.

Just as mom ducked out to get the meds, my cell beeped. I dug it out of my pocket, saw that it was Claire, and quickly answered the call, cussing myself for doing so.

"Hey, gorgeous," she said.

"Hey back at you."

Mom came back in with two red pills and a small paper cup of water. She pretended she wasn't listening.

"Same time, same place?" Claire asked and my gut tightened.

"I'm . . . a little tied up tonight. But how 'bout I drop by the ranch tomorrow?" I did need to find out more about her hiring practices. My body parts had their own agenda.

"Oh." Claire didn't take well to being turned down for anything. "Okay . . . what time tomorrow?"

"Lunchtime?"

She laughed. "I'll plan a picnic."

I closed my eyes and was taken back twenty years to other picnics, blankets under trees, sun-kissed skin. . . . "That sounds good," I whispered. "I'll see you then."

I slipped my phone back into my pocket. I glanced up at my mother and swore I saw Rhonda standing there. She slammed the pills in my hand then shoved the cup in the other. "The *ranch*? As in the *K-Bar Ranch*?"

I quickly downed the pills, then took a long drink of the water.

Mom shook her head. "Rhonda told me you saw her the first night you were back."

Rhonda needed to get her facts straight. I saw Claire the *second* night I was back in Wink. "Not that it's any of your business, but I've actually got a reason for seeing her, *Mother*. Since her dad had a stroke, she's been managing the ranch and—"

"Carroll had a stroke? When?" There was far too much concern in her voice.

My mother had despised everything about the Kinleys since as far back as I could remember. Why all the concern now?

"When did Carroll have a stroke?"

"I don't know. Claire just said she was managing the ranch because her dad had a stroke. Why is Carroll Kinley's health so important?"

She waved me off. "Don't get an attitude. I went to school with the man. We're the same age. It's a little unsettling when you start seeing people you went to school with in the obituaries."

"He's not dead. He had a stroke."

She rolled her eyes, then pulled a handful of red pill packets from her pocket and handed them to me. "Take two every four hours. I've got to get back to work."

It was a little troubling seeing my mom's world stop, too, at the mention of a Kinley.

"We've got a weird family," I told Rodney. We were on the back deck waiting for a much anticipated thunderstorm, finishing off the two six-packs Rhonda had bought the night before. Two bottles were unaccounted for and I suspected Gram, who had conveniently passed out after dinner.

Rodney didn't say anything but grunted his agreement to the weird family comment.

"My mother freaked out when I told her Carroll Kinley had a stroke. I thought for a minute there she was going to have one.

What's up with that?" I was feeling buzzed and chatty. "Since Rhonda and I were kids, Mom has all but called an exorcist to rid the Morans of anything Kinley."

"Maybe she used to date him."

I shook my head. "Mom and the old man got married their senior year. I was a backseat baby." I couldn't stop the chuckle that bubbled up into my throat along with the beer. After a moment, I finally said it. "Claire's married." I was certain he already knew; I just wanted to see if I could say it.

"Yep. Senator Steven Sellars."

Sellars. So that was it. Claire *Sellars*. It didn't roll off the tongue with ease; it was cumbersome. Heavy. She deserved better. I sighed and pressed the cold bottle to my forehead. The temperature had dropped to an almost bearable 85 degrees as a cold front moved in from the northwest. So far it had brought with it a lot of thunder, some impressive lightning, but little rain.

"I think the K-Bar Ranch might be involved with the missing girls." I finally said that, too.

Rodney turned quickly and stared at me. If I had been completely sober, I could have probably seen the wheels turning in his bald little head.

"Oh my God . . . it makes perfect sense." He pulled his chair closer and hunkered down for a meeting of the minds.

"What makes perfect sense?"

"Claire's husband, Steven Sellars—his sister's married to Mark Peterson. Peterson's Claire's brother-in-law."

A crack of lighting exploded north of the tree line followed by a churning rumble of thunder. Normally, that would have been my cue to head inside, but I couldn't move. I felt like my heart was tied to an anchor. A sinking anchor. She couldn't be involved. Claire toyed with people's hearts, she took them to dizzying heights of ecstasy, she was the strongest-willed person I had ever known—but she wouldn't be involved in something like this. She was a protector. She protected the unpopular girls at school. She protected the fillies and geldings that didn't make the rodeo cut from slaughter. She protected the land, and the ranch. It was her nature.

Could they be using the ranch as a pipeline? I laid my head back against the chair and waited for the coming storm.

Rodney went inside and returned with two fresh bottles. He handed me one, then sat back down and leaned in close. "How do you think Claire's involved?"

"Two of the missing girls' fathers work at the K-Bar. Sophia Ortez is looking into how many others there might be."

"They were working at the K-Bar when their daughters went missing?"

I slowly nodded. "But I don't know who hired them. I don't know how long Claire's been managing the ranch. Years ago, Sam Amos was the ranch foreman—he did all the hiring back then."

Rodney settled his weight in the chair. "Okay . . . so the K-Bar hires these illegals and then their daughters go missing. There's got to be someone sending them the workers . . . someone who would know these men were, one, illegal, and two, had teenage daughters."

I popped the top on the new bottle and downed half of it in one long swig. "Peterson and McCoy worked for the Border Patrol. Maybe there's someone there feeding them these poor bastards."

"More likely a coyote they've hooked up with."

I drank my beer. My heart ached for the missing girls. Maybe after I proved Ryce was murdered, I could dig a little deeper into the pipeline. And after that, I was going to have to find a paying job.

CHAPTER 15

How's the nuts?" Gram asked. She slurped her oatmeal, leaving a trail of soggy oats dribbling from her wrinkled chin.

Nothing like discussing your private parts with your eighty-year-old grandmother over morning coffee. "Still working." I looked at Rhonda and rolled my eyes.

"You know your grandpa got hit there once. Put him out of commission for a month. Thought I was goin' to have to take a lover."

I hurriedly got up and topped off my coffee, anxious to nip that conversation in the bud.

"You need to finish your oatmeal, Gram," Rhonda said. "We're going to the senior center today."

I winked at Rhonda, a small gesture of appreciation for rescuing me.

"Oh joy, joy," Gram said, not the least bit enthused about her field trip. Couldn't say that I really blamed her.

I took my coffee out on the deck and called Sophia.

"Good morning," she said, obviously recognizing my number now on caller ID.

"Morning to you, too. I found a set of tire tracks at Ryce Mc-Callen's yesterday."

"Hmm. Interesting."

"Does Odessa PD have a forensics lab?"

"Why do I get the feeling this is going to involve me?"

I wiped a stream of sweat from the back of my neck. "That's what I like about you, Sophia. You're one of the few women I know who doesn't want the world to revolve around them."

I thought I detected a slight chuckle. "Yes, the Odessa Police Department has a crime lab. It's not state-of-the-art but it can probably handle matching tire tracks."

"Can you get me in?"

There was a slight hesitation on her end. Finally, she asked, "When?"

"Either late this afternoon or in the morning." I still had to get over to McCoy's and hopefully get some shots of his truck. I also had a lunch date with Claire.

"Let me make a call and I'll call you back." She hung up like she usually did, without saying good-bye.

Rhonda stuck her head out the back door and looked more concerned than I was comfortable with. "Hey—there's a call for you. It's a Detective Chip Adams from Las Vegas."

I forced myself to breathe, then followed Rhonda back inside. I stared at the phone a moment after she handed it to me. I took another deep breath then answered. "Chip?"

"Guess you made it down to Texas okay."

"Long drive but I made it. What's up?"

"Gilleni was arrested two days ago. No bond."

I let out the breath I'd been holding since leaving Vegas. "Murder one?"

"And conspiracy to commit."

"Good. There should be enough evidence there to make it stick." I had dropped off a nice, neat little package for Adams before leaving, tying Gilleni directly to Gina and her lover's murder. The best defense attorneys Gilleni's money could buy would have a hard time making this one go away.

"Gypsy—if we can't work a deal, you may have to come back to testify."

I squeezed my eyes closed. That was not what I wanted to hear. Even if I took the Fifth, I'd never make it out of the courthouse alive. "If I have to testify, I might as well put a bullet through my own head and save him the trouble."

Rhonda's eyes widened to the size of the mismatched saucers she had in the cabinet. I turned away and she grabbed my arm, staring at me with raw fear.

"Besides," I said, "if I testify against a former client, I'll lose every ounce of credibility I ever had as an investigator. You know that, Chip."

"I'll see what I can do. This a good number to reach you at?"

I gave him my new cell number. "You're the only one who has the house number and it doesn't exist, right?"

"What number? I'll be back in touch. And Gypsy . . . take care of yourself. It took some balls to do what you did. You're an all-right guy."

I hung up and immediately met the wrath of Rhonda. "What do you mean, *put a bullet through your head*? Gypsy, what was that all about?"

My mouth was open but nothing was coming out. I didn't want to get into the whole sordid tale; I prayed for Sophia to call back and rescue me.

"Sounds likes your brother's in trouble," Gram said. "That's what the hell it was all about." She waddled over to the sink and dropped her empty oatmeal bowl into the dishpan.

Rhonda closed her eyes and let out a quick, short breath.

"Gram, why don't you go get dressed? We'll be leaving in a few minutes."

"Whatever. That boy was born in trouble if you ask me." Gram shuffled down the hallway to her bedroom.

"No one asked you, Gram," I shouted after her.

When she was out of earshot, Rhonda shoved me toward the table. "Sit. You're going to explain this whether you're ready to or not."

"Don't you have to be leaving soon?" I asked, hoping for the best.

She bobbed her head toward the bedrooms. "It'll take her a good thirty minutes to get dressed. Now, tell me what's going on."

I guessed she deserved to know. I *was* staying at her house. "A couple months ago, a guy named Frank Gilleni hired me to find out if his wife, Gina, was having an affair. Gilleni owns a couple of casinos and everyone suspected him of being tied to the mob but no one could prove it."

"Was he?"

I laughed. "Is Jimmy Hoffa still missing?"

She looked at me with uncertain eyes. "Who's Jimmy Hoffa?"

God love her. If it didn't happen in Wink, it never happened. "Never mind, it's not important. Anyway—yes, he was very involved in organized crime."

"And you agreed to work for him?"

I gawked at her. "At least he paid me. Very well, I might add."

"How could you work for him if you knew he was involved with the mob?"

"Rhonda, you're missing the whole point here. He hired me to find out if his much younger wife was having an affair. And she was. With her high school sweetheart. They were planning on running away, changing their identities, and starting a new life together. I started kinda pulling for them, wanting them to make a break for it and live happily ever after. Anything to get away from Gilleni. He's a real sonofabitch. I mean *sonofabitch*."

She shook her head. "Gypsy—you are such a sucker for stuff like that. Look at you and Claire. The woman's toxic but it's never stopped you from believing she's the love of your life."

I glared at her. What the hell did Claire have to do with any of this? "Would you like for me to continue or are you going to bitch some more?"

She rolled her eyes. "I was just pointing out your weakness. You're a hopeless romantic. So what happened with the wife and her boyfriend?"

I continued. "Gilleni started bugging me about what I knew and when was I goin' to give him my report."

"Couldn't you have just made something up?"

"I did. Apparently, he had gotten suspicious because it was taking so long so he had one of his men trail me. And I led them straight to her. Gina and her boyfriend had arranged to disappear the Fourth of July. Sometime around ten the evening before, Gilleni paid them a visit at the boyfriend's apartment. The maid found their bodies the next morning. He'd been shot in the head; her throat was cut ear to ear."

Rhonda let it sink in before saying anything. "And you know it was Gilleni?"

I slowly nodded. Other than knowing how much I loved and hated Claire Kinley, I'd never been more sure of anything in my life. "I spent the next few weeks putting together a package of evidence of everything I knew against Gilleni and left it with Chip Adams."

"The detective you just spoke with?"

I nodded again. "He'd been working Gilleni for years. Just never could get anything to stick."

She gnawed the inside of her lip. "And you trust him?"

There were few people in the world I trusted. I was sitting at the table with one of them, and I had just hung up with another. "He's good people. We've worked together on several cases."

She changed from gnawing on her lip to biting a fingernail. "But if he could track you down here . . ."

"I gave him the number before I left. I knew I'd have to get a new cell phone when I got here, so it was the only number I had to give him."

She nodded. But I could tell her mind was still bouncing in a thousand different directions. "And you're sure this Gilleni guy doesn't know where you are?"

"Few people in Vegas know my real name. Fewer know where I'm from and I don't think Texas would be the first place they'd look. Rhonda, I never would have come here if I thought for even a second Gilleni could track me down. I wouldn't put you in that kind of danger."

She nodded again, then sighed heavily. "I know that."

Gram shuffled back into the kitchen wearing nothing but a raincoat. And it wasn't a pretty sight. "Gram! What do you think you're doing?" Rhonda leapt up and closed the raincoat.

"Hopefully giving Otis Dinkins a thrill. Besides, weatherman said we might finally get some rain this afternoon."

"Otis Dinkins doesn't need a thrill. He has a pacemaker. And it's not going to rain, Gram. You go put some clothes on right now."

I prayed for Sophia to call, and lo and behold, she did. I quickly took the call and turned away from my naked grandmother.

"Four o'clock. The lab's not at the police station. It's at the corner of Baylor and Fourth Street."

"You got an exact address? My GPS doesn't do corner-ofs very well."

"Five-sixteen Baylor. Meet me in the parking lot."

"See you there." I hung up first, beating her in the hang-up game. I grinned, imagining what she'd be wearing today. Now, that I'd like to see in nothing but a raincoat.

"So are you going to have to testify at Gilleni's trial?" Rhonda asked. She had an annoying way of slamming me back to reality.

I rubbed my hands over my face and decided I should probably shave sometime today. "I can't testify. I wouldn't make it out of the courthouse."

Rhonda looked at me. The fear in her eyes broke my heart. "Then what are you going to do?"

"Pray Gilleni takes a plea deal."

After a shower, I swung by Burke's and picked up Tatum. Since this particular assignment called for more photographs, I figured he might want to tag along.

"You know where Averitt McCoy lives?" I asked as he climbed into the van's passenger seat.

He gave me the address. He seemed quiet and reserved today. I wasn't sure if it was preteen moodiness or if he wasn't sure about seeing the truck that was used to help kill his father.

"You don't have to go if you don't want to." I sat in the driveway a moment, giving him the opportunity to change his mind.

He looked at me as if he didn't understand. "No, I want to. I like taking pictures."

"Okay. Just making sure."

I keyed Averitt McCoy's address into my GPS and headed out. McCoy had been so far in debt, I was lucky his address was attached to a rental house and not a cardboard box. The rental was near Kermit, and it being a rental, I was banking on a dirt driveway. Not many landlords are going to pave a drive they don't use themselves.

We drove in silence for a while, then Tatum finally spoke. "Dad had scheduled a vacation day today. He was supposed to take me to the dentist this morning and then he was going to take me over to the sinkholes to take some pictures."

My heart grabbed in my chest. I felt for the kid. My ol' man wasn't much for family vacations but he did take a day every now and then to take me camping. We'd head down to Big Bend and sleep out under the stars and fish the Rio Grande. Even when I got older and preferred to sleep under an air conditioner, I never begged out of a trip.

"How 'bout if I take you by the sinkholes one day when all this is over?"

He glanced at me and I saw a hint of a smile. "Would you?"

"Might even let you use one of my cameras."

"Oh, man . . . that would be like, so cool. See, it's for my seventh grade science project and I was going to get an early start on it and—"

"You're doing your science project on sinkholes? During your summer vacation?"

"I wanted to get an early start. And sinkholes are pretty cool."

I glanced over at him. "If you say so."

I found Averitt McCoy's street and decided it was going to be a grand day indeed—the little house was the only house on a dead-end, unpaved street. No nosy neighbors wondering why some guy in a van was taking pictures of McCoy's driveway. There were a couple rotting barns and abandoned outbuildings scattered around the end of the road, but other than that, McCoy had the whole road to himself.

The truck, an older model Ford, was parked near a small side stoop leading into the house. I parked along the road, grabbed my camera, and hopped out. Tatum and I walked along beside the driveway, not wanting to disturb any tracks. "Do not touch anything, you got it?"

He nodded and followed my every step.

Last night's storm dropped just a spattering of rain, so the tracks were still very visible. I spotted two different sets; I assumed the smaller set was from the department's cruiser and the larger ones from his truck.

I took several shots of the tires, the truck, and the tire tracks.

"Gypsy . . ." Tatum was at the back of the truck, staring into the bed.

"What?"

He slowly raised his arm and pointed to the bed.

I walked around to where he was standing and saw what he was pointing at.

A yellow nylon rope was tossed into a heap at the back of the bed. Tatum just stood there, staring at the rope, seeing things in his mind he didn't need to see again. "Why don't you go get back in the van?" I said, imagining the thoughts and images flooding his head at that moment.

He moved slowly back to the van carrying the weight of the world on his scrawny shoulders. I went around to the side of the truck and peered over into the bed. The rope had definitely been cut. One end was frayed, the other still sealed with factory glue.

I called Rodney on his cell. "I think I found the rope they used to hang him with."

"Where are you?"

"At Averitt McCoy's. There's a nylon rope in the bed of his truck. One end's been cut."

"Don't touch it!"

"Rodney, I'm not stupid. I've been doing this sort of thing a few years, you know."

"I know . . . but, Jesus, Gypsy. Let me see if I can get a warrant."

"You don't need a warrant—it's in plain view. Just get over here and tag it yourself. You're on duty, right?"

"What if McCoy comes home for lunch?"

"Then maybe he'll offer us a sandwich. Just get over here, Rodney. And bring an evidence bag." I gave him the address, then hung up.

I checked the time on my cell and it was close to eleven o'clock. I hadn't considered McCoy coming home for lunch. Of course I hadn't expected to find a key piece of evidence lying in his truck bed, either. I went back to the van and drove to the end of the road. I then pulled the van around behind one of the old barns.

"What are we doing?" Tatum asked.

"I don't know if Averitt McCoy comes home for lunch and if he does, he's probably not expecting guests. Stay here."

I got out and crouched beside the barn and waited for Rodney, or McCoy, praying they didn't arrive at the same time. A few minutes later, Rodney's cruiser turned onto the road. I stepped out and flagged him down, directing him to pull in behind one of the outbuildings. The poor guy was already red-faced and frazzled.

"You know we're trespassing," he whispered after he got out. "You've got Tatum with you?"

"Yeah. I wasn't planning on finding the freakin' murder weapon. You got the evidence bag?"

He nodded. "Evidence bag, gloves, and department camera. I wasn't sure we could use your pictures."

I sprinted toward McCoy's truck, with Rodney in tow. Rodney handed me the bag and gloves, then took a couple pictures from the back of the truck of the pile of rope in the bed. I asked him to get a wide shot of the rope that also showed the decal on the back window of the cartoon kid taking a whiz. With the gloves on, Rodney then reached over the side and gathered the rope, dropping it into the evidence bag.

"Let's get outta here, Superman," I said.

A satisfied grin spread across his face. We were within a few feet of the barn when I heard a car turn onto the dirt road. I shoved Rodney behind the barn, then dove headfirst out of the way. I knew how to take a dive, drop and roll, all that avoiding-disaster stuff, but every ounce of knowledge left me. "Ouch," I groaned, spitting out a mouthful of west-Texas sand.

"You okay, man?" Rodney's famous words.

I'd live. I reconsidered when I heard the ominous rattle. It was a Western Diamondback coiled and ready to strike.

"*Holy shit* . . . don't move," Rodney whispered.

Don't move? Was he fucking crazy? It all happened so fast. I was scrambling to get the hell away when I felt the white-hot pain rip through my ankle. *"Motherfucker! I'm bit!"* I was on my back, kicking frantically at the sand to put distance between myself and the pissed-off viper.

Rodney started firing and emptied a clip into the ground before actually taking out the rattler. The snake exploded into blood and guts.

I don't know who was more frantic: me, Rodney, or now Tatum. "Where'd he get you?" Rodney asked, on the verge of hyperventilating.

"Ankle," I screamed, unashamed of the panic surging through me faster than the deadly venom. The pain was more intense than anything I'd ever felt in my life.

"It was the mailman," Tatum said. "The car—it was the mailman. It wasn't McCoy."

I threw my head back and screamed out again in unadulterated agony.

"Gypsy, you've got to stay calm!" Rodney was yelling as loud as I was screaming. "We've got to get you to the hospital."

"You need to wrap it near the puncture wound," Tatum said, the only voice of reason. "Like a tourniquet, but not as tight."

"We can use the tape on your ribs," Rodney said, grabbing me underneath my arm to help me sit up. He jerked my shirt up and Tatum ripped the tape from around my chest.

My entire body was on fire. I felt like there were a million bees trapped underneath my skin, stinging from the inside out, pushing their way to freedom.

As Tatum wrapped the tape around my calf, Rodney pulled me up. "Come on, come on . . . ," Rodney said, hurrying Tatum along. "We've got to get to the ER."

I started to hobble toward the van but Rodney was heading toward his cruiser. "You can't drive. You're either going to start throwing up or you're going to pass out."

"I'm not leaving the van! Do you know how much equipment I've got in there?"

"Well, I can't leave the cruiser."

"I'll drive the van," Tatum said. The kid was in it before either of us could object.

Rodney hurried me to the cruiser, mumbling something about getting fired. He loaded me into the backseat, then yelled at Tatum to stay close behind him and not to stop for anything. He hit the lights and siren when he got out to the main road.

He keyed the department radio. "Dispatch, this is Officer Walker, car 416. Notify Kermit Regional ER I'm on my way in with a rattle bite to the left ankle. Victim is a thirty-eight-year-old male, in good health. No known medical conditions. ETA six minutes." He clicked off the radio then glanced over his shoulder at me. "You hanging in there? Man, you're sweating."

"I think I'm goin' be sick."

"Ahh, *Jesus*."

My head was spinning. Every nerve in my body had turned into a raging inferno. I tried to remember everything I could about rattlesnake bites but kept coming back to amputated limbs, multiple surgeries, useless muscles, organ damage, and death. I did remember the mortality rate was something like less than 5 percent, which was a good thing I supposed. I wasn't ready to die. I had lunch plans with Claire. I kept repeating the 5 percent statistic to myself; it kept me from screaming.

I heard Rodney punch a number into his cell phone. "Hey—I don't want you to panic, but call your mom and see if she's on duty. I'm on my way to the ER with Gypsy. A rattler got him on the ankle. Rhonda, calm down. It was a big snake and their venom's not as powerful as a young snake's. I'm hurrying, Rhonda. I'm pushing ninety now."

I thought of Tatum behind us in my van and thought I really was going to be sick.

A minute or two later, I was slung from one side of the backseat to the other as Rodney whipped into the hospital parking lot on two wheels. He pulled up outside the emergency department, where a small platoon of trauma personnel were waiting. I was pulled from the backseat and thrown on a gurney in one fluid motion. Rodney ran alongside the stretcher giving the doctor the low-down on the killer snake as they rushed to a treatment area.

"It was about four-and-a-half-feet long, Western Diamond-back. I only saw one puncture site. Left ankle." He was covered in blood. My blood.

The next thing I heard was my mother burst into the room, her panicked voice more unsettling than the oxygen tube they were cramming up my nose. My mother doesn't panic. She was over me, her worried face in full view, brushing the sweat-drenched hair from my forehead. "It's goin' to be okay, Gypsy. We're mixing the antivenin now." The quiver in her voice betrayed the comfort she intended.

Five percent . . . five percent . . . five percent. . . .

The pain was beyond excruciating. I wouldn't wish it on my worst enemy. The hit I had taken to the nuts was small potatoes.

"Does he have an advanced directive?" someone in scrubs asked.

Sweet Jesus . . . use the fucking paddles! Shove whatever you need to down my throat. I have lunch plans with Claire!

"Pupils are constricted," one of the techs said. "BP's eighty over sixty-four, pulse rate ninety-two."

Five percent . . . five percent . . . five percent. . . .

"Cut his clothes off and start a double line IV. Let's get an IM injection of Dilaudid in him," the doctor ordered.

A minute later I was butt naked with only a cold sheet covering parts my mother hadn't seen since I learned to pee in a toilet.

"He's wearing a St. Christopher. Should we call a priest?"

Hail Mary, full of grace . . . blah blah blah . . . Jesus Christ . . . why couldn't I remember that simple prayer? Holy Mary, mother of God, pray for us sinners now and in the hour of our death. Five percent . . . five percent . . . five percent. . . .

A tech who needed more practice was butchering my arm with an IV until my mother jerked it away from him. She jabbed it in the vein on the first try. It took her less than a few seconds to get the second line in.

"Let's get two more vials of CroFab antivenin up here stat," the doctor said.

I lifted my head just enough to get a glimpse of my ankle. It was already swollen to three times the size of the other one. I had blue lines from a ballpoint pen drawn across my lower leg, monitoring the level of swelling and time notated. My toes looked like short, stubby sausages.

My stomach lurched. I instinctively tried to roll to my side—I'd had my share of booze-induced nausea—but between the IV, the oxygen tube, the blood pressure cuff, and the small army of scrubs working feverishly around my leg, I couldn't move. I grabbed my mother's arm and she immediately recognized the warning sign.

"Roll him. He's goin' to vomit."

There was a mind-numbing flurry of activity going on, including some projectile vomiting, but I recognized Rhonda's frenzied scream above the chaos.

"Get her out of here, Rodney," Mom shouted. "Now!"

Hail Mary, full of grace. . . . Five percent . . . five percent . . . five percent. . . .

"Could we keep the family hysterics to a minimum, please?" the doctor asked.

Rhonda took that as her okay to stay and pushed past Rodney. She assumed Mom's previous position of hovering, gently wiping my face and forehead with a cool rag. She was crying and I wanted to tell her that whatever happened, it would be all right. At this point, at least dying would relieve the pain.

I wanted to tell Rhonda I loved her. I wanted to tell her I was as proud as any older brother could be. I wanted to tell her to tell Claire I didn't care if she was married. Tell her I'd never loved anyone as much in my entire life as I loved her.

Obviously, I wasn't going to make our lunch date. She wasn't going to be very happy about being stood up. Maybe dying was a reasonable option.

Or maybe Rhonda would, just once, show me some pity where Claire was concerned and call her to let her know I'd be a little late. "Call Claire," I mumbled before the stinging pinch jabbed in my hip put me under.

CHAPTER 16

I had graduated Wink High School a month ago and here I was, still shoveling horse shit. I tossed the last shovel onto the trailer and cussed. I cussed the sweat stinging my eyes, I cussed the fucking horses that dumped more crap than biologically possible, I cussed this godforsaken town, and I cussed Carroll Kinley and the K-Bar Ranch for offering the only jobs available.

It was either shoveling horse shit at the K-Bar, learning how to run a pump jack, or unloading trailers at the Walmart in Odessa. Those were the options. I wasn't big enough (or good enough) for a football scholarship to Texas A&M; my fastball wasn't fast enough for a tryout with the Rangers' farm team; I barely squeaked by academically so an academic scholarship wasn't even plausible.

Thunder reverberated off the barn's metal roof and vibrated the ground underneath my feet. The boots pinching the shit out of my toes was enough discomfort. I walked to the edge of the barn and watched the storm roll in. The sky was the color of fresh charcoal; the wind kicked up small cyclones of sand and dust. I twitched my nose, trying to pick up the scent of rain, but all I smelled was hay and horse shit. My ol' man could smell rain coming from miles away. The sonofabitch. Sometimes I wondered what he was doing, where he was. Why he left. And sometimes, in the very far reaches of my brain, I envied him.

In the distance, I saw Claire's truck jerk along the dirt road, heading toward the barn. The closer she got, the more I could hear the gears grinding. I couldn't help but laugh. Her father gave her the old farm truck to get around the ranch, unconcerned that she didn't know how to drive a stick shift. I taught her the best I could but after the fifth lesson ended with us screaming at each other, I gave up. She'd learn it sooner or later. I did take a step inside the barn just in case she got the clutch mixed up with the brake again.

She jerked to a stop, then got out, her face lit up with the most beautiful smile I'd ever seen. She was wearing a pale yellow skirt that fell just inches below the tops of her thighs, and a sleeveless white top. She'd complained earlier about having to have lunch with her mother at the country club. She didn't like the country club women and liked their daughters even less. "Thought you might need some water," she said, carrying a large thermos.

I grabbed her arm and pulled her to me, kissing the inside of her neck. She smelled like honeysuckle. "I've got all I need right here."

"Mmm," she moaned, then dropped the thermos, wrapped her arms around my neck, and drove her tongue deep into my waiting mouth. She hiked her leg up and wrapped it around my thigh, pressing herself against me.

I pulled back slightly and smiled. "Careful . . . I don't want to get you dirty." I was sweaty, dirty, and reeked of manure.

"Mmm . . . down and dirty . . . I like the sound of that." She kissed me again playfully, then pulled away and took my hand. She led me over to a stack of hay bales, then lifted herself up and sat on the top bale. She pulled me to her. "Guess what," she said, grinning ear to ear.

"What?"

"I talked to Daddy last night and he's going to tell Sam to start letting you go to the auctions with him."

Well, I supposed the good news was she didn't tell me she was pregnant. Going to the auctions with the ranch foreman was just slightly below hearing I was going to be a daddy in the list of things I didn't want to hear.

I swallowed hard and didn't say anything.

"Aren't you happy? It'll get you out of the barn a few days a month."

"Claire . . . I don't know anything about . . . I mean, they're horses and cows." I could tell the difference between a stallion and a gelding, a steer and a bull, but other than that . . . all I knew was they were big, could kill you with a kick, and crapped a lot. And the fact was, I didn't care to know more.

She chuckled, but it had an uneasiness to it. "You'll learn. By next summer, you could be the K-Bar's junior foreman and chief buyer."

She said it like it was really something to look forward to. We'd had this conversation since we were in junior high and she still just didn't get it. I slowly pulled away and walked to the edge of the barn. It was starting to rain. Big, fat drops splattered against the brown dirt, creating miniature mud puddles. Thunder rolled in over the mountains to the west like angry ocean waves. Bolts of lightning zigzagged across the sky. I watched the storm for a moment, wondering what one would look like over the Pacific.

"Gypsy . . ." She was beside me now. I could feel her breath on the back of my neck. "You could be a junior foreman before you're twenty. That's pretty rare."

I closed my eyes. "Claire . . . I don't want to be a junior foreman. I don't want to be a foreman." I turned around and looked at her. "You've known that since we were thirteen years old."

Her chest rose and fell with each deep breath as she calculated her next move. I knew her too well. "Okay . . . if you're happy here in the barn, I'll just tell Daddy—"

"Claire—I'm not happy *here in the barn*. I'm not happy in this *town*. Haven't you ever wondered about what's on the other side of that fence?"

Her eyes widened and she looked at me like, honestly, the thought had never crossed her mind. "But what's wrong with the life we have here?"

I sighed heavily. "It's your life, Claire. It's not our life."

"Well, what do you want to do? Do you want to go to college? Maybe Daddy can give you the money—"

"I'm not goin' to ask your daddy for money!"

"Gypsy—you're being unreasonable." Her voice was getting louder, competing with the thunder.

"Unreasonable? What good would going to college do if shoveling horse shit's the only job around? Even with a college degree, I'd have to go somewhere else to find a decent job."

"But you don't have to go anywhere else. There's plenty of other jobs you could do here on the ranch."

God! She could be so frustrating! I stormed away from her and stood outside in the rain, hoping it would cool my rising temper.

"I just don't understand what it is you're looking for," she said, arms flaying in the air.

"Claire," I yelled, "I can't stay in this town another day. I don't want to be one of those old men in the diner talking about the things they wished they'd done."

"What is it you want to do?" She'd stepped outside, too, standing a few feet from me, the rain clinging to her lashes.

"I don't know . . . but there's got to be something more. There's got to be." The rain was coming down harder now, soaking through my clothes. "Come with me . . . one year . . . that's all I ask. We'll travel, we'll sleep under the stars, we'll see what's out there. If we can't find something better out there, we'll come back. One year, Claire . . . that's all I'm asking."

"No!" She screamed and covered her ears with her hands, shaking her head back and forth.

I grabbed her hands and pulled them away from her ears. She was going to listen to me whether she wanted to or not. "We can do it, Claire. I've got money saved. I can work odd jobs when that runs out. We can go to San Francisco, Seattle, Las Vegas. I'll even take you to Montana. Wouldn't you like to see Montana, Claire?"

She jerked away from me and took off running, away from our own private storm and into nature's fury. I took off after her and finally caught her nearly a hundred yards from the barn. The ground was rain slick and muddy and I scrabbled to keep upright as I hooked one arm around her waist. "Are you fucking crazy?" I screamed. "You're going to get killed out here!"

She fought to get free and despite every attempt to not fall, I went down, taking her down underneath me. She was sobbing and gasping for air as she grabbed my face between her muddy hands. "Please don't leave me, Gypsy. Please don't go."

I'd never loved her more. Or hated her more. My mouth found hers in a fury of passion. I jerked her skirt up as she tore open my jeans. We came together at the same time in an explosion of ecstasy, the rain washing over us, the storm at its peak.

At first I thought it was a bird chirping. The high-pitched *beep beep beep* droned on for what seemed like hours. I forced my eyes open to get a look at the source of the annoying sound, wishing I had the Glock with me. If I had, whatever was making the noise would be history.

Then my mother came into a blurred view as she moved around the end of the bed and twiddled with one of the machines I was apparently hooked to. The beeping stopped. "His antibiotic's out," she said, poking her head out the door of the room.

The whole left side of the room was glass, giving a front-row view of a massive nurses' station on the other side of the glass wall. Mom turned and padded quietly back toward the bed, then froze as she caught sight of me watching her. "Well, glory be. Welcome back to the world," she said, her lips parting into a broad smile.

A nurse in pink scrubs came in carrying a replacement bag. "He's awake," she said, smiling almost as broadly as my mother. "I'll let Dr. Merrick know."

As she replaced the bag, Mom moved around to the other side of the bed and scooted a chair closer. "How's your pain? On a scale of one to ten."

I wasn't feeling much of anything other than an incredibly heavy head. I tried to say "not bad" but all that came out was a dry, raspy whisper. On second thought, on a scale of one to ten, my throat was pushing a twelve. "My throat . . ." I whispered.

"That's from the ventilator."

"I'll get him some ice chips," the nurse said. She replaced the bag, then did a quick check of the array of monitors. "Need anything else?"

I shook my head slightly. Everything was still hazy at the moment, but I was certain given an hour, I could rattle off a list.

"Well, I'm Laurie. I'll be your CCU nurse tonight and if you need anything, just press the button on the side of the bed rail. But I think you're in pretty good hands. She hasn't left your bedside." She winked at my mother. She then pulled a heavy curtain across the windowed wall before she left.

"CCU?" I said, painfully, then forced myself to swallow.

"Critical Care Unit. You've been in a drug-induced coma for three days. They just removed the ventilator yesterday and started weaning you off the drugs this morning."

I nodded, afraid to try and say anything more. Laurie came back in the room with a small Styrofoam cup of ice chips and handed it to my mother. Mom scooped out a tiny bite with the plastic spoon and placed it carefully in my mouth. "You gave us quite a scare."

I held the ice in my mouth until it melted, then slowly swallowed. The cold actually felt good going down. I opened my mouth for more like a newborn bird.

"What happened?" I managed to squeak out after the third round of ice chips.

"You had a reaction to the shot of Dilaudid they gave you in the ER. You stopped breathing, then went into respiratory failure, then full cardiac arrest."

Wow. They shoved a tube down my throat and used the paddles. Fuck the advance directive.

Mom pretended to brush the hair off my forehead, but I think she just needed to touch me. "Father Sean O'Reilly gave you last rites. And we gave Rhonda valium." She laughed.

I held back a chuckle myself, envisioning the chaos I knew my kid sister could cause. And then I remembered the reason for the chaos. Panicked, I grabbed the sheet and jerked it away from my leg, fully expecting to see nothing but a bandaged nub. But my leg was there, and my foot was there, and five swollen toes were all still there. I dropped my head back on the pillow and fought off the urge to cry. I was not going to cry in front of my mother.

A doctor in a white lab coat came in, winked at my mother, then poked around on my leg. He was old enough to be experienced, and still young enough to be up on current medical procedures.

"I'm Dr. Merrick. It's nice to see you awake. You're a lucky man, Mr. Moran."

"My foot . . ."

"Your foot's going to be fine. The envenomation was quite minimal given the severity of the toxin. You're going to have two nice, rather large fang scars, but other than that, give it a few weeks and you won't even know you were bit. The pain should be controllable now with a pain reliever."

I nodded, relieved. "I've never been in so much pain in my life."

"It's understandable. Rattlesnake bites are incredibly painful to begin with but in your case, you're both fortunate and unfortunate. Fortunately, for your foot and ankle, the toxin went straight to your nervous system. I can say without a doubt, it saved your foot. Probably your whole leg. On the flip side, because of the neurotoxin, you suffered some serious pain, and had some pretty severe complications. Inducing a coma was the only way to control the pain. It gave your body time to settle back down into its own rhythm."

"They gave you eleven vials of antivenin," Mom added. "They had to fly some in from Dallas because we used all we had. You do have insurance, don't you? That stuff's a thousand dollars a bottle."

I would have choked but my throat was too sore.

"Rhonda was talking about maybe doing a fund-raiser—"

"Whoa!" I really did choke. After I caught my breath, I set my mother straight. "No one's doing any kind of fund-raiser. I have insurance. Very good insurance." Considering the fact I was self-employed and in what the insurance agency liked to call a somewhat "dangerous" occupation, it was rather expensive, too.

Dr. Merrick smiled, probably relaxing now that he knew he was going to get paid. "I'm sure we can work all that out later," he said. "Right now, I want you to stay in CCU tonight, then we'll see how you're doing tomorrow. If all goes well, we'll move you to a regular room for a day or two, then send you home. You may be on crutches a few weeks, depending on the swelling."

I nodded but was not real happy with the idea of staying in the hospital another couple of days nor hobbling around on crutches. I guess, given the alternative, I still had my foot and Father Sean O'Reilly's services were no longer needed, so I wasn't going to complain. As long as this thing didn't drag on too long. I had a job to get back to. Whether I was getting paid for it or not. I wondered if this qualified for workmen's compensation?

Dr. Merrick excused himself, saying he'd check back in the morning. My mother watched him leave, then, once sure he was gone, leaned in closer to me. "I think I can get him to reduce his bill." She winked at me.

"Mom—really . . . I have insurance. Quit worrying about the bill."

She shrugged. "I'm just saying . . . neurologists don't come cheap. If I can get his services for free, what's the harm?"

I glared at her suspiciously. I knew of professional courtesy, but there were always limits. She smiled a wicked smile. "He's asked me out a couple times."

Oh my God. My mother was going to prostitute herself to pay my hospital bill. "Mom, really . . . I have *damn* good insurance."

She patted my hand. "You don't worry about a thing. I'm goin' to run down to the ER for a little while and get a couple hours in."

I forced a smile and slowly nodded. My head was starting to hurt. I didn't know if it was from the snake bite, the coma, the thought of my sister planning a spaghetti dinner fund-raiser, or my mother doing it with my doctor.

The sooner I could get out of here, the sooner life could return to normal. Whatever that was. I had no idea where my cell phone was but there were calls I needed to make. I didn't know whose wrath at getting stood up was going to be worse: Sophia's or Claire's. At least I knew what to expect from Claire. Sophia was still a mystery.

Just as I was about to call for the nurse to see if my phone was even in the hospital, Rodney poked his head in the room. "So you are alive?" He was grinning ear to ear. He came in and went around to the chair Mom had sat in earlier. "Saw Mom in the hallway and she told me you were finally awake."

"No offense, but next time you and I go anywhere together, I'm going to go ahead and file workmen's comp."

He laughed. I was halfway serious.

"How's Rhonda?" I asked as he sat down.

He bobbed his head up and down. "Doing better. When they removed the ventilator yesterday and you didn't croak, I think she was finally convinced you were going to be okay. Enough about Rhonda . . . boy, that Sophia Ortez . . . that is *one hot mama*." He waved his hand like he was fanning a flame.

I stared at him, wondering what I had missed in my three-day coma. "And just how did you meet Sophia?"

"I remembered you said she was going to have someone in Odessa run a comparison on the tire tracks for you. I found her number in your phone and called her to let her know what happened. After a pretty chilly reception, she warmed up a little and did ask if you survived."

Ahh . . . so she was concerned. I couldn't help but grin. "Still doesn't explain how you met her," I said, all the more curious.

"I took your camera over to Odessa so she could pull the pictures off. She's not the friendliest woman in the world, but by God, she just might be the best looking."

Thoughts of Sophia in her low-cut blouses and that gorgeous

bronze-colored skin suddenly took a backseat to a more urgent thought. "Where's my camera? That's a three-thousand-dollar camera, Rodney."

"She's got it. She said she'd run the comparison then bring the camera back when you were out of CCU."

I had no reason not to trust her, but I still wasn't comfortable with my camera in the hands of someone I knew so little about. I didn't need a complete background check but I would at least like to know where she lived. That little desire probably wasn't totally business related but I had a headache from hell creeping up the back of my neck so I pushed those thoughts to the side.

"What did you do with the rope?" I asked, remembering what got me into this mess in the first place.

"Well, that's kind of interesting."

"Where's the rope, Rodney?" I almost died for that damn rope. It better be in his possession.

"Well, actually, we got more than we thought we did. Remember how you said one end was frayed and looked like it had been cut? Well, it had. And the second piece was coiled up in the bigger piece."

My heart skipped a beat and I don't think it had anything to do with the snake bite. "The noose?"

He nodded and smiled. "We think. Sophia's having the lab in Odessa run some tests on it. I haven't heard back from her yet."

"And if they find skin on it, we can do a DNA comparison. . . ."

"We'll need to get a hairbrush, a toothbrush. Anything we can pull a DNA sample from."

I sighed and laid my head back against the pillow. "If Denny's not in control, I'd like to know what they've got on him."

"In due time. You just concentrate on getting out of here." He stood up to leave. "And oh . . . Claire called. She called your cell about ten times so Rhonda finally called her back."

The creeping headache found its way into my brain and exploded into a giant throb. I hit the nurse call button in dire need of a pain pill.

"Rhonda was actually very nice to her. She told her she'd keep her updated. I think she called her last night to tell her you were off the ventilator. She said it'd be awhile before you were up to visitors, though."

I'd die of old age before Rhonda would tell Claire I felt up to visitors.

CHAPTER 17

The next morning I was moved to a regular room. My barbaric mother checked in on me before her shift. She ripped every hair on my chest out by the root when she tore off the little sticky pads the CCU nurse had left on, just in case. Just in case *what*? I wasn't planning on flatlining again and I sure wasn't interested in keeping them as a souvenir.

Rhonda had brought my cell phone, along with a pair of cargo shorts and a T-shirt. The lovely little hospital gowns with the open back weren't exactly my style.

"I don't think you're allowed to wear regular clothes," she said, turning her head while I slipped the shorts on.

"What are they going to do? Throw me out?"

My foot was still the size of a deflated basketball and it hurt like a bitch to put any weight on it. I unsnapped the shoulders of the hospital gown and dropped it to the floor. I stared at the IV tube still connected to the back of my left hand. Putting the T-shirt on was going to require some thought.

"I'm going to need a little help," I said as I took the IV bag down from the hanger.

Rhonda turned around and stared at me with a scowl on her face. "Gypsy . . . why can't you just once follow the rules?"

"I'm supposed to start walking down the hall today with crutches and I'm not wearing a gown that shows my ass. Hold the bag."

"You show your ass all the time."

I smiled sarcastically, then fed the bag through the sleeve of the shirt.

"What happened to your chest? You've got little red blotches all over it." She poked at one of the round blotches.

"Remember how mom used to rip off Band-Aids?"

"Ouch."

I had my left arm with the IV line through the sleeve and was fighting to get the shirt over my head when Rhonda stopped helping and said, "Oh. Hello."

"Hi."

I recognized that voice. I hurriedly pushed my head through the shirt, then smiled sheepishly at Sophia.

"Well, damn. Looks like you're going to make it," she said. "I thought I was going to inherit myself a pretty nice camera."

I pulled the shirt down over my red, blotchy chest, then introduced Rhonda to Sophia.

"Oh. So you're Sophia," Rhonda said. I detected a slight bit of uneasiness in her voice. "My husband's told me a lot about you."

Like what? The only thing Rodney knew about her was how damn good-looking she was and if he had at least one brain cell in his head, he'd keep that opinion to himself.

"Speaking of my camera . . ."

Sophia patted a leather book bag slung over her shoulder and smiled. "Haven't let it out of my sight."

Now that my mind could rest a little easier, I could bask in her glorious glow. I took a minute to soak up every ounce of her before getting down to business. "Feel up to working a little?" I got up, hobbled over to the bed tray, and pulled it over to the bed, my portable desk.

"You're asking me if I feel up to it? What about you? You're the one who was snakebit."

I laughed. My foot was killing me but in Sophia's presence, I was going to man up. "He may have got me but there isn't much DNA left of him." Then the pain from hobbling got to me. It was time for a pain pill. I wanted to cry. Maybe Sophia wouldn't stay too long. Male pride wouldn't let me even grimace in front of her.

Rhonda sat down on the side of the bed and scooted over to my portable desk. Sophia and I both glanced at her, then at each other. I shrugged. Sometimes it was just easier to not put up a fight against the Moran women. Sophia grinned, then pulled up the guest chair. She unloaded the camera, which I was overjoyed to see, and several eight-and-a-half-by-eleven color photos.

"First off," she said. "They're a perfect match."

I knew they would be but it was still nice to hear it. We examined the pictures closely as Sophia pointed out something that the naked eye missed. "The rear passenger tire has a screw or maybe a nail embedded, which is causing a slow leak. With each rotation, you can see where the tread skips."

"Like a hiccup," Rhonda said. She pointed out the "hiccup" in the pictures.

"Exactly. Did you notice the tire needing air?" Sophia asked, glancing up at me.

I slowly shook my head. "No, but it's been several weeks since Ryce was killed. McCoy's probably had it patched since then. What about the rope?"

Sophia smiled. "Rodney told you about it?"

"He said you were having the lab in Odessa analyze it."

"There was definitely epidermis on the smaller portion. And even a trace of blood."

"Was that the noose?" Rhonda asked.

Sophia and I looked at one another. "Yeah," I said. I pushed my hand through my hair, wondering how I was going to tell Tatum the rope he saw in the back of Averitt McCoy's truck was the rope that killed his father. Truth was, the kid probably already knew it.

"So what's next?" Rhonda asked.

"What I do best . . . surveillance work. I want to find out who's pulling Gaylord Denny's strings, and why. Would you like to join me?" I asked Sophia. It beat the hell out of spending several hours in the van with Rodney.

"How soon do you think you'll be ready to get back to work?" Sophia asked.

"As soon as they turn me loose. Probably another day or two."

"Now, wait just a minute," Rhonda said. "You've been through a major trauma. The doctor said you'd need physical therapy. Plus, you're supposed to have blood drawn every few days to check for organ damage—"

"The physical therapy is getting used to walking on crutches, which I've done before. And the blood work is outpatient. Besides, there's not a lot of physical work required in putting a tail on someone. All that's required is a lot of sitting and a lot of coffee."

"Gypsy, I'm not so sure—" Rhonda started, then stopped. "Ooh . . . hi, Claire."

I looked up at the door and thought I was going to need the ventilator again. Her smile nearly took my breath away. Her smile turned into more of a smirk as she eyed Sophia.

Sophia turned to get a look at my other visitor. Her brows

raised with surprise. She stood and offered Claire her hand. "Mrs. Sellars. It's a pleasure to see you again."

Claire ignored Sophia's outstretched hand but did smile. "Ms. . . . I'm sorry . . . I don't remember your name."

"Ortez," I said before Sophia had the chance.

"Ah, yes. I didn't realize you two knew each other." She waved her hand in our direction like she was shooing away a fly.

I gathered the pictures that were spread on the bed table and handed them to Sophia. "Sophia's helping me with an investigation."

"Oh. How nice of her."

The tension in the room was growing at a very uncomfortable rate. Claire was showing her true colors and it wasn't a pretty sight. I was within seconds of pressing the nurse-call button for a little something to knock me out.

"Well, I think I'll run down and see Mom, then grab something to eat," Rhonda said, anxious to get the hell out of there.

"I need to be going, too. I'll walk down with you," Sophia said. She put the pictures back in the book bag, then smiled at me. "Call me." She smiled at Claire, then waltzed out of the room with Rhonda in tow.

Claire watched them leave, waited a moment, then pushed the bed table out of the way, leaned in, and kissed me hard on the mouth. After she pulled away, she stood gazing at me. "I was worried I wouldn't ever be able to do that again. Rhonda said it was touch and go for a while."

I grinned. "You know Rhonda. She tends to be a little dramatic."

She sat down in the chair Sophia had sat in. "Last rites and a ventilator *is* a little dramatic."

My mind was bouncing like a Ping-Pong ball. I wanted to

grab her and love her. I wanted to know how she knew Sophia. I wanted a pain pill.

"Are you going to tell me how you got snakebit?" She was smiling again and the Ping-Pong ball was bouncing toward option number one.

"Oh . . . I was just in the wrong place at the wrong time."

She leaned forward and examined my foot. The scent of her jasmine shampoo seduced my olfactory nerves. "It actually looks pretty good, considering."

"So, how do you know Sophia Ortez?" I finally asked, curiosity getting the better of me.

She threw her head back and laughed. "I was going to ask *you* the same thing."

"I asked first."

Her laugh settled into the infamous Claire smirk. "She covered Steven's campaign. She was determined to find a skeleton in his closet, but always came up short." She shrugged.

I wondered if the shrug meant her husband was clean or if Sophia just didn't dig deep enough. I wondered if it involved hiring illegals?

"Your turn. How do you know her?"

Now I shrugged. "Like I said earlier, she's helping me with an investigation."

She lowered her brows and crinkled her perfect nose. "I didn't realize your trip home was a working visit."

"It didn't start that way. I'm just doing a favor for a friend."

She smiled devilishly. "And I'm sure the fact your working partner is absolutely beautiful doesn't hinder this investigation at all."

I fought back a grin. "Oh . . . Sophia? I hadn't noticed."

"Don't make me stomp on your bad foot."

We both laughed until I started wondering what was wrong

with this picture. Claire was the one who was married. I hadn't asked Sophia if *she* was seeing anyone, but to my knowledge, we were both free agents.

Claire got up out of the chair and sat close beside me on the bed, nuzzling my neck. I hadn't shaved in five days. I didn't want to imagine what her porcelain skin was going to look like. "I'm glad you're okay," she whispered, and I believed her.

Still, it irritated me that here was the wife of a state senator, recognizable to some in the general public, sidling up to me in my hospital bed like she was ready to see how okay I really was. I turned my head only slightly, but it was enough to cause her to pull back and glare at me.

"*Okay*," she said, and judging by her tone, I braced myself for the coming storm. "You want to tell me what's going on?"

I was wanting that pain pill something fierce. "Actually . . . I need to talk to you about your husband."

She stared hard at me with questioning eyes. "Steven?"

"Unless there's another one I don't know about."

She laid her hands in her lap like a schoolgirl and smiled softly. "Steven's the only man I ever married. The only man I ever *wanted* to marry loved Las Vegas more than he loved me."

Oh, that was a low blow. The same could be said for the only woman I ever wanted to marry who loved horses and cows more than she loved me. "Why'd you marry him if you didn't love him?"

She blew a heavy sigh. "He needed a wife for his career, and I needed a husband to keep the ranch."

"What do you mean to *keep the ranch*?"

She rolled her eyes. "Daddy and his stupid ideas of what a woman can and can't do. After his stroke, he was going to sell the ranch. He didn't think a woman could run it. Even if that woman was his own daughter."

"Does Steven know anything about running a ranch?"

She looked at me and grinned. "About as much as you do."

I returned the smile but something wasn't adding up. She had told me the night at the motel that they had been married twelve years. Carroll Kinley suffered his stroke four years ago. They were married long before Daddy threatened to sell.

"But weren't you and Steven already married when your dad had the stroke?"

She stared at me for a long time, then finally looked away as her eyes filled with tears. "What do you want me to say, Gypsy? That I got tired of waiting for you to come back? Steven was nice, he was convenient."

I'm sure Senator Sellars would like to know he was convenient. "Do you love him?"

She turned to me, her lips arched in a sweet smile. "No."

I took a deep breath, wanting to avoid what I knew was coming next.

"I've never loved anyone like I love you."

I called that one as if she were reading from a script. Probably because I was reading from the same script, reciting the same lines.

"And a divorce wouldn't be good for his political career," I said quietly.

She shrugged slightly. "That's a part of it. If I divorce him, I lose the ranch."

I stared at her, uncertain of what she meant. "The ranch is in Steven's name?"

"It's in both of our names. Daddy transferred ownership a few years ago."

"You could buy him out."

"Do you know how much the ranch is worth? Where would I ever get that kind of money?"

I hated that ranch with a passion but because I knew what it meant to her, I was suddenly scrambling for ways for her to never lose it. "You could use your share as collateral."

"A loan against the ranch? With Carroll Kinley still alive?" She chuckled.

"I guess killing him's out of the question."

Her mouth dropped as she gently punched my shoulder. "Gypsy!"

God knows the man had thought about killing me enough. I simply returned the thought. I lightly touched the scar on my lip. "I'm just kidding," I finally said so she wouldn't get any ideas. I had enough blood on my hands. I wondered how much blood Claire had on her hands? "How involved *is* Steven with the ranch?"

She looked at me as if she didn't understand the question, then slightly shook her head. "He's not involved at all. I oversee most of the day-to-day operation. Sam—remember Sam? He's still the foreman so he helps a lot."

"Who does the hiring?"

She cocked her head and stared at me, grinning slyly. "Why? You need a job?"

I laughed. "I tried that once. It didn't end very well."

"Yeah, I never did get the mud out of my blouse."

She had the most annoying ability to change the subject, or totally distract me. I pushed the memories of our rain-soaked lovemaking out of my mind. "No, I don't need a job," I said and smiled. "But my current job does have a couple questions about the ranch."

"Your current job? You're investigating the ranch?" She turned away and stared straight ahead, nodding angrily. "She won't give up."

She'd lost me. "Who won't give up?"

"That Mexican reporter. The one that was just in here. Did she put you up to this?"

"Claire, no one put me up to anything. I was hired by a family to investigate a suspected *murder.*"

She sprang from the bed and spun around to stare at me. "A murder? At the K-Bar? When?"

I shook my head and quickly raised my hands to calm her rising anger. "It wasn't at the ranch. The ranch isn't even involved, not directly anyway."

"What do you mean 'not directly'?" She was getting louder, and angrier.

"Claire, calm down. No one is investigating the ranch."

"Then why all the questions? Who does the hiring . . . how involved is Steven . . . you were interrogating me."

She always did have a flair for the dramatic. "I wasn't interrogating you. I had some questions because there were some things that came up during the course of the investigation that jumped out at me."

"What kind of things?"

I took a deep breath and figured I might as well put it out on the table. "The K-Bar employs several undocumented workers. I didn't know if you were aware of that."

She looked away, her mouth twisted into a tight knot. She didn't say anything for a long while and I could see the words tumbling around in her head as she contemplated what to say. Finally, she looked at me, then sat back down on the bed. "I don't know that much about your business, Gypsy, but I imagine you work by yourself most of the time. I doubt in your line of work you've ever had the need to hire someone. The Mexicans who work at the ranch are good men. They're hard workers. It's not an easy job. I mean, you lasted what . . . one summer?"

"Claire, I'm not saying they're not good men. But it can't look good for a state senator to knowingly be working illegals."

She sighed again then spoke in a soft voice. "He doesn't know."

That's *not* what I wanted to hear. I wanted her to tell me her husband was the mastermind behind everything and she was totally mortified at his unscrupulous behavior. But it's not a perfect world.

"Did you hire them or did Sam?"

She closed her eyes and spoke in a sad voice. "I did. I think part of me did it out of spite, thinking how it might even benefit me for the good senator to be caught in a scandal. He couldn't really make too many demands for a divorce settlement if his career was at stake."

"And what about the other part?"

She stiffened her back and set her jaw. "It was strictly business. It was financially beneficial to everyone involved."

Everyone except the eight missing girls.

She sniffled back tears, then laid her head on my shoulder. "So what do we do now? Is your pretty Mexican girlfriend going to expose Senator Sellars's dirty little secret?"

"It's not *his* dirty little secret."

She wiped at her face, then glanced up at me. "You know, this might not be a bad thing. If he thinks his political career is in jeopardy, he might be willing to negotiate a more reasonable settlement."

That was my Claire. Always thinking. Always thinking about how she could benefit from someone else's problems.

"She's not my girlfriend. She's a business associate," I said, referring to Sophia.

She pulled away and looked at me. "I hope you're not one to mix business with pleasure."

I put my arm around her and pulled her to me. "Only at the company Christmas party, sweetheart."

CHAPTER 18

I wanted to kill Rhonda as soon as Rodney pulled into the driveway. I had the sinking feeling my sister was throwing a coming-home party and I was the guest of honor. Rodney parked behind Tatum and Burke's truck. My mother's two-seater sports car was parked in the yard and a shiny red Mercedes convertible was parked behind my van.

"Rodney . . . what is she doing?" I asked, staring at the bright yellow balloons and yellow ribbon tied to the porch rail.

"Don't be mad at her, Gypsy. She means well."

He closed the passenger-side door after I got out. I maneuvered the crutches along the walkway, still unable to put any weight on my left foot. I stopped and stared at the Mercedes, praying Dr. Merrick hadn't taken my mother up on her offer.

Inside, a "Welcome Home" banner stretched across the top of the archway between the living room and the kitchen. Clusters of yellow balloons were taped to each end of the banner; a few strays had escaped and were floating around the ceiling.

I was more than pleasantly surprised, and a bit embarrassed, to discover the Mercedes didn't belong to Dr. Merrick. It was Sophia's. She was sitting beside Tatum on the sofa and smiled coyly at me.

"He's here!" Tatum squeaked as he leapt up. He ran over and awkwardly wrapped his arms around my waist.

"We can see that, Tatum," Burke said, and shook his head, grinning. He was parked in his chair near the television. "Don't knock him down or he might need this ol' chair before the night's over."

Rhonda, Mom, and Gram all gathered at the doorway. Rhonda was wearing an apron, Mom had an oven mitt on one hand, and Gram was holding a wooden spoon. With this collection of women in the same kitchen—the house hadn't burned to the ground yet—I was impressed.

Rhonda squealed like she was meeting a rock star. "Welcome home!" She hugged me, then kissed me on the cheek.

"How's the foot?" Mom asked.

"Good," I lied. I wasn't going to say it hurt like hell in front of Sophia.

"Damn lucky they didn't cut it off," Gram huffed, then went back to the kitchen mumbling something about Grandpa and a nest of rattlers.

"Gram—keep that spoon out of the spaghetti," Rhonda said, and hurried to follow her back into the kitchen. "You're goin' to make it gummy."

Mom looked at me and shrugged. What did she know about spaghetti? She turned and headed back into the kitchen to referee.

I smiled apologetically at Sophia. At least, to my knowledge, Rhonda's spaghetti dinner was a family-and-friends affair and not a community-wide fund-raiser.

"Tatum, help him over to the sofa while I put his bag away," Rodney said.

I didn't need the help but humored Tatum anyway and let him think he was my rock of stability.

"I sure am glad they didn't have to cut your foot off," he said, his arm still wrapped around my waist.

I grinned. "So am I."

I eased myself down beside Sophia onto the sofa and laid the crutches across the coffee table. She still hadn't said a word but her presence was undeniable. She was generating enough electricity to power a small city.

"Well . . . this is kind of embarrassing," I mumbled.

Her perfect nose twitched as she controlled a small smile. "I think it's kind of sweet," she whispered, leaning toward me as if sharing a secret.

Tatum sat down in an old recliner Gram had brought with her when she moved in years ago. It had once smelled like cigar smoke. In recent years, it had taken on an old-person, menthol smell. "So, what do we do now?" Tatum asked. "We have the proof we need, right?"

"Will you let the man enjoy his first night at home?" Burke said. "The evidence isn't going anywhere. Is it?" He looked at Sophia, then at me.

"Rodney has everything secured, and properly tagged. And I do plan on getting back to work tomorrow." I grinned at Tatum.

"Great. What are we doing?"

"Tatum," Burke scolded.

I laughed and Sophia giggled softly. "It's okay, Burke. He has other motives. He wants to put this thing behind him so I can take him up to the sinkholes to take some pictures."

"You didn't forget," he said, beaming.

Whatever his reasons, I couldn't blame him for wanting it to be over. But I wasn't going to be the one to tell him it would never, ever really be over. Whether dead or absent, the first birthday that comes and goes without an acknowledgment is the hardest. After that, you just become numb to it. But it's always there.

Rhonda popped her head into the living room. She looked overwhelmed. "Dinner's almost ready."

Poor Sophia. Subjected to all three Moran women and their nonexistent cooking skills at one time. I hope she didn't consider this a date.

After dinner, Sophia, me, Rodney, and Burke went out to the deck. Tatum remained in the kitchen, giving the Moran women cooking advice. Rodney quickly brushed off a chair for Sophia, then pulled his chair beside her, leaving me to fend for myself. I leaned a crutch against the rail, then struggled with one arm and one good foot to position the other chair within hearing distance.

"So, how long have you been a reporter?" Rodney asked.

"Since junior high," she said, offering nothing more.

"A whole three years, huh?" He cackled at his own joke.

I groaned, expecting him to say something about heaven calling because they were missing an angel. If he was going to flirt, he at least needed to come up with some decent lines.

I cleared my throat to remind him I was there. "Sophia, why don't you tell Burke about your meeting with Sheriff Denny?"

"Gypsy told me you thought he had dementia," Burke said.

She told him what she had told me. "He just seemed to be a doddering old man who didn't even know what day it was, let alone being the ringleader of a human trafficking ring."

Burke leaned forward in his wheelchair, resting his elbows on his knees. "Maybe you just got him flustered. He always did have an eye for a pretty woman." He winked at her and I closed my eyes.

Jesus. Not him, too. Sophia took the compliment in stride, smiled softly, then shook her head. "No, this was much different. He went from talking coherently to me one minute to not even remembering I was in the room the next."

"Now *that's* impossible," Rodney said, and laughed himself silly.

I felt sorry for her. And I wanted to whack my brother-in-law in the head with a crutch.

"Sophia and I are going to put a tail on him tomorrow," I said, and casually threw a smile in Rodney's direction.

"Oh. What time? Maybe I'll tag along as backup."

"Oh, I don't know. Sometime tomorrow afternoon. You'll probably still be on duty."

The look of disappointment on his face made me feel a slight twinge of guilt. It faded quickly.

"Besides, it'll be pretty close quarters in the van," I added just for spite.

"What are you hoping to find by running surveillance on Denny?" Burke asked.

"Who's pulling the strings and why Denny's letting them."

"You know who's pulling the strings," Rodney said. "The guy who shoved his knee in your crotch." He turned to Sophia and slowly shook his head. "Thought Gypsy was going to be out of commission for months."

Sophia looked at me with raised brows. Much more and I was going to remind Rodney that his wife, *my* sister, was a few feet away in the kitchen. I didn't want this to turn into an all-out war.

"Mark Peterson," I said.

She nodded. "The same guy who gave you the busted lip?"

I smiled sarcastically and slowly nodded.

"No wonder you want to take him down."

Rodney and Burke laughed like they were front row at a comedy show with the poor schmuck sitting next to them the target of some smart-ass comedian. I let them have their moment, then turned the conversation back to business.

"I know Peterson is pulling the strings, but I want to know why Denny's letting him. Peterson's got to have something on the old man. You worked with him, Burke. Is there something in his past Peterson might be using?"

"You said he had an eye for pretty women," Sophia said. "Maybe an affair?"

I liked that . . . teamwork. And she was on my team. The ten-year-old in me wanted to stick my tongue out at Rodney.

Burke leaned back in his chair and rubbed his chin, thoughtfully considering her question. "If there was an affair, or affairs, he was discreet. Sure, there were rumors, but he was the sheriff. Everyone just looked the other way."

"What if Peterson decided he wasn't going to look the other way any longer?" I asked.

Burke scrunched his face and rubbed his chin again. "I don't know, Gypsy. I don't think men play by the same rules as women do when it comes to things like that."

"Meaning men don't usually rat out one another when it comes to affairs," Sophia said.

"But Mark Peterson's not most men. He doesn't seem to play by anyone's rules but his own," I added.

"That's true," Rodney added. "Most men would never shove his knee into another man's crotch hard enough to take him down to the ground."

I smiled at him, silently thanking him for the reminder. Silently plotting how I was going to dispose of his body after I killed him.

"Well, I guess Sophia and I'll just have to spend some time in the van until we find out what Denny's hiding."

I was pleased with myself. Torture was always preferable to killing.

CHAPTER 19

I spent the next morning with my foot propped on a pillow in a chair at the kitchen table reviewing the evidence we had, and what we still needed. Rhonda played nursemaid, refilling my coffee before the cup was empty and asking every fifteen minutes if I needed anything for pain.

"Are you sure you're going to feel up to doing this surveillance thingy this afternoon?" she asked for the third time.

"Rhonda, surveillance really isn't hard work. It involves a mind-numbing amount of sitting. I think I can handle that."

"Leave him alone for crying out loud. He said he'd be fine," Gram said. She circled a word in her *Word Search* magazine and smiled at her accomplishment.

"Excuse me, Gram, but Gypsy *died* a couple days ago. I'd like to make sure we don't have a repeat performance."

"We all got to go sometime. Hot damn! Finished another one." She flipped the page with an arthritic hand, then began a new puzzle.

I wasn't sure if I should thank her for telling Rhonda to stop hovering, or worry about her lack of concern over my flatlining experience.

"Besides, he's probably just using this surveillance *thingy* as an excuse to get in that little Mexican chica's panties. If she wears any."

Rhonda and I both stared at her for a long moment.

"Isn't it about time for your nap?" I finally asked Gram.

She looked up over her bottle-thick glasses at me. "I ain't been up but an hour."

It seemed like so much longer.

Rhonda sat down in the empty chair and started tugging on her right ear, a sure sign she was worried about something. "I think Sophia's very . . . nice. I mean, she seemed . . . pleasant enough."

"I thought she was a bitch," Gram said.

"Gram!" Rhonda's mouth fell open as wide as her eyes. "That's a horrible thing to say."

"She's not a bitch. She's an . . . observer," I said.

"Well, whatever you want to call her, she sure ain't warm and fuzzy," Gram said.

"Can we stop talking about Sophia?" I asked.

"Well, since we're talking about her," Rhonda said. "Are you seeing her?"

I sighed heavily. "At the moment, we're business associates."

"At the moment . . ." Rhonda tugged on her ear again.

"It means when they're through working together he's hoping to get laid."

"Gram!"

"Okay—as of right now, my personal life is off-limits. We're not discussing it anymore."

"It's not that I'm not happy for you, anything to get you away from Claire, it's just—"

"Rhonda! Off-limits—no more discussion. Period."

"Talk about bitchy," Gram mumbled.

I jerked up the laptop and the files, shoved the crutch under

my arm, and hobbled back to the bedroom where I could half-ass
concentrate on what I was doing. I either needed to find an apartment, or Gram needed to break a hip and go to rehab in a nursing
home, or school needed to start back so Rhonda would have something else to spend her time on, or one of us was going to disappear.

I propped a pillow against the headboard, then set up shop on
the bed. Averitt McCoy wasn't a go-to man; he was a follower.
Which meant McCoy was the weak link in Peterson's food chain.
So far, I could connect every piece of evidence I had back to Mc-
Coy, not Peterson. Something told me Peterson planned it that
way. That in itself wasn't a bad thing. If McCoy was as weak as I
suspected and was hit with the mounting pile of evidence against
him, he might roll over on Peterson with a gentle nudge.

How Sheriff Denny fit into all this was still a mystery. He owed
someone something and my bet was on Peterson. I keyed the Kermit
County Board of Elections into the laptop and searched candidates'
financial records. Denny had quite a coffer of campaign contribu-
tions. If Peterson had made a donation to the cause, he kept it
low enough they didn't have to attach his name to it. But the K-Bar
Ranch had made a sizable donation, along with Mrs. Claire Kinley
Sellars herself. It wasn't enough to raise a red flag—unless you had
something to tie it back to. I stared at the name for a while, wondering how deep she really was involved.

Maybe Peterson had conned her into hiring the illegals, then
threatened her with it? Maybe she had just gotten in over her head
and didn't know how to get out?

I logged in to the banking program and keyed in Claire's name,
then minimized the screen. I didn't know if I really wanted to see
it or not. I sat there for the longest time staring at the screen saver of
the Bellagio, afraid to know the truth, ashamed I even suspected it.

Finally, I took a breath and maximized the screen. I found her records of deposits and withdrawals. I pulled out the copies of Peterson's accounts I had printed earlier and started comparing line by line. If I was right, Peterson was paying Claire to hire the illegals. Maybe that was the extent of her involvement? Maybe she didn't know anything about the missing girls? And if I were right again, Claire would be making a sizable deposit days after Peterson made a withdrawal. Sure enough, there was a pattern. My stomach knotted as I highlighted the dates and the amounts. Then I sat staring at the ugly truth, the bitter bile slowly creeping into my throat. I had it backward. Peterson wasn't paying Claire. Claire was paying Peterson. The sonofabitch was blackmailing her.

Mark Peterson was selling teenage girls; he'd taken Tatum's father from him; he'd tried to take me out on a basketball court; and he was putting the pinch on Claire. I was really harboring a strong dislike for this guy. I had to figure out a way to take him down without Claire getting caught in the cross fire. If he was using her husband's career as the bargaining chip, she could shed a few tears for the camera, say how truly sorry she was for her lack of judgment, and come out of it looking like a victim.

I worked through lunch and into the early afternoon charting a timeline and fitting pieces of the puzzle into the bigger picture. I wondered if Ryce had any idea of the scope of what he was uncovering?

Although the bedroom door was open, Rhonda knocked anyway. "Hey . . . Sophia's here."

I tried to get up off the bed but a searing heat shot up from my foot, running the length of my leg. I grabbed my thigh and grimaced at the suddenness of the pain.

"You okay?" Rhonda asked, stepping into the room. "When's the last time you had a pain pill?"

"I'm fine," I lied. "Just a cramp." I grabbed the crutch and

forced myself up but the pain was intense. I laughed, then eased myself back down onto the bed. I was not postponing this tail we had
planned on Denny. "Why don't you escort Sophia back to my office?"

"You want me to bring her back here?" She looked around the
bedroom disapprovingly.

"Is Gram still living?"

She huffed and rolled her eyes. "You can be so cruel, Gypsy."
She turned and left, shaking her head as she went.

I took the bottle of pain pills from the nightstand drawer,
popped two, then downed them with a swig of leftover morning
coffee. A moment later, Sophia, in all her splendor, was standing at
the bedroom door. She was wearing a plain white T-shirt and plaid
shorts, perfect for a night of sitting in a van. She was carrying the
same leather bag she had brought to the hospital.

"Hi," she said, a small grin dancing across her perfect lips.

"Can I get you something to drink?" Rhonda offered, playing
the good hostess.

"I'm fine, but thanks anyway," Sophia said.

She wasn't a bitch. She was quite pleasant. Quite pleasant
indeed.

"Can I get you a chair?" Rhonda asked.

Again, Sophia smiled. "No, really, I'm fine."

"She can sit on the bed. I promise, we'll keep the door open."
I scooted over and made room for Sophia to sit down.

Rhonda's face turned bright red. She quickly shook her head.
"Oh, no, I didn't mean it like that. I mean . . . I just thought she
might be more comfortable . . . okay, I'm going to go now. If y'all
need anything, just yell." She turned and hurried out of the room.

Sophia's lips were locked tight as she fought hard not to burst
out laughing. I patted the side of the bed. She glared at me a moment,
those mocha-colored eyes searching my every intention.

"Trust me. I'm harmless." I grinned.

"For now." She chuckled, then sat down facing me, keeping one foot on the floor. She sat the leather bag between us, then opened it up and removed a file folder. "I've got Denny's work and civic-related schedule and according to my research assistant, he does attend the board of alderman meetings. He did miss the April meeting and the undersheriff sat in for him." She handed me a printout of Denny's schedule.

Rotary Club, Lions Club, Jaycees, Winkler County Democratic Committee, and various law-enforcement organizations. If the man's mind was wandering, it was because the poor guy probably couldn't remember where he was supposed to be and when.

Sophia handed me another printout. "I went ahead and pulled some basic background info. I'm sure it's not as detailed as what you can gather, but hey, I'm not getting paid for this." She smiled.

I chuckled. "Neither am I."

She stared at me for a long moment. "You're kidding?"

I laughed again. "It's a long story."

She offered a wicked smile. "You're a crusader for justice?"

"I wish I was that noble. I felt sorry for Tatum. He deserves to know what happened to his dad. No kid should have to go through life wondering."

Her smile vanished as she studied me. I felt the heat of her thoughts boring into my soul, going places I wasn't comfortable with her seeing. "So, Denny's married," I said, quickly turning my attention to the background information. "Wife's name is Martha. She's more civic-minded than he is. President of the Junior League, chairwoman of the Safe Haven for Domestic Violence Victims . . ."

"She also volunteers twice a week at the elementary school as a reading buddy."

I read further. The Dennys had two daughters, neither was married and both lived in Tulsa. Why would both daughters live out of state? They both graduated from Texas universities, so an out-of-state college wasn't the reason. Neither was married so there weren't husbands to consider. Sons moved away; daughters usually stayed closer to home unless careers, school, or significant others took them away. It was pretty sexist in theory, but it was the truth.

"Mrs. Denny's avoiding something at home," I said.

Sophia glanced at the printout, then looked to me to explain. "Why do you say that?"

"Look at all the stuff she's involved in. She's either making amends for something that's going on at home or she's avoiding having to be at home. Or maybe both."

Sophia was skeptical. "Why can't she just be a good person with too much energy?"

I shrugged. "She could be, I suppose. But if I were a betting man, I'd say she's making good to make up for something bad. The daughters moved out of state. They live close to one another but left Mom and Dad in the dust."

"Maybe their jobs took them out of state."

I pulled the laptop over and keyed in the first daughter's name. Within a few seconds, I had her complete profile. "She's a restaurant manager. She could do that in Texas." I pulled up the second daughter's info. "The youngest one is a graphic artist. There's plenty of design firms in Texas."

Sophia gnawed on the inside of her lip, not wanting to admit my theory had a basis. "Maybe they just raised independent daughters."

"Possibly. But I don't think so. The oldest daughter is thirty-five, the youngest is thirty-two. Their baby-making clocks are ticking and neither really has the kind of career you'd have to choose between family or work. Why no kids? Why no husbands?"

Her eyes narrowed into tiny slits. "Do you *even know* how sexist that is?"

I think we were about to have our first real fight. But I wasn't going to backpedal to soften the truth. "Yes—I know it's sexist and archaic. But it's the truth, Sophia. There's a reason these two women are living where they're living, aren't married, and have no children."

"Yeah, and the reason may be they simply don't want to be married and don't want kids. Not every woman dreams of the white picket fence and a dozen snot-nosed kids running around."

I threw my hands up to calm the storm. "I'm just saying there's usually a reason *why* they don't want it."

"Yeah—they just don't want it." Her voice was raised. I'd not only touched a nerve, I'd severed it. "Wow. I'd never have guessed you to be so blatantly *chauvinistic*."

"All I'm saying is, where the Denny sisters are concerned, I'd be willing to bet the reason has something to do with Daddy. There's a reason people want or don't want things. Do you have kids? A husband?"

She sprang up off the bed and I actually flinched. I thought for a moment she was either going for the jugular or upside my head. "Whoa," she said, jamming her hands on her hips. "Ground rule number one, we're not going there. Have I asked you how long you've been screwing Claire Sellars?"

I could hear my heart beating in the silence. We stared at each other for a long while, each trying to grasp what had just happened. Was she trying to make a point that I had treaded into a topic that was off-limits? Or was the investigative journalist in her curious because she had investigated the senator and his wife? Or was she actually a little interested in who I was sleeping with?

I finally looked away from her and pretended to read Denny's schedule again. "Okay . . . it looks like he's got a Rotary Club meeting tonight. So, um, here's the game plan. We pick up the tail at the Sheriff's Department, and stay with him until he's tucked away nice and safe at home."

She nodded quickly, then casually sat back down on the bed. "And how long do we do this?" I thought I detected a slight quiver in her voice. Miss Cool-as-a-Cucumber was flustered. It was kind of cute. It took every ounce of restraint I could muster to not comment on it.

"We'll do it a few nights and if nothing happens, we'll switch gears and go to plan B."

"And what's plan B?"

I grinned. "Well, if plan A works, we won't need plan B, will we?"

She nodded. "You don't have a plan B, do you?"

I shook my head. We were easing back into our comfort zones and I liked it. Maybe it was going to be a good night after all.

CHAPTER 20

Sheriff Gaylord Denny left his office at 6:15 P.M. He drove straight home, disappeared inside his comfortable brick ranch-style house and emerged twenty minutes later. He had changed out of his coat and tie and into a pair of ill-fitting athletic pants, ball cap, and a golf shirt that looked like it had been pulled from the bottom of the laundry hamper.

"I don't think Rotary Club meetings are formal, but it seems he'd at least make himself presentable," I said.

Sophia didn't say anything as she watched Denny through the tinted windshield. She was in the passenger seat with her long legs pulled up and feet pressed against the dashboard.

I had parked two houses down on the intersecting street with a clear shot of the Denny homestead just beyond the backyards. Denny left the department-issued vehicle in his driveway and climbed into an older model Cadillac with a busted taillight and scratched rear bumper.

"Peterson's got something on him." I cranked the engine and followed the Cadillac out of the neighborhood. He drove about two miles, then picked up the main road and headed back into town.

"Why do you say Peterson has something on him?"

"If he was an active participant, he'd shell out the money to have his car fixed. A man that drives around in a Caddy likes the status that comes with it. They usually have the car in the shop the next day."

"I still say he's just a doddering old man with some issues."

I threw a glance at her and grinned. "Uh-huh. Then why are you tagging along on this ride? It's not that you simply like my company."

She glared at me a moment, then turned back to the windshield. "I'm tagging along to prove you wrong." I thought I saw a hint of a grin.

"He's turning into that burger joint." She pointed toward the fast food restaurant on the corner. "He's going through the drive-thru."

I pulled into the opposite turning lane and headed into the gas-station parking lot across the street. "Why the hell is he going through a drive-thru? Don't they have dinner at Rotary meetings?" I pulled the van out of the way of the gas pumps and parked near the curb where I could keep an eye on the restaurant.

"Maybe he doesn't like what they serve."

"Or maybe he's not going to the meeting." I hoped he wasn't going anywhere he wanted to make an impression. Not how he was dressed.

A few minutes later, he pulled out of the drive-thru and back onto the main road. I let a few cars pass, then picked up where we'd left off. About three miles later, he turned into Kermit's definition of a mall and drove around to the south entrance.

"He's going shopping?" Sophia was as perplexed as I was.

"Maybe he's shopping for a new outfit."

The parking lot was nearly empty. Denny parked, got out, and strolled inside. I parked a row over. "Can you follow him?" I asked Sophia.

She looked at me with a tiny amount of fear in her eyes. "Me?"

"I'm going to tag along behind you but I'm afraid we're going to lose him if you don't go now. I'm still kind of hobbling." My voice took on an urgent tone as Denny neared the entrance.

Sophia hurried out of the van, giving me a look like she didn't know if she should trust me. What did she think I was going to do? Drive away and leave her there? She sprinted toward the same entrance Denny had just gone through. Damn, she looked good in shorts.

I climbed out of the van, then pulled a crutch from the back. When I finally got to the entrance, I called Sophia's cell. "Where are you?"

"At the Dollar Movie Palace."

"He's seeing a movie?"

"*Toy Story 3.*"

"Seriously?"

"Ah . . . yeah."

He's meeting someone. "Buy two tickets and I'll be there in a minute."

Before she could respond, I clicked my phone off and hobbled inside. She was standing at the theater entrance and didn't look happy.

"The least you can do is buy me popcorn." She handed me the tickets.

I happily obliged and even bought her a drink. The movie was showing on screen six of six, which meant it was at the farthest end of the theater. By the time we made it down the hallway, my foot was throbbing.

The trailers for upcoming attractions were already playing so the theater was dark, illuminated only by the flickering on the giant screen. The theater was stadium seating with a few clusters

of people scattered here and there, no one wanting to invade anyone's space. Denny was sitting by himself on the third row from the
back. I gritted my teeth and struggled with the crutch until we
made it to the back row. From this vantage point, we had a great
view of the back of Denny's head.

There was a couple sitting on the opposite end of the top row
and three teenagers in the middle of the next row within whisper-
ing distance to Denny. Other than these few, we had the top half of
the theater to ourselves.

"Did you see one and two?" Sophia asked in a hushed voice.

"One and two what?"

"*Toy Story.*"

I glared at her, then shook my head slowly. "No, I'm afraid I
missed those."

She stared, mesmerized, at the trailer for a romantic comedy,
slowly moving individual pieces of popcorn to her mouth. "They
were great," she said between bites.

"Uh-huh. I try not to make it a habit of lurking around kiddie
movies. Especially if I don't have a kid with me. Otherwise
people look at you weird—kind of like we're looking at Denny
right now."

She lifted her chin and looked at the back of our subject's head.
"Maybe he just likes great animation. You know, people with dementia or Alzheimer's do sometimes revert back to childhood."

"That's true, but he drove himself here. He dressed in comfortable clothes and knew exactly where he was going when he
left the house. And ten to one, Mrs. Denny thinks he's at the Rotary meeting."

"Probably." She turned her attention back to the screen and
settled in for the movie.

It was obvious by her interest in a plastic cowboy named Woody that I was going to be the one to keep an eye on Sheriff Denny.

"This movie's about talking toys?" I asked, thirty minutes into the movie.

"*Shhh.*"

I went back to watching Denny and let her watch the movie in peace. When it was over, Denny wandered the mall for half an hour, then bought an ice cream cone and sat on one of the benches. Sophia and I pretended to be interested in a cell phone display a few stores down from where Denny sat enjoying his melting ice cream. I popped a pain pill and took a swallow of Sophia's watered-down soda to wash it down.

"Did you like the movie?" she asked, in all seriousness.

I shrugged. "Not really."

She looked taken aback. "How can you not like *Toy Story*?"

"That doll with the messed-up eye gave me the creeps."

She stared at me a moment, her lips puckered in question. Finally, she pointed a finger at me. "There's a named phobia for that. I can't think of it at the moment, but fear of dolls is a real phobia. Probably goes back to something in your childhood."

I couldn't help but grin. "Don't try to analyze me. You'll die of frustration."

Denny stood up, wiped the chocolate from his mouth with a napkin, then dropped the napkin in a wastebasket. He glanced around the mall, then headed out.

"Whoever he was meeting didn't show." I nudged Sophia in Denny's direction and we tagged along at a safe distance.

"How do you know he was meeting someone? Maybe he was just observing, keeping an eye out for trouble. He is the sheriff."

"How can you keep an eye out for trouble in a dark theater?"

"Okay, with him being the sheriff, would he actually meet someone in a public place like a mall?"

"Dark theater, dear. He just spent two hours in a dark theater alone watching a kid's movie. Now that's creepy."

It was dark when we got outside the mall. We climbed back in the van and followed Denny back to his neighborhood. I drove by the entrance street and circled back around. The Cadillac was parked in the driveway beside a black Lexus I assumed was Mrs. Denny's. I drove around the neighborhood a couple times to make sure Sheriff Denny was home for the night.

"So much for the Rotary Club." I turned back on to the main street and headed to Rhonda's.

"So what do we do now?"

"The same thing tomorrow night."

"I'm telling you he's just a doddering old man."

"And I'm telling you he was meeting someone."

And whoever that someone was, was one of the reasons Denny's daughters lived out of state. But I wasn't going to broach that subject again. Not yet anyway.

She glanced at me and shook her head, a tiny smile playing on her lips. Damn, she *could* read my mind.

At Rhonda's, we climbed out of the van and stood in the driveway a long moment. I caught a glimpse of the blind in the living room pull aside, then drop back in place. Eat your heart out, Rodney.

"Same time tomorrow?" Sophia asked.

I nodded. "I'll check the movie schedule and see what's playing."

She threw her head back and laughed, then said, "I still don't understand how anyone could not like *Toy Story*. It's a classic."

"No—*The Godfather,* one and two, are *classics.*"

"It's the doll thing, isn't it?"

"I don't want to talk about it. I'll have nightmares."

She laughed hard again, and then a comfortable silence settled on us like a setting sun. I wanted to kiss her so bad I could already taste her.

"Okay . . . same time tomorrow," she said, then hopped into the Mercedes. She gave me a little wave, then disappeared into the darkness.

I stood there for a long time staring at the spot at the end of the street where I lost sight of her. I wondered whom she was going home to. Lucky bastard. I wondered if she lived in an apartment. A condo? Maybe a house with a yard.

I could find out everything I wanted to know with one click on the laptop, but somehow, it felt like an invasion of her privacy. Of course, in the grand scheme of things, it was. It just didn't seem right where she was concerned. She'd tell me everything I needed to know in time.

Inside, Rodney and Rhonda hurried away from the window and headed into the kitchen as soon as I opened the front door.

"Y'all are so busted," I said.

"What?" Rodney turned around and looked at me with this goofy expression that made me want to laugh rather than kill him. "What do you mean *we're busted?*"

"We were just going into the kitchen to grab a beer," Rhonda said. "You want one?"

I slowly shook my head and grinned, following them into the kitchen. Beer my ass. Rhonda hadn't had a beer since high school when she threw up all over the floorboard of my Camaro.

"How'd it go?" Rodney asked. "Anything out of the ordinary?"

I eased myself down into one of the chairs and propped the

crutches against the wall. "Depends on what you call ordinary, I suppose. He was supposed to go to a Rotary Club meeting but ended up at the movies instead."

"He went to the movie alone?"

I shrugged. "Personally, I don't think he intended to be alone. But whoever he was meeting was a no-show."

"How do you know he was meeting someone?" Rhonda asked. She handed me a beer, then handed one to Rodney.

I unscrewed the cap and downed half the bottle in one swig. "He was seeing some kiddie movie. Grown men usually don't go to kiddie movies by themselves."

"Really?" She looked to Rodney for confirmation.

He shrugged. "Unless they're a movie critic, it is kind of weird."

"What movie?" Rhonda asked.

I took a smaller swallow of the beer. "I don't know, something about talking toys."

"*Toy Story 3*," they both said in unison.

"Ah, man . . . we wanted to see that," Rodney said. "I didn't think it was still playing."

I stared from one to the other. Had the world gone completely mad? I pushed thoughts of that creepy baby doll with the bad eye out of my head before a nightmare became a real possibility.

The only doll baby I wanted to dream about tonight was Sophia.

"So he skipped out on a Rotary meeting to see a movie," Rodney said. "Maybe he's just a member of the Rotary but only attends a couple meetings?"

"Could be. But as an elected official, you'd think he would want to rub elbows with as many constituents as possible."

Rodney finally took a drink of his beer. Rhonda hadn't touched hers.

"What do you want to do about Averitt McCoy?" Rodney asked.

"Bring him in for a formal interview. Hopefully, he'll roll over on Peterson and everything will be hunky-dory."

"And if he doesn't?"

"We've got the evidence. Evidence doesn't lie."

"And what are you going to do about Denny?"

The beer and the painkillers were doing a tango in my head and my thought process was moving in slow motion. "Tail him again tomorrow. Peterson's got something on him and I want to know what it is. The more evidence we have against Peterson, the better."

And the sooner I knew how everyone was connected in this sick game, the sooner I could move on to a paying job.

The next morning, the sound of a car engine woke me. I fumbled for the alarm clock and was surprised to see it was after nine. I rolled over and peered out the bedroom blinds in time to see Rhonda's car heading down the street. Today was volunteer day at the adult enrichment center, which meant she had Gram with her.

I sat on the edge of the bed a moment and examined my foot. It was only about a quarter size larger than normal now so I took that as a sign the swelling was going down each day. Another couple days and I might be able to wear something other than sandals.

I hobbled into the kitchen to find Rhonda had left the coffee on. Hot coffee, a quiet house, no Gram. It was starting out to be a pretty good day. I poured a cup of coffee, then took it and my phone out on the back deck. I scrolled to Claire's number in my contact list, then punched send.

"Good morning, gorgeous," I said when she answered.

"Good morning to you, too. How's the foot?"

"Better. Still a little swollen but at least I can tell I have five individual toes now."

She laughed, then asked, "Feel up to lunch?"

"I thought you'd never ask."

"Can you drive yet?"

I thought it best not to mention last night's surveillance work. "Oh, yeah. I'm good. Where and when?"

"Well, if I remember correctly, we had plans for a picnic here at the ranch."

"Yeah, we did, didn't we? Around noon?"

"I'll see you then. When you come in, drive past the main house. My house is about a mile and a half past Daddy's. "

"He's not going to come out and shoot me, is he?"

She laughed. I was serious. I touched the scar on my lip.

"He won't even know you're here. Just like old times."

She hung up and I sat staring at the phone for a minute or two after. I wasn't sure yet how I was going to approach the subject of the money transfers or her connection to Mark Peterson. I wanted to give her the benefit of the doubt. But I wasn't stupid.

I finished my coffee, then grabbed a shower.

CHAPTER 21

I was purposely ten minutes late. I didn't want to give her the impression I was sitting around watching the clock, counting off the minutes until I saw her again. The games Claire and I played with one another's hearts and minds were sometimes beyond comprehension. I didn't understand why we did them, and I didn't think she did, either. I loved her more than life and I know she loved me the same, but we didn't trust each other further than we could see one another. And sometimes, even when she was within sight, in full view, I trusted her even less. That's when she was the most dangerous. At least when she wasn't within arm's reach, I could push her out of my mind.

I drove through the wrought iron gate welcoming me to the K-Bar Ranch. The main house was about two hundred yards past the entrance. It was an eight-thousand-square-foot, two-story colonial with a front porch and a manicured lawn. Claire's bedroom had been upstairs, the last room on the right. The bedroom window faced the side lawn and there used to be a massive tree close enough I could climb and sneak in. Kinley got wise and had every tree within a hundred feet of the house cut down.

I followed the driveway like Claire had said and finally, a mile and a half later, pulled up to a cedar-sided log house not quite as

large as the main house. I couldn't help but grin—that was my
Claire. She'd always dreamed of a log cabin. How could two people
who were such polar opposites be so in tune with one another?

She bounded out onto the front porch, grinning like a giddy
teenager, and motioned for me to park near the steps. I did as she
wanted and parked about ten feet from the steps leading to the
porch. I got out, turned and stared at the van parked haphazardly
in the yard, then turned back to Claire. "Is that the handicap
spot?"

She smiled. "I figured it would be easier for you. The swelling
really has gone down, hasn't it?" She looked at my foot and nodded approvingly.

I spread my arms and laughed. "Look, ma, no crutch." I had
no idea how I was going to make it up the stairs without it but I
was going to give it my best effort. Heaven was waiting for me at
the top.

I was able to put a little weight on my toes and probably looked
like a creatively challenged dancer clumsily prancing about. It took
a minute or two but I made it up all seven steps. I wrapped my arms
around Claire's waist and locked her in a tight embrace. Partly for
support, and partly because she just looked so damn good standing there.

She pulled back slightly then kissed me hard on the mouth.

"Hello to you, too," I said.

She wiped a transferred smudge of lipstick from the corner of
my lips with the tip of her index finger. She sighed contentedly,
then took my hand and led me into the house, adjusting her usually fast-paced steps to my gimping gait.

The house was large, but not a ridiculous show of wealth. It
was open and airy and decorated in standard west-Texas flair,
complete with bleached cattle skulls and Navajo-inspired blan-

kets. The furniture was worn brown leather, purposely distressed and softer than a cloud.

"You want a beer or a drink?" She headed toward a wet bar in the corner of the family room.

"Whatcha got?" I'm a picky drinker.

She ducked behind the bar, then popped back up a minute later with a smile and a full bottle of Johnnie Walker Black. "That'll work just fine," I said, my mouth watering with anticipation.

She fixed us each a drink, then brought them, and the bottle, over to the sofa. She sat close to me, tucking one leg under her perfect ass so she could face me. She was so close her warm breath lightly tickled my neck. Despite every nerve ending in my body on pleasure high alert, I reminded myself this really needed to be a business call. It was easier to be objective if our clothes stayed on. Besides, I reminded myself, she *was married*. And I don't make it a habit of doing married women. Not even if that woman was Claire Kinley.

"Claire," I said after a stout swig of my drink. "We really need to finish the conversation we started in the hospital."

She ran her finger lightly around the collar of my shirt, gently tickling my neck. "About me and you, or you and that Mexican reporter?" she said, her voice a breathy whisper.

I gently clasped her playful finger and moved her hand to her lap. "I was talking about the investigation and the ranch."

She frowned. "You said you weren't investigating the ranch."

"Not directly. But some things have come up that I was hoping you could explain."

She sighed heavily, then finished her drink in one long swallow. She refilled both our glasses, then sat the bottle on the coffee table. "I've already explained the illegal workers. I'm not sure what else there is to talk about."

"Tell me about Mark Peterson."

For a second, I thought I was going to have to smack her and force her to breathe. Her gaze darted all around the room, focusing on everything and nothing, avoiding looking at me altogether.

"I know he's your brother-in-law. But I want to know about the business deal you have with him."

She still wouldn't look at me. She took a sip of her drink, then sat the glass on the table. "I thought this was going to be a picnic. I wasn't expecting an inquisition."

"Claire," I said with a sigh. "It's not an inquisition. Mark Peterson may be involved in things that would not be good for you to be involved in. I'm trying to find out where you fit into this picture."

She finally looked at me. Her eyes were blue as ice and just as cold. "What kind of *things*?"

I swallowed the rest of my drink, then poured myself another. "I can't really say yet."

She guffawed. "Oh. Let me see if I've got this straight. You come in here and tell me my brother-in-law is involved in some kind of criminal activity, but you can't tell me what, and oh, yeah, it may involve me. Is that about the gist of it?" Her voice was rising in pitch, which meant her temper wasn't far behind.

"Claire . . . I'm trying to protect you. I can't do that if I don't know what's going on."

"Seems like you do know what's going on. Why don't you tell me, then we'll both know." She sprang up from the couch and paced back and forth in front of the picture window. I imagined if I could hear the thoughts running through her head at that moment, it would sound like crashing ocean waves.

"Claire, I know you have business dealings with him—"

"How would you know that unless you've . . ." She stopped pacing and glared at me so hard I caught a chill. "You've pulled my financial records? *Oh . . . my . . . God.* You sonofabitch!"

"Claire, wait a minute. It's not like that." I hobbled over to her, keeping an arm's-length distance between us just in case.

"You knew about the illegals, you knew about Steven when you *fucked* me. What else do you know about me, Gypsy? Is there something else you want to know? Ask me, I'll tell you. You don't have to dig it up."

"It's not you I'm investigating. But damn if you don't have a lot of connections to Mark Peterson. I know money's changed hands between you and Peterson, Claire. If he's got something on you, you've got to tell me."

Her icy stare bore a hole straight through to my soul. Finally, after a long moment, she sighed and pushed her hand through her hair. "Gypsy—he's my brother-in-law. He's married to Steven's sister. He doesn't manage their money very well. We're always having to bail them out of one financial crisis after another." She turned away and stared out the window. "What are you investigating him for?" Her voice was low, somber.

I closed the distance between us. "I can't tell you that, Claire. You know that."

"How involved is he?" She continued to look out the window, her back to me.

"He's involved. That's all I can say right now."

I watched her shoulders rise and fall with a deep breath, then she turned around and looked me in the eyes. "And I don't know what to tell you. I don't know if he's gambling it away, or if he's using drugs . . . I don't know what he's using the money for."

It wasn't adding up. There were too many dollars changing

hands. Claire was too shrewd to be her brother-in-law's personal bank. "How much is he into you for?" I knew the exact amount that had been exchanged. But I wanted to hear what she had to say.

She pushed her hand through her hair again, then slowly moved back to the sofa. She poured herself another drink then sat down. "Couple thousand, maybe."

Closer to a quarter of a million but who was counting? "You said that y'all were always having to bail them out—does that mean Steven knows about it?"

She glanced at me, then took a sip of her drink. She swallowed slowly, then slowly shook her head. "I meant we, as in me and the ranch. I gave him the money from the ranch account."

"And Steven doesn't know?"

She shook her head again. "He doesn't have a clue what goes on at the ranch and he wouldn't know how to read a ledger sheet if it came with instructions."

That was worthy of a little concern considering the man was involved with the state's budget. "Why'd you keep paying Peterson? Why not just cut him off?" I sat back down beside her on the sofa.

"He's married to Steven's sister."

"But Steven doesn't know anything about it."

She stared at me, her eyes searching mine. "And I'd like to keep it that way."

Was she protecting her husband . . . or herself? I fixed myself another drink and took a slow sip, steeling my nerves. "Claire . . . the undocumented workers you have working for you . . . how'd you find them?"

She looked confused, like she didn't understand the question. "What do mean, how'd I find them? I needed help. They applied for the job. I don't understand what you're getting at."

"How'd they know to come here?"

She thought about it a moment, then shrugged. "Word of mouth, I suppose. I don't understand why you're asking these questions." The hurt in her eyes was real.

I wasn't sure how much to tell her, how much I could trust her with. Or not trust her was more like it. "The men that work for you . . . do you know anything about them?"

She shook her head. "Not really. I mean, I know they're hard workers. It may sound cold, but I try not to get real involved with the employees' lives outside the ranch. I figure what they do after hours is their own business." Her eyes then narrowed and she turned a sharp gaze at me. "Why? Has one of them done something?"

I shook my head. "Other than come here illegally? No. They haven't done anything wrong, Claire. They're the victims."

She was taken aback. "Victims? What do you mean?"

"You have at least three illegals working for you whose teenage kids have gone missing."

Her face twisted with concern. "When? Recently?"

"Pretty recent, yes."

She got up again and slowly moved around the room, her face etched with concentration. "Do you think they're connected?"

"I don't know yet." I didn't trust her enough to play all my cards.

"Do you think maybe they ran away?"

"I don't know what to think."

She stopped in front of the window and gazed out at the ranch she loved more than life itself. "That's terrible. Your daughter disappears and you never know what happened to her. And you can't report it to the police because you run the risk of being deported."

How did she know they didn't file police reports? How did she know the missing kids were daughters? My heart felt like it had been coiled in a cable and tossed overboard with a cast-iron anchor. No matter how much I tried to convince myself she wasn't involved, this boat was going down and it was taking Claire with it.

CHAPTER 22

That evening, Sophia and I followed Sheriff Denny home again, waited while he changed clothes, then tailed him to the Grove Street Methodist Church. He was dressed in the same ill-fitting athletic pants and another golf shirt more wrinkled than the one he had worn last night.

Sophia looked over the printout of Denny's schedule. "It's Tuesday night so that counts out church service. Maybe they have men's Bible study or something?"

I glanced over at the schedule. "Boy Scouts."

"They meet at churches?"

I slowly nodded, remembering my six months of wearing the uniform. I can't remember if I got kicked out or if Mom was the one they didn't want back. Her one attempt at being involved in her kids' lives ended with her receiving a certified letter and threat of a lawsuit.

We were parked across the street with a clear shot of the church parking lot. Something about Denny being involved with a scout troop made me uncomfortable. The man had two daughters, but no sons. Yet he was an assistant leader for a Boy Scout Troop. He went to a kids' movie by himself with, at least in my opinion, the intention of meeting someone. I wasn't sure I liked the direction my thoughts were going.

Neither did I like the direction my thoughts were going with Claire. She was in too deep for me to pull her out.

"Foot hurting?" Sophia asked.

"Pardon?"

"I asked if your foot was hurting. You're kind of quiet to-night."

I didn't say anything for a moment, then shook my head. "Nah, the foot's fine. Just a lot on my mind, I guess." I probably should have let Rodney handle tonight's surveillance; he would have thought he'd died and gone to heaven. Especially with the shorts and tight T-shirt Sophia was wearing tonight.

She nodded, watching me for a moment, then turned her attention back to the parking lot.

Silence settled over us like a comfortable blanket, not too heavy or cumbersome. We were content to leave the other alone in thought. And my thoughts kept going back to Claire. "Why did you investigate Senator Sellars?" I asked.

Sophia turned to me, then shrugged. "Routine campaign stuff. Why?"

"Did you find anything?"

She shook her head. "Not enough to keep him from getting elected. Why do you ask?"

"Just curious." It was a lame answer, but it was all I was willing to give up at the moment. I gnawed on my bottom lip wondering how much I should tell Sophia. I didn't want to see Claire's name strewn across a headline. I still needed time to figure out if there was a way to keep her out of it.

"How long do Boy Scout meetings usually last?" Sophia asked, her voice was growing bored senseless.

WINK OF AN EYE

"I don't remember. About two hours, I guess."

"Surveillance work sucks." She went back to watching the parking lot.

"Yeah. Sometimes it does." I hesitated a moment, then said, "You asked me how long I'd been sleeping with Claire Sellars."

She turned and glared at me, even lifting her sunglasses to get an unobstructed view. "I don't believe those were the exact words I used."

I laughed lightly. "Claire and I have history. We go back to when we could do it in a backseat and not worry about a leg cramp."

She lowered her glasses, then turned back to the parking lot. "And you're telling me this because . . ."

"You asked. And I have a favor to ask."

Without taking her attention from the parking lot, she blew a deep breath through her nose. "Isn't a *favor* how I got involved in this in the first place?"

She had a point. And a memory like a freaking elephant. "The K-Bar Ranch may be more involved with this whole thing than I originally thought. Until I know the depth of Claire's involvement, I'd appreciate it if you can keep her out of it."

Her jaw tightened first, then her whole body followed. I thought I saw a plume of smoke shoot from her nostrils like a raging bull's. "That wasn't part of the deal, Gypsy. I don't tell you how to run your investigation and you don't tell me what to write. *That* was the deal."

I scratched at the back of my neck. It was hot in the van. And getting hotter. "I'm not telling you what to write," I said, my voice taking on an unintended whiny tone. "I'm just asking if you can keep Claire out of it. That's all."

She turned and glared at me hard. Her eyes were so cold they could have caused hypothermia. "You're asking me to keep your girlfriend out of it but you're *not* telling me what to write?"

We stared at each other for a long moment, the reality of my request sinking deep into my steel-encased brain. I slammed my hand hard against the steering wheel. "Dammit!"

She shook her head, then looked away, blowing more air out of her nose. "You know, if she's that involved in this whole thing . . . why is she someone you would *want* to protect?"

I pushed both hands deep through my hair and sighed. I could remember only a few times in my life that I was truly confused, and each time involved Claire. "I don't know why I want to protect her. If she is involved, then she deserves whatever comes to her."

Sophia looked at me and her features softened. The rock-hard jaw went slack. "Gypsy—despite what you may think, I don't have some proverbial ax to grind with Claire Sellars. Whatever I write will be fair. That I can promise you."

I supposed that was all I could really ask.

She turned her attention back to the parking lot. "Finally," she said with a huff.

A cluster of boys in their khaki-and-green uniforms spilled out of the church, laughing and playfully punching one another while their mothers and fathers hurried them along to their individual cars. They were as anxious as Sophia and I to call this meeting over. A few minutes later, Denny and a short, squat man with calves bigger than my thighs came out of the church. The bulldog turned and locked the door behind, then he and Denny chatted a moment. There was some head nodding, some bobbing from one foot to the other, a clap on the back. They parted ways and Denny climbed into his Caddy. The bulldog climbed into a shiny Ford 350 and drove away. I cranked the van's engine and waited for Denny.

He pulled out of the parking lot, and instead of turning back toward home, he turned left.

"Where's he going?" Sophia asked.

"I guess we'll soon find out." I waited for the few passing cars that constituted Kermit's heavy traffic, then picked up Denny's trail as he turned onto Highway 302.

After twenty minutes of driving, I was fairly certain he was headed to Odessa. "What's he got going on in Odessa?" I asked quietly, more to myself than to my partner.

"Maybe he's got another meeting."

I threw a glance in Sophia's direction and frowned. "*Really?* It's almost nine-thirty. Why don't you want to believe this *doddering old man* could be up to something?"

"Why does every odd behavior have to be criminal? You're too tainted."

Tainted? I'd been called a lot of things in my life but couldn't remember ever being called tainted. Cans of rotten tuna were tainted.

"Bet I can prove you wrong," I said. "Your doddering old man isn't as nice as you want to believe he is."

"Yeah? What's the bet?" One corner of her mouth turned upward in a slight grin.

I shrugged. I had a lot of things I could think of but didn't want to risk being slapped while I was driving. "Dinner. And drinks. Lots of drinks."

She gnawed the inside of her lip. "You're on."

Oh, I was so going to enjoy this.

We drove for another thirty minutes, straight into Odessa. Denny drove through the heart of downtown, passing the *Odessa Record,* then went two blocks north and hooked a right. He turned into the entrance of the municipal park, the same park Sophia and I had walked to the day I approached her about the case.

"What's he doing?" she asked with honest bewilderment in her voice.

"He's looking for drugs or sex. My guess is sex. Is there another entrance to this park?"

She pointed ahead, then craned her neck to keep an eye on Denny's Caddy. "Next block, take a right. It's the first drive on the right."

"Do the parking lots connect?"

She nodded excitedly. "I lost him behind the trees. Hurry up."

The last thing I wanted to do was draw attention and go barreling into the park on two wheels. So I drove her crazy and poked along five miles under the posted speed. I opened the center console and fished out the key to the locked storage bin mounted on the wall behind the driver's seat. "Do me a favor," I said, handing her the key. "There's a lockbox in the bottom drawer on the left. I need the camera out of that box."

"Won't you need a flash?" She crawled over the console, her ass momentarily brushing my right cheek. Rodney would have had a freakin' heart attack.

"It's a night-vision camera." I forced my attention back to Denny. He had parked at a picnic shelter tucked into the far southwest corner of the park. I had a clear-enough view of him without getting any closer so I turned the van off and settled in. Within a matter of seconds, the temperature in the van felt like it was inching upward of 90 degrees or better. I didn't want to roll down the window; any sound, even the most hushed conversation, would carry through the night air. Sweat beaded at my hairline and trickled down the back of my neck.

Sophia climbed back into the passenger seat. She had a frown on her face and my most expensive camera in the palm of her hand. "This is really a camera?" She turned it over, checking out all sides.

"Night vision, baby, Mil-Spec. Cool, huh?" I took it from her and powered it up.

"What's Mil-Spec? Sounds like some kind of mill worm."

"Military specifications." I looked at her and grinned. "You know, for a modern-age journalist, I'd have figured you for a gadget geek."

"Most of these gadgets are nothing more than big boy toys."

"And your point is?"

She rolled her eyes and tried not to grin but her lips weren't cooperating.

"Okay, so I collect cameras and other gadgets. What do you collect?" I was afraid to offer suggestions. Everything I could think of would classify me as sexist. My sister collected old cookbooks. Rhonda had obviously never used one but liked the way they looked in the kitchen. Kitchen, cookbooks, barefoot and pregnant . . . Sophia would consider it an insult and we were jammed together in a minivan. Not a good time for me to be stupid. "So, are you a collector? Of anything other than men's hearts?" The speed of light, speed of sound, breaking the sound barrier . . . nothing was faster than the regret I immediately felt. I only used really horrible, cheesy lines when my blood-alcohol level was floating near double digits.

She glared at me. "Please tell me you've never actually *used* that line."

"It was pretty bad, wasn't it?"

"And you've used it, haven't you?"

I opened my mouth to defend myself but couldn't find the words.

"Oh my God . . . you have. You've used the worst pickup line I've ever heard!"

I threw my hands up in surrender, confession, whatever she

wanted to call it. I was at her mercy. "Maybe once. I might have used it once. It does require an enormous amount of alcohol for it to work."

She gazed at me a moment and shook her head, trying hard not to grin. Leaning forward, she propped her arms on the dashboard and stared out the windshield at the picnic shelter. "You really think he's here for sex?"

"Well, it's a little late for a picnic, don't you think?"

She scrunched her lips, then nodded slowly in defeat. "Suppose it's more likely he's here for sex than drugs."

"Have you ever heard anything about the park being a local pickup spot?"

She shook her head. "Odessa PD runs a raid every now and then at an underpass near Austin Drive. But I've never heard anything about the park."

The back of my shirt was drenched with sweat. My hair was damp and I was suffocating. I scanned the area around the picnic shelter for any sign of life other than Denny's. He hadn't moved from the front seat of the Cadillac. His green ghost image was still behind the wheel, scrunched down in the seat. From what I could make out, both palms were on the steering wheel so at least he hadn't taken business into his own hands yet. I took a couple shots of Denny behind the wheel, then zoomed out for some shots of the car.

Sophia leaned in, watching the camera, then followed the direction of the lens to hopefully see what I saw.

"Can you see him in the car?" I asked.

"I can see a figure but it's too dark to make out any features," she said, breathy and soft.

I handed her the camera and leaned back so she could get a better look. She tried from different vantage points but still couldn't get an unobstructed view. She was all but sitting on the center console, leaning forward, leaning back, leaning to the side—every way she possibly could—but it was hard to see anything through the windshield. The heat outside and sweat inside joined forces to layer the windshield with a thin fog. I leaned farther back, pressing my wet shirt against the seat, trying to give her more room. She handed the camera back, then, to my surprise, swung her leg over mine and slid over onto my lap. She took the camera and focused it on Denny. "Wow," she whispered.

I couldn't agree more. The scent of her took me to places that reminded me of fields of wildflowers. Deep, strong scents mixed with soft and delicate, like the spot on a woman's neck, just below her ear. I felt her breathe, slow and steady. Watched the back of her shoulders rise and fall with each breath. Slowly, she lightly pressed her back into my chest, my stomach, lightly pressing her ass into my crotch until the tightening in my shorts became almost painful.

I gently took the camera from her, reached around her, and laid it on the dashboard. Her hand remained there, suspended in midair, suspended in the moment. I lightly ran my fingers up the length of both her bare arms, moving so slow and light, she shivered under the touch. She arched her back, dropping her head backward until it rested at my shoulder, offering me the sweet spot of her neck. I tasted her sweetness, tasted the sweat beading around the collar of her shirt. She moaned lightly and I softly whispered "shhh." I moved my hands up her arms, barely touching her, lightly brushing across her breasts. I ran my fingers along the outline of her waist, of her hips, moving them so slowly to the tops of her thighs, then to the insides, then inside the openings her shorts offered. I gently moved her legs apart while running my tongue softly up the length of her neck, to the sweet spot, just below her ear.

Then a car door shut. I jolted back to reality and scrambled, reaching around her for the camera. She leapt out of my lap and back over to the passenger seat, staring straight ahead out the fog-covered windshield. I aimed the camera at Denny's Cadillac and clicked off several shots before it dawned on me what I was taking pictures of.

It wasn't Ryce McCallen who had a fondness for teenage boys.

CHAPTER 23

It was after midnight when I pulled the van into Rhonda's driveway. Sophia and I sat in silence for a while, staring at the house. It was past Rodney and Rhonda's bedtime. Gram had probably gone to sleep hours ago so there were no quick peeks between the blinds. The house was totally dark. I wondered if I should wake Rodney to show him the fruits of our labor. Or the spoils of one man's life would probably be more like it.

"What now?" Sophia asked.

I was pretty sure she was referring to the situation with Denny and not our own almost-front-seat action. "I'll print a couple of the pictures, then pay him a visit tomorrow."

"I'd like to go with you."

I grinned. "Enjoying my company that much, huh?"

She glared at me a moment with her brows lowered, perfect lips fighting back a smile. "Um . . . no. My editor's given me a deadline."

"Deadline? You can't—"

She held her hand up to shush me. "I'm not going to jump the gun. But writing about it was kind of my purpose on this whole thing, remember?"

I sat back in the seat and nodded. It seemed a little strange

knowing this investigation might be over in a few days. "I'll probably be ready to turn everything over to the Rangers' office by the
end of the week. I'll show you what I've got if you'll show me
yours." I looked at her and winked.

She tossed her head back and laughed. "I have a pretty good
idea what you've got. I could feel it through my shorts."

She laughed again, then climbed out of the van. I hurriedly
caught up to her as she was reaching for the door of the Mercedes.
I blocked her with my good leg from opening it, then wrapped my
arm around her waist and turned her toward me.

"Gypsy . . ." She whispered so softy I wondered if I imagined it.

I lightly kissed her chin, then her cheek, and when she didn't
resist, I kissed her lips.

"Gypsy . . . I can't." She was saying one thing but her body
was telling me something different. She brought her arms up, wrapping them around my neck, digging her fingers through my hair,
pushing her tongue deep into my mouth. "I have a partner," she
said between gasping breaths.

Jesus. Another freaking husband to deal with. She kissed me
again hard, biting at my lip. I'd worry about the husband tomorrow.

Hands started moving so fast it was hard to keep up with who
was doing what. We moved backward toward the van, stumbling
over each other's feet. I would have died before screaming out in
pain when she stepped on my snake-bitten foot. We crashed nois-
ily into the side of the van with me on the outside pressing her
hard against the closed door. She ripped open my shorts as I
worked the button on her own. A few weeks ago, prior to a Western Diamondback trying to take my foot off, I would have lifted
her, balanced her legs on my hips, and drove it home. But things

being what they were, it wasn't working out that way. Dammit! This gimpy foot was cramping my style.

"Shit!" I pulled her away from the van and pushed her toward the Mercedes.

There wasn't much distance between the van and her car but when you're trying to get there with your pants around your ankles, it's a wonder we got there at all.

The back of the van was still loaded with my case files. Her Mercedes was a sharp-looking little car but had no backseat. And there was no way in hell this was going to happen in the front seat. I lifted her onto the shiny red hood. It was the perfect height. She'd lost her shorts somewhere in the shuffle and all was right with the world.

If there had been a soundtrack, just about the time the music swelled into a crashing crescendo threatening to send us both into another hemisphere, I moved my foot a fraction of an inch and stepped on her shorts, smashing the keys in the pocket into the hard ground.

A prison break alarm couldn't have caused more noise. There were so many bells and whistles, I didn't know if I was having an orgasm or if I'd won the grand prize at the county fair.

A woman can stop at any time. A man's different. A man reaches a point, come hell or high water, bells or whistles, there just ain't no turning back. Not even when the floodlights in the yard come on, every light in the house flashes on, and your brother-in-law barrels through the front door with his service weapon drawn wearing nothing but tight white briefs and cowboy boots.

"Gypsy? Ah, Jesus . . . Christ Almighty! What in the hell are you doing?" Rodney shouted over the alarm. He paced in small circles in the dirt yard, one hand on his head while the other partially covered his eyes.

Rhonda was on the front stoop, arms folded tight across her chest. "Can you at least shut the alarm off?"

I jerked my shorts up and was trying to get them fastened while Sophia was dancing around trying to get her shorts back on. She finally snatched her keys up and hit the right button and the little car fell silent. It was like someone had pressed the mute button on the whole world as there wasn't even a cricket chirping. After a short spell of dead silence, the screaming resumed.

"What the hell were you doing?" Rhonda screamed, arms flaying about.

"What the hell do you think he was doing?" Rodney asked.

Gram joined Rhonda on the stoop and peered out into the yard. "Why's your husband out here in his drawers?"

"Everything's fine, Gram. Go on back to bed."

"Gypsy finally get some from that cute little Mexican?"

"Gram, please go back to bed."

Sophia jerked the keys from my hand. "I'll meet you at the sheriff's office in the morning. Tenish?"

I quickly nodded and helped her into the car. I was going to kiss her good-bye but she had already backed out and was moving at a quick clip down the road before I had even bent over. Given the way the night had gone, maybe a good-bye kiss wasn't necessary. At this point it probably wasn't even desired.

Rhonda threw her arms up in the air. "And what the hell were you *doing* out here? Jesus! Why didn't you get a room?" She spun around and pushed past Gram. "I'm going in. Rodney, come in before someone sees you standing out here in your underwear. Geez."

Gram chuckled and followed Rhonda inside. Rodney stomped up the steps. He made sure Rhonda was safely inside, then turned and glared at me. "Yeah, why *didn't* you get a room? You've gone and ruined every fantasy I could have ever had."

"What? How'd I—"

"Sophia. You think I can ever fantasize about her again without seeing your shiny white ass banging her?" he whispered.

"Oh." We stood there for a moment with neither saying anything. Although I didn't understand why, I felt the need to apologize. "Sorry, man."

He shrugged. His lips were knotted in a silly-looking pout. "S'okay. Probably would have done the same thing if I'd been given the chance. And if I were single."

"Yeah," I said slowly then sighed. "It's getting late and you're still . . . standing out here, in your underwear. And that's not exactly a pretty sight, either. Much longer and I'll be traumatized."

"You want to talk about *traumatized* . . ."

CHAPTER 24

The next morning, after I grabbed a quick shower, I set up office at the kitchen table. I hooked up the camera and photo printer to the laptop then loaded the glossy paper in the printer.

Gram was sitting at the table slurping her morning coffee, watching me through her thick glasses. Her bony shoulders' sharpness were visible through a bathrobe older than me. "Did you at least use a rubber?"

I pulled my attention away from a shot of Gaylord Denny with his tongue halfway down a kid's throat and glared at my grandmother. I wasn't going to even humor her with an answer. I went over to the coffeepot for a refill. When I returned to the table, Gram was scrutinizing the pictures. "Looks like you weren't the only one getting some action last night."

"Let's just forget about last night. It wasn't one of my better moments."

She chuckled. "Probably what she was thinking, too."

"Thanks, Gram." I turned my attention back to work. I printed four glossy five-by-sevens of various actions, then saved the pictures to my hard drive, then to a flash drive. The pictures were graphic, leaving little room for misinterpretation. I was curious if Mark Peterson had similar pictures.

Rhonda came into the kitchen, hauling a laundry basket full of dirty clothes. Gaylord Denny's world was about to come crashing down around him, and life went on. "Gram, how many times have I told you not to stuff your dirty clothes under your bed? Takes me forever to dig 'em out." Rhonda dropped the basket at the laundry closet. "Tatum called last night, Gypsy. He wanted to know if you could take him out to the sinkholes tomorrow."

"I did tell him I'd do that, didn't I?" And hopefully, by this time tomorrow Tatum could rest easier knowing someone was finally going to be held accountable for his dad's death. I stuffed the pictures of Denny into an envelope, then slipped it into a folder I had made containing copies of the files I wanted Denny to see. "Tell Tatum I'll pick him up around ten tomorrow morning."

I snapped a micro-mini video recorder onto the outside arm of my sunglasses, looked at Gram, and told her to smile for the camera.

"Who are you, James Bond?"

"Wow . . . that's really cool," Rhonda said, her face within inches of my own as she stared directly into the camera.

"Can you see the camera? Are there any lights flickering?" I asked.

"You mean that light glowing beside your head?" Gram asked.

I took off the glasses and tested the camera again.

"There was no light, Gypsy." Rhonda rolled her eyes. I wasn't sure if the gesture was for me or Gram.

I didn't trust either of them. I rested the glasses on top of my head, then checked out my reflection in the glass door of the microwave. From what I could tell between the nuked-on grease spots, they looked like any other pair of shades.

I shut down the laptop, then gathered the files. It was 9:20. I was meeting Sophia around ten at Denny's office. Exposing Denny's dirty little secret wasn't near as nerve-racking as facing Sophia again after last night. Did I dare ask if it was good for her? Or should I act like nothing ever happened?

What was it about Sophia Ortez that had me so far out of my element that I morphed into some stupid schoolboy every time I was around her? I wasn't used to being nervous around women. It confused me.

"Good luck today," Rhonda said as she stuffed a wad of Gram's clothes into the washer.

I started out but Rhonda's lack of housekeeping skills got the best of me. Luckily she hadn't added the detergent yet nor turned on the water so I dug the clothes out of the washer and quickly sorted them into three piles on the kitchen floor. "Okay, look . . . whites in one load, colors in another. And I like to wash things that wrinkle easily, like all cotton, together in one load. That way, when you dry them, you can set the heat on high."

Rhonda looked at me like I had lost my mind. "You've got three little piles there. That's three loads. Scoop it all together and it makes one big one." She scooped up the three little piles and stuffed it all back in the machine, then smiled like Satan's spawn. "There. Laundry's done."

Twenty minutes later, I was sitting in the parking lot at the sheriff's office waiting for Sophia. My palms were sweaty. I checked my forehead in the rearview mirror, feeling a pimple gestating under the skin. Damn her.

I closed my eyes and took a deep breath, pushing any thought that involved Sophia's glory out of my head. Today was Tatum's day. I had to have a clear head when I confronted Denny.

A moment later, there was a rap at the window. Sophia was standing there, a questioning smile turning one corner of her lip upward.

"Sorry to interrupt your Zen," she said as I got out. She was holding a small basket creatively filled with brownies, cookies, and little packets of hot chocolate and fancy teas.

"Another gift basket?"

She shrugged. "You have a better way of getting in there?"

"I was going to tell his secretary I had something I thought he'd want to see." I opened the file and teased her with a glimpse of the pictures.

"That ought to get his attention."

As I closed the folder, a burgundy unmarked car drove by the parking lot so slowly a turtle could have beaten it to a finish line. The windows were tinted but I had no doubt it was Mark Peterson.

"You ready?" I asked, not waiting for her answer. I gently led Sophia by the arm toward the front door. For some reason, I wasn't comfortable with her standing outside in the open with Peterson on the prowl. I glanced over my shoulder as he turned into the south end of the parking lot.

The sheriff's office was an old three-story brick building that housed Denny's office, the criminal investigation and patrol divisions, and the administrative offices. The county jail was banished to a separate facility on the outskirts of town. I held the door and ushered Sophia into the small lobby.

A secretary who looked as old as Gram was seated behind a massive oak desk that dominated the lobby. Two hard-back chairs occupied the front corner. Visitors obviously weren't encouraged to hang out. I pushed my sunglasses up on top of my head, triggering the recorder in the process. I cleared my throat to get the ancient secretary's attention. She stared over the rims of her glasses, expressionless.

"Can I help you?"

"We'd like to see Sheriff Denny."

She gave us each a stern glance-over. "And you are?"

"Baskets to Go—Sophia's Custom Creations," Sophia said, smiling broadly while proudly displaying her custom creation. "I'm Sophia Ortez, and this is my partner Michael Moran. We're working with the sheriff on an upcoming retirement party." She leaned in against the desk and lowered her voice. "It's a surprise party, so . . . you know . . . you might want to keep it quiet for a little while longer."

Damn, this girl was fast on her feet! Miss Older-than-Dirt's whole demeanor changed. The old woman even blushed. "A surprise party? That old coot," she said, and chuckled. "He's in his office. I'll let him know you're coming in."

Sophia shot me a devilish grin, then beckoned me to follow her. Denny's office was a few steps off the lobby down a short hallway. The door was partially open so Sophia knocked once, then gave it a little push. The office was the size of a small apartment. The walls were pale yellow stucco with professionally placed artwork and photographs of the sheriff in various photo ops. Floor-to-ceiling bookcases lined one of the walls with various collectibles and more reference books than were in the library. Denny's desk had a light cherry finish and was complemented by dark red leather guest chairs that faced it. The office was much more inviting than the lobby.

He was at his desk with his nose inches from a laptop screen. He glanced up and smiled. He closed the laptop and I wondered what he had been looking at. Denny stood and offered his hand. "I remember you—the basket lady. Or were you a reporter?"

Sophia gently smiled and shook his hand. "Actually, I'm both. Sophia Ortez, the *Odessa Record*. And this basket, I made just for you." She gnawed on her bottom lip as she handed him the simple gift, looking almost like she felt sorry for him.

I didn't feel sorry for him. Less than twenty-four hours ago he was fucking a boy not much older than Tatum. This was one noose I'd enjoy tightening. I quickly cleared my throat and introduced myself. And I didn't use a cover. I made my intentions clear. "I was hired to investigate Ryce McCallen's death. And I've got a couple questions I'd like to ask."

"Ryce McCallen . . . what a tragedy." He made a *tsk-tsk* sound and shook his head. "Please, have a seat. How's the family doing?"

Family? Like there was a host of relatives to pick up the slack. "You mean Tatum and Burke? They're coping."

He nodded as if he were truly filled with compassion for the twelve-year-old fatherless boy. I wanted to slap the shit out of him. "Why was there never an autopsy performed on Ryce McCallen?"

Denny looked at me a moment like a game show contestant who had drawn a blank on the million-dollar question.

"I think in every state in the country, an autopsy is performed in suspected suicides. Why wasn't one performed on Ryce Mc-Callen?"

Denny's mouth puckered like a fish. "Well, Mr. Moran . . . an autopsy wasn't ordered because we didn't want to cause the family any more stress. They've been through an awful lot the last few years. And—the cause of death was pretty obvious."

"That's bullshit."

"Beg your pardon?"

"I *said* that's bullshit."

Both Denny and Sophia shifted in their seats.

"Mr. Moran, Ryce McCallen hanged himself. I wanted to save

the family from the rumors and gossip. From what we learned after his death, he had some deep *personal* issues that were going to be exposed."

"Let's talk about being exposed. . . ." I removed one of the glossy pictures from the folder and tossed it on his desk.

He stared at it for the longest time, never touching it, turning his head to different angles like the movement would alter the photograph. He stared at it like he wasn't sure he understood the bigger picture. I removed another photo, a close-up, and tossed it on top of the other.

"I have more. Would you like to see another?" I tossed a third picture onto the pile.

Denny laced his fingers together, then folded his hands behind his head and leaned back in his chair. He sighed and looked away from the pictures.

"Now would you like to talk about *deep personal* issues?"

He unfolded his hands and leaned into his desk. "I suppose this is going to be tomorrow's headline?" He waved his hand over the pictures.

"Oh, the dirt in this department goes a lot deeper than your preference for teenage boys." I tapped my finger on the top photograph. "This—is connected to Ryce McCallen's death. And Ryce McCallen's death is connected to two of your deputies and eight missing girls. *That's* what's going to make the headline."

"I see." The words were clipped, but not angry. More matter-of-fact. For someone facing a life-altering crisis, Denny was so collected he could have been discussing dinner plans. "And you have proof of these allegations?"

"Your two deputies aren't the brightest bulbs in the lamp, Sheriff. They left a pretty decent trail."

He slowly nodded and looked at Sophia. "Miss Ortez, there's a

statue of a bucking bronc on the bookshelf. Taped to the under-
side of it is a key. Would you mind getting it for me?"

Sophia glanced at me, unsure what to do. Instinctively, my
arm went across the front of her chair and blocked her from getting up. "What does a key have to do with anything?"

I thought I saw a slight shadow of a smile. This visit was getting weirder by the minute. "It's the key to a lockbox at Fidelity
Bank, Mr. Moran. Everything you'll need to know is in the box."

I went over to the bookshelf, found the horse statue, and removed the key from underneath it. Something was very odd about
this man and his businesslike attitude. He was talking in future
tense and I don't think that future included him.

Then the panic surged through me as fast as my heart was
pumping. As I spun around, I saw the gleam of the .45-caliber
Glock. I dove for Sophia at the same time Denny raised the gun to
the side of his head. The *bang* was almost as deafening as Sophia's
hysterical scream. Blood and brain matter spattered us both before
we hit the ground. It looked like a scene from a bad horror movie,
but it wasn't. It was real. Sophia was frantically trying to get away
while I was trying just as frantically to shield her from the grue-
someness.

The ancient secretary came rushing in. *"Oh my God!"*

"Call an ambulance!" But I knew from the amount of blood
and brain matter on Sophia and me there was little a paramedic
could do.

The scene quickly escalated into pure pandemonium. I was
slammed face-first onto the floor by a swarm of deputies who apparently thought shoulders were detachable. My arms were yanked
behind my back with enough force to crack bone while at least one
knee was driven hard into my spine as they slapped a pair of cuffs
around my wrists. "I'm Michael Moran, a private investigator," I

sputtered, trying desperately to catch my breath. "My ID's in my back pocket."

There was a collection of voices yelling commands but there was no one in charge. I couldn't see Sophia but I could hear her sobbing above the melee.

"My ID's in my back pocket," I said again in case they missed it the first time. "Michael Moran, private investigator."

Someone heard me above the noise that time. I could have flown the friendly skies with less groping. They finally fished my wallet out of my pocket, then shortly after that heaved me to my knees with my arms still cuffed behind my back.

The whole scene was major chaos. It reminded me of a colony of confused and angry bees swarming around a destroyed nest. Their queen was dead, sunk down in his leather chair with half his head blown off.

"You want to tell me, Mr. Moran, what the hell happened here?" a lieutenant asked. His face and neck were splotched red.

"I confronted Sheriff Denny about an investigation I'm working. Next thing I know, he's got his Glock at his head."

His eyes narrowed and I knew he wasn't sure if he should believe me. From a purely objective point of view, I couldn't say I blamed him. Redface stared at me, then yelled at the bevy of officers around Denny's body. "Check his hands for GSR."

One of the officers slowly nodded, acknowledging the gunshot residue covering Denny's right hand.

Redface turned more red, like a kid in school suffering from anxiety-driven hives. "And who is she?"

"Sophia Ortez. She's a reporter with the *Odessa Record*. She's working with me on the investigation."

I caught a glimpse of her when the crowd parted for a moment. She was shaking so bad her hands could barely hold a cup of water.

Black mascara streaked her face, mixing with her tears and Denny's blood. Her cheeks looked like a child's finger painting project. I wanted to go to her, to hold her. I wanted to gently wash the blood, his blood, from her face and tell her everything would be okay.

Suddenly, Mark Peterson was there wrapping a thin blanket around her trembling shoulders. My gut knotted, forcing the surging panic into my throat. *Please Sophia—don't tell him anything. Don't mention anything about a key, about a deposit box, about the—*

"Hey, Lieutenant, you better take a look at these."

Pictures. Sweet Jesus.

Redface stepped around me and went over to Denny's desk. He'd look at a picture, look at me. Look at a picture, look at me. He finally gathered them all up and motioned for another deputy to get me to my feet. He then motioned for a small entourage to follow him, and to bring me with them.

We stepped aside near the door to give the paramedics room to bring in their stretcher. One of them asked if the medical examiner had been called.

"You'll have to check with the captain," a deputy said. He then shoved me around the stretcher and out into the hallway where Redface was waiting.

His face was beet-red now, his eyes two tiny drills boring straight through me. He turned on his heel and headed down the hallway with the entourage in tow. I was steadily growing a little concerned with the situation. I was surrounded by a small army of pumped-up cops flying high on adrenaline. Their nerves were on edge. They didn't know what the connection was between me and Denny, but they knew there was a connection. And my hands were still handcuffed behind my back. If I were a betting man, I'd bet I was going to come away from here with a few bruises.

CHAPTER 25

You want to tell me again what kind of *investigation* you were running on Sheriff Denny?" Lieutenant Redface said, the anger turning his face the color of a bowl of cherries.

One of the deputies shoved me hard toward the table for emphasis. His uniform bore sergeant stripes. Great. I was locked in an interview room with a fucking sergeant, a lieutenant, and twelve angry cops.

Panic mode was setting in. I could feel my heart throbbing in my temples. I stumbled my way around the table, trying to keep the officers in sight. Not that I could do anything with my hands still cuffed behind my back; it was the psychology of knowing what was coming. "Look, you checked his hand. It was covered with gunshot residue. There wasn't any foul play involved."

"I didn't ask you if you killed him. I asked you what kind of investigation you were running on him." He tossed the pictures on the table. The glossy paper skittered easily across the gray metal, each picture separating from the other until the entire table was partially covered with images of Denny pounding some poor kid's ass.

"Looks like blackmail pictures to me," the sergeant said. His breath was sour and warm in my face.

I had no way of knowing if he or any of them were part of Peterson's little crime circle. My brain was scrambled while remnants of Denny's were still splattered on my arm. I thought of Sophia. She hadn't bargained for all this. All she wanted to do was write her story, a story I goaded her into pursuing.

My cell phone buzzed, stopped, then buzzed again several times. I'm not sure what the deputies were expecting me to do—I couldn't answer the phone with my hands behind my back.

"You're that PI from Vegas, aren't you? The one Mark Peterson nailed the other day on the court." The deputy speaking had dark curly hair and a scar under his right eye. He was the guy who gave me a bottle of water after Peterson's castration attempt. He didn't look as sympathetic now as he did then.

"Were you blackmailing the sheriff, Mr. . . . . *Moran*?" Redface referred to my ID, which he hadn't bothered to return.

I was beginning to feel like a wounded antelope surrounded by a pack of snarling wolves. "I wasn't blackmailing the sheriff."

Redface cocked an eyebrow and looked at the sergeant, then at me. "Were these pictures part of your investigation?"

There was only one way out of this that I could see that didn't involve broken bones. "I think it would be in my best interest to not answer any more questions without an attorney present."

"You're lawyering up." The sergeant sounded defeated.

There was a collective round of groans from the pack.

I didn't actually think of it as lawyering up, but there wasn't a term for Rangering up. Besides, I didn't think they'd be welcoming to an outside agency right now and saying I'd like for them to call the local Rangers' office would guarantee a broken bone.

Redface's whole demeanor changed. "Moran, look . . . I just want to know what type of investigation you were working on that includes pornographic pictures of the sheriff. I mean, look at it from our point of view."

"I am looking at it from your point of view. And that's why I'm requesting an attorney." I've never claimed to be a genius but I'm not stupid.

Sophia and I were the only two people who knew what happened in Denny's office. I'd offer up the video recording of what transpired before going as far as actually being arrested. But the video would also show the conversation about the safety-deposit box, and I wasn't ready to share that knowledge just yet. I had no idea whom in Denny's department I could trust and who would slit my throat at the first opportunity. Until I figured that part out, I wasn't talking.

Redface bobbed his head toward the door and dismissed the uniforms. "You boys go see if they need any help processing the scene."

The deputies grumbled as they shuffled out, leaving me, the sergeant, and the lieutenant standing there staring at one another.

"My phone's in my left front pocket," I said after a long moment.

Redface chewed on the inside of his lip before finally motioning for the sergeant to remove the handcuffs. The sergeant wasn't happy about it and retaliated with a strong twist before releasing my wrists. My shoulders ached at the newfound freedom. I rolled them a couple times, then dug my cell out. Obviously Redface and the sergeant weren't going to give me any privacy.

The display showed five missed calls, one from Rhonda and four from Rodney. I punched in Rodney's number.

He answered on half a ring. "Gypsy? What the hell is going on? Where are you?" There was so much commotion going on around him, it was hard to hear.

"Sheriff's office."

"The same. With half the town. Were you here when it happened?"

"In the room." I wiped a fleck of Denny's brain from my shirt. "Look, I'm going to need——"

"*Oh Jesus.*"

"Yeah, him too. Look, I'm in an interview room on the first floor. Can you get back here?"

A minute later, there was a loud rap at the door as Rodney burst in.

"Rodney Walker's not an attorney," the sergeant said. I couldn't distinguish if his expression was perplexed or amused.

"Rodney's involved with the investigation."

"Of this department?" Redface asked. He wasn't impressed.

Rodney held his hands up in his own defense. "Hang on, Jim, we're going to get all this straight. But first you need to get someone out there running crowd control. The public's crowded around the front entrance."

Redface looked more gloomy than ever. He spoke to the sergeant. "Dale, go see what you can do out there. Until we've established otherwise, the office is a crime scene. Handle it like one, please."

Sergeant Dale glowered at me before clapping Rodney on the back in a strained show of solidarity. As soon as the door shut behind the sergeant, Redface went over and locked it. I wasn't sure what was going on but I felt a lot better with Rodney there as a witness.

"Can one of you please tell me what the hell's going on?" Redface turned around and looked at us with more confusion than authority. "Rodney?"

Rodney nodded in my direction. "I'm assuming you've met my brother-in-law, Gypsy Moran. Gypsy, meet Lieutenant Jim Oshay."

Oshay plopped down at the metal table and scratched his bald spot. He stared at the pictures of Denny, then disgustedly shook his head.

"Did you know that was going on?" Rodney sat down across from Oshay. I sat down beside Rodney.

Oshay scrubbed his face with his hands and let out a deep sigh. "I'd heard rumors. We'd all heard rumors over the years. I still don't understand what these pictures have to do with your investigation. Looks an awful lot like blackmail, Mr. Moran."

"I prefer to think of it as leverage. There's some dirty cops in the depart—"

"Dirty cops?" He bowed up like a goose on a rampage. "You got any proof of that?"

I waited on him to finish the question with the word *boy,* saying, of course, in a slow country drawl. When he didn't, I continued. "Ryce McCallen was conducting an investigation into the department when he died. He'd gathered a lot of evidence before he was killed. I was hired to finish the investigation. And to prove Ryce's death wasn't a suicide."

Oshay studied me for a long while before speaking. "Ryce was a good cop." He didn't say anything more, or anything less. Everything I needed to know was in the tone of his voice. I could trust him.

"Mark Peterson and Averitt McCoy hung him like a horse thief in his own backyard. His twelve-year-old son found him," I said, purposely implanting the mental image of Tatum trying to save his father.

"We found the rope in the back of McCoy's truck that they used to hang Ryce with," Rodney said.

Oshay sighed, sounding like a tire with a slow leak. "And you've got proof?"

Rodney nodded. "DNA proof."

"But why?" Oshay shook his head.

"Mark Peterson and Averitt McCoy are trafficking teenage girls. Ryce was on to it and had gathered a lot of evidence before he was killed."

Oshay held a hand up. "Wait a minute. You're saying Peterson and McCoy are involved with human trafficking?"

"Over the last three years, eight girls have gone missing from around the area. All Hispanic. All illegals," I answered.

"And their parents are too scared to push the police for a report—" Rodney began.

"So there's no paper trail," Oshay said, finally seeming to understand. "How did Ryce know about this?"

"The younger sister of one of the missing girls told Tatum McCallen she was afraid that what happened to her sister would happen to her. Tatum asked Ryce if he could do anything to help."

"And you think the sheriff was involved?" Oshay glared at the ugly pictures still spread on the table.

I raised my shoulders in a slight shrug. "I don't know how *involved* the sheriff was—but I believe he did know what was going on. I think Mark Peterson knew about the sheriff's fondness for young boys and used it as a way to control him."

Rodney cleared his throat. "Jim . . . we don't know how deep this thing goes. We don't know how many people in the department may be involved. And we don't even know who's in charge out there right now. For that reason, Gypsy's going to turn the evidence over to the Rangers' office. The entire department may be under tight scrutiny for a while."

Oshay sighed again and the tire had gone flat. At that moment, he had given all he could give. Except my ID.

I held out my hand and smiled sympathetically. "Can I have my ID back now?"

We spent the next four hours in Denny's blood-spattered office with Rick Ramirez from the Rangers' division office. Ramirez had sent Rodney to Fidelity Bank to collect the contents of the lockbox after I handed over the key. The dearly departed Sheriff Denny had been right—everything we needed to prove Mark Peterson was a scumbag was in that metal box. Recorded conversations between Denny and Peterson, some with mentions of Claire accepting money for providing the girls, along with pictures of Peterson and Averitt McCoy handing off black-haired girls to greasy looking thugs, and an obviously forged letter from Burke McCallen to the sheriff requesting no autopsy on Ryce. There was also a small evidence bag with a spent slug in it. I didn't need to test it to know it was the slug they accused Hector Martinez of firing into Burke's back. Rodney had also brought in the rope retrieved from McCoy's truck while I handed over Ryce's files along with the financial records I had accumulated. As far as I was concerned, my job was done. There was enough evidence in Ramirez's hands to reclassify Ryce's death as a homicide, which meant insurance would pay out and Tatum and Burke could stay in the house. The missing girls were a much deeper issue. For Tatum's sake, I figured I might take a closer look at Alana Esconderia's disappearance. Her family, like the others, deserved an answer. Even if it was one they didn't want to hear.

The early signs of a pounding headache were creeping up the back of my neck as Ramirez, Oshay, and Rodney watched the video of Denny blowing his brains out. They watched it over and over and over again as if each new viewing would change the out-come. Each time I heard the *pop,* I saw the white explosion turn crimson red in my mind. Saw the horror on Sophia's face as she came to realize what happened. I blamed her for the oncoming headache. I was worried about her.

Ramirez and Oshay interviewed her briefly but wouldn't let me talk to her, taking the "separate the witnesses" game a little too far for my liking. While Ramirez, Oshay, and Rodney watched the video, I peered at the growing crowd through the side of the blinds covering the windows in Denny's office. The wooden-planked blinds were drawn to deter the photographers and overly curious from seeing parts of Denny's brain embedded in the yellow stucco wall.

I could see my van through the crowd but Sophia's little red Mercedes was gone. I wondered if she went home or if she was at the *Odessa Record* begging the editor for front page above the fold.

I tried her cell for the hundredth time and again it went to voice mail. I'd already left enough messages to classify myself as a stalker, so I ended the call. I finally called the office. The receptionist trans-ferred me to Sophia's desk, then came back and told me the call was going straight to voice mail; did I want to leave a message? No, I didn't want to leave a message. I wanted to talk to her. I wanted to see her.

I turned away from the window and looked at Ranger Rick. "Do you need me anymore?"

He scanned over everything we had presented, then slowly shook his head. "I think you're good for tonight. I'll probably bring McCoy in for questioning tomorrow morning."

McCoy was the weak link and even Ramirez could see it. If he could get McCoy to roll on Peterson, Peterson's fate would be sealed.

"Peterson might try and run. Especially if he thinks he's boxed in." I didn't want to question Ramirez's ability but I didn't want Peterson vacationing in the south of France, either.

Ramirez smiled. "We've got him. I've got your cell number if I need you. By the way, there's some good work here. Get licensed in Texas and we can use you."

I laughed. If I had worn a hat, I would have tipped it as I left.

CHAPTER 26

I pulled away from the mayhem surrounding the sheriff's office and drove to a mom-and-pop store about a mile away. I parked near the side of the building but left the motor running with the cold air blowing straight into my face. The temperature outside had to be in triple digits and I was supposed to take Tatum to the sinkholes tomorrow to take some pictures? How drunk was I when I agreed to that?

I opened the browser on my cell and opened my most frequently used app. I carefully keyed in the tag number on Sophia's Mercedes and within seconds had her address. I plugged it into the GPS, then settled in for the ride to Odessa.

The whole "partner" thing did concern me. The last thing I needed this evening was to come face-to-face with a significant other. But dammit, I was worried about her, and she wouldn't answer her freaking phone. If he was there, maybe we could mumble our way around an awkward situation. After all, Sophia and I had worked together on this investigation, so it was technically a business visit. If I kept telling myself that, maybe by the time I got to Odessa I'd believe it.

Highway 302 had to be one of the loneliest places on earth. Or maybe it was just west Texas in general. The forty-minute ride seemed like four days. I drove into town and circled around the *Record* to see if her car was there. It didn't surprise me that it wasn't. I rekeyed Sophia's address from the current location. ETA eight minutes.

The Arbor Crest Luxury Apartments was a sprawling complex spread out on several acres. A lush green lawn and flowering shrubs gave it the appearance of a country club. Beside the office that doubled as a clubhouse was a well-kept tennis court. Like someone was really going to play a round of tennis when it was 115 degrees. The majority of cars in front of the clusters of units were high dollar, free of soccer ball decals or "my kid's an honor roll student" at blah-blah elementary. Sophia's neighbors were, like her, professionals who made decent salaries, probably preferring to keep to themselves than to attend the once-a-month social at the clubhouse.

Sophia's apartment was one unit from the back of the complex. I parked in the empty spot beside her car, hoping that one, her husband/boyfriend/significant other usually parked in the same spot, which meant he wasn't home or didn't live there altogether, or two, there was only one designated spot per apartment, which meant I really was parked in someone else's spot. I took the steps leading up to her apartment on the second floor by twos and knocked hard on the door.

"Sophia—it's Gypsy." No response. I knocked again. "Sophia. I need to talk to you. Please open the door."

I heard shuffling around inside the apartment but the sound wasn't moving toward the door.

"Sophia. Come on, I just want to make sure you're okay."

A text alert came through on my cell. It was from Sophia. *I'm fine. Go home.*

At least I knew it was her shuffling around inside. I sent a reply. *Not happening. Open door.*

After a few minutes, I knocked again, more gently this time. "Sophia . . . please open the door. I'm not leaving until you do."

A few minutes of silence went by. I leaned against the door and took in the surroundings. The stairs leading to the second floor ended at a landing large enough to classify as a deck. A large cluster of potted plants dominated a corner near the railing overlooking the parking lot. A thick strand of ivy wove around the railing and climbed a gutter spout like a trellis. I could see Sophia took great care of the plants as their leaves were vibrant and shiny. It might cause her great pain to lose one. Not that I wanted to cause her any more pain—I just wanted her to open the door.

I went over to the corner and hoisted one of the pots to the railing, tipped it just to the point of dropping it, and snapped a picture with my phone. I sent the picture to Sophia with the text: *Open the door or else.* I returned the plant to its nesting place and patiently waited for a reply. Several minutes went by and no response. She either cared nothing about the plant or she wasn't in any mood for joking around. I banked on the latter.

I sat down and leaned against the door, deciding I was going to wait her out. I held my phone out in front of me and snapped another picture, typed *not going anywhere,* and hit send. About thirty minutes passed before I heard movement in the apartment.

She finally opened the door and stared down at me. "You don't give up, do you?"

I stood and stretched my legs. "Not without a fight."

She looked horrible. Still wearing the blood-spattered clothes she was wearing in Denny's office, the whites of her eyes were as red as the bloodstains. Small splotches of dried blood were still caked on her face like bad makeup. She was barefooted.

I followed her in and closed the door behind us. She sat down on the floor in front of the sofa, pulling her legs up and wrapping her arms around her knees. "What are you doing here?" Her voice was indifferent, almost robotic. She wasn't angry; she was still in shock.

"I was worried about you." I sat down in one of two wingback chairs across from the sofa. I wasn't sure of the situation with the partner and I didn't want the visit to be any more strained than it was.

She gently rocked back and forth, her arms still wrapped tightly around her legs, staring at something only she could see. I had a pretty good idea of what it was she was seeing over and over again.

There was an open laptop on the coffee table with a pile of notes beside it. "Goin' to make your deadline?"

It took her a moment to answer. She pushed a hand through her hair, then shrugged. "It's going to take more than one article to tell this story." She sighed heavily. "I'm sorry—I'm not much of a hostess. Would you like a beer or something?"

"Sure." Truth was, I didn't want anything but for her to be okay.

She pulled herself up like it required a great deal of effort, then shuffled over to the kitchen area. The apartment was industrial-style with brick walls and exposed duct work overhead. The kitchen gleamed with stainless steel. Custom-matted and framed black-and-white photographs were the decoration of choice. The overstuffed sofa and the two wingback chairs were the color of expensive vanilla ice cream spotted with bean flecks, not the cheap shit that's sold in a plastic bucket.

I moved over to the sofa to take a look at what she had written and stared at an empty white page in a blank Word document. I don't really know what I was expecting, but the coldness of the empty page was jarring. I skimmed idly through some of her notes while waiting.

The kitchen couldn't have been more than thirty feet away, separated from the living room by a white brick wall. Sophia could have run down to the local store for the amount of time that had passed.

I found her leaning into the counter beside the refrigerator, her back to me, her shoulders softly shaking as she quietly cried. She jumped when I touched her, then turned and fell into my arms. The crying soon became hysterical as she kept repeating *the blood, all the blood*. I held her tight, softly stroking her hair, telling her it was going to be okay.

I could feel the sharpness of dried blood still in her hair, and the slickness of specks of brain matter. She still had Denny's blood on her arms and hands. I scooped her up, forced her legs around my waist, and carried her to the bathroom.

The shower was a stand-alone with a frosted-glass door. She was still propped around my waist, her arms clinging tightly around my neck, still crying when I carried her into the shower and turned on the water. I adjusted the temperature until the water lightly beating against her back was just a shade cooler than hot. She relaxed slightly and it was enough to allow me to pry her legs lose from around my waist and help her stand. Gently, I removed her blouse and tossed it behind me as I batted back the water spraying straight into my own eyes. The water swirling around the drain had a reddish tint as Denny's blood washed away.

I removed her pants, then my own shirt and pants, adding them to the growing pile of blood-stained clothes in the back of the shower. There we were, standing in her shower, warm water washing over us, her in her bra and panties, me in my boxers, and I *didn't* want to make love to her. I wanted to take care of her, to wash the blood off of her, to hold her.

The crying settled into an occasional sniffle as I washed her hair, then her face, then her arms and hands. She reached out and lightly ran a finger across my cheek, then sadly looked at her finger. The streak of dried blood turned bright pink, then faded and disappeared.

I quickly scrubbed the remaining blood from my arms, then lifted my face to Sophia, batting the water out of my eyes. "Clean?"

She slowly nodded. At that moment, my heart couldn't have been any larger. It encompassed my entire body, my whole being. I could feel it exploding in my head and throbbing in my toes.

I lightly ran my hands over her wet hair, smoothing it down, pushing the slick strands behind her ears. Wetness glistened on her bronze-colored skin like tiny jewels. Her warm, mocha eyes were now heavy-lidded and tired instead of panic-filled and horror stricken.

I reached behind her and turned off the water, then gently removed her bra. I held her arm for balance as she stepped out of her panties. I tossed my boxers onto the bloody laundry pile at the back of the shower.

After I stepped out of the shower, I found towels in the laundry cabinet behind the bathroom door. I wrapped one around my waist, then wrapped Sophia in one. She was like a small child after a full day of hard play, exhausted and relaxed, allowing me to dry the wetness from her body with no protest. I ran the towel over her hair and asked if she wanted to blow dry. She shook her head slowly. I left her for a moment to find her some comfortable clothes, returning with fresh panties and a white tank top I found in a tallboy dresser in the bedroom. After helping her dress, I carried her to the bed and tucked her under the white down comforter. When I started back to the bathroom, she grabbed my hand.

"Don't go."

"I'll be right back. I promise."

I went back into the bathroom and rung out the pile of laundry as best I could. I found her washer and dryer in a hallway utility closet. I dropped the clothes in the washer and hoped the blood would wash out without leaving a stain of bad memories.

I wondered what size her partner wore and if he kept any clothes at her place. From what I had seen of the apartment, Sophia lived alone. It was definitely a woman's place.

I went back to the bedroom and was going to ask about the partner but she reached behind her and pulled back the comforter. I dropped the damp towel and climbed in behind her. She was curled into a fetal position, and pushed herself backward until she was snuggled against me. She pulled my arm across her, our fingers wrapped around one another's.

She smelled so clean, so innocent. Like it was really possible, I tugged her closer and nuzzled her neck. I felt her breath settle into a steady rhythm, a rhythm that matched my own. Once I knew she was sound asleep, I closed my own eyes and drifted off to a world that included Sophia Ortez.

I wasn't expecting her to snore. Unless I've got a bottle of Black Label in me, I'm a pretty light sleeper. Comes with the territory. And I've *slept* with my share of women. Even woken up in the middle of the night and crept out unnoticed. But Sophia Ortez, possibly the sexiest woman on earth, took the prize for snoring. Deep, lip-smacking, wet gasps that rattled the blinds. It was not a Barry White moment.

I was happy she was sleeping so soundly. I wished I could catch an hour or so before daybreak. I was picking Tatum up at ten and taking him to the sinkholes. After that, I figured I'd check in with Ranger Rick. And somewhere in my schedule for the day, I was going to have to include a nap.

My stomach was past empty and protested unheard above Sophia's sleep apnea. I eased out of bed, wrapped the towel around
my waist, then headed to the kitchen in search of food.

There were a couple cans of soup in the pantry, a few cans of
tuna, some wheat crackers, and a box of Cocoa Puffs. I checked the
fridge for milk. Bingo. I checked the expiration date. Still good.

I poured myself a bowl of cereal and ate as I checked out the
apartment. I was curious about this partner she had breathlessly
mentioned while ripping my pants off the other night in Rhonda's
front yard. I thumbed through a few pieces of mail she had in an
organizer in the corner of the counter. All addressed to Sophia
Ortez. The apartment's décor wasn't ultra-feminine, but it definitely wasn't masculine, either. It wasn't even middle-of-the road
compromise. It was all Sophia. No two people can have the same
taste in *everything*. The flat screen television was moderate, connected only to a cable box and DVR, no PlayStation 3 or other
game consoles to raise the testosterone level. The bookshelf was
jammed with reference and self-help books geared toward wom-
en's interests. The few fiction titles were thick paperback romance
novels, their spines frayed and faded. I grinned as I imagined Sophia propped up in bed, that fluffy down comforter covering her
bare legs, thoroughly lost in a book that had a guy in a white pi-
rate shirt on the cover.

There was no indication anyone other than Sophia Ortez lived
in this apartment. Maybe it was one of those friends-with-benefits
relationships? Maybe he was a fellow journalist, someone she
worked with—like a *partner* in crime?

The snoring could explain a lot. Maybe he had tried to stay
over, maybe even move in, but valued a good night's sleep over
good sweaty sex. What an idiot.

I went back into the kitchen and spotted a coffeemaker tucked into the corner of the counter. I scrounged around the cabinet until I found a can of coffee and a bag of filters. While the coffee brewed, I dug our clothes out of the washer, then tossed them into the dryer.

I rinsed out the cereal bowl, poured a cup of steaming coffee, then took it out on the small deck to enjoy. It was a wooden deck, maybe twelve by six, with a wrought-iron table and two chairs. The sun was still an hour away from creeping over the treetops, but darkness was already fading, giving way to a brand-new day. I watched a rabbit dart in and out of a row of bushes then disappear into the darkness. I wondered if it was running back home, or away.

I wondered why *I* ran home. When the whole Gina Gilleni case went south, I headed straight for the one place I fought so hard to leave. It wasn't a family thing—I talked to Rhonda or Mom on the phone sometimes once a week. They came out to Vegas fairly often. When they came, I showed them a good time. Gram loved the nickel slots and Rodney loved the complimentary drinks in the casinos. Rhonda and Mom loved the shows and the shopping. Me—I loved riding up into the mountains at night and looking down at all the lights. There wasn't a hooker in Vegas flashier than the grand whore herself. Never understood why I despised the loneliness of west Texas but fled to the mountains overlooking Vegas every chance I got. I probably needed to see a shrink.

I went back inside and refilled my coffee, then turned the television on, the volume on low. The early-morning news was in full swing as the heavy-eyed anchor thanked Tom the weatherman for another blistering forecast. Frank, the anchor, looked like he needed an IV line of Starbucks's strongest.

As he turned and faced the camera head-on, a graphics box containing a picture of crime-scene tape popped onto the screen over his left shoulder. "Winkler County is still in shock over the apparent suicide of Sheriff Gaylord Denny," he said, reading from the teleprompter.

Apparent, my ass. The man blew his brains out. There was no *apparent* about it.

"Authorities are being tight-lipped about the investigation," Frank continued, then introduced a video. "Megan Gruber has more from outside the sheriff's office in Kermit."

The video had been shot yesterday with a crowd gathered in front of Denny's office. Megan Gruber looked like a summer intern who had been thrown into a live shot of the most explosive story of the year because everyone else was on vacation. She spit her words out like she was blowing out birthday candles. "Authorities haven't ruled out foul play but did say it does appear the sheriff did take his own life. What we do know is at approximately ten A.M. a man and a woman, identified as Private Investigator Michael Moran and Sophia Ortez, a reporter with the *Odessa Record,* were with the sheriff in his office when the death occurred. The reason for Moran and Ortez's visit isn't known at this time but it is believed to concern an investigation Moran was conducting involving the sheriff."

"So it wasn't just a bad dream," Sophia said.

I glanced over my shoulder. "Afraid not."

She sighed heavily, then padded into the kitchen, her bare feet falling lightly on the slate floor. "I see you found the coffee." Her voice was gravelly and full of morning hoarseness. Probably had something to do with the snoring.

"I kinda made myself at home." I followed her into the kitchen and pulled her to me, lightly kissing the top of her head. She didn't pull away. She laid her head on my shoulder.

"Thanks for staying last night," she whispered. "And for not . . . you know . . . expecting anything."

"Today's not over."

She playfully smacked my shoulder, then shook her head. "You're such a jerk." She poured herself a cup of coffee, then topped off mine.

"I'm sorry you didn't get the scoop. I wasn't expecting it to end that way."

She made an exaggerated expression, then laughed sarcastically. "I don't think anyone could have predicted that." She held her coffee mug—it was pink with green embossed ivy wrapping around it and up the handle—blowing lightly into her coffee as if to cool it. "I've seen dead bodies before. I'm not a total rookie. But I've never seen . . ."

"You've never seen it happen. It can be a jolt to the psyche."

She finally took a sip of her coffee. "Will I ever *not* see it?"

I slowly shook my head. I wasn't going to lie to her. "You just won't see it as often."

She looked so small standing there, barefooted, in nothing but a tank top and her white cotton panties. Her hair was a mess, flat in places and mussed up in others. She had a faint pillow impression on one cheek. I'd never wanted her more.

I was still only wearing last night's towel. The stirrings down below were going to be noticeable soon. I turned away and went into the living room before confirming her claim I was a jerk. "So . . . even if you didn't get the scoop, you're going to have the best exclusive, right?" I asked over my shoulder.

"I suppose. I guess being a witness would give me a leg up on the competition." She followed me into the living room and sat down on the sofa, her gloriously long legs pulled up and crossed Indian style.

I smiled. "Yes, but a real journalist doesn't put themselves in the story."

She cocked an eyebrow. "A *real* journalist? *Excuse me?*"

I sat down beside her and stretched my legs out, propping my feet on the old luggage trunk she used for a coffee table. "You're the best journalist in the field. That's why I chose you."

She burst out laughing. "You chose me because I was the only one who wrote an article, if you can call it that, on Burke McCallen's shooting."

"You were a girl after my own heart even then."

She tossed her head back and laughed deep and loud. I was expecting a snort to escape any second. She was a classy broad, this Sophia. And I was falling hard and fast.

"This . . . um . . . *partner* you mentioned the other night in my sister's front yard. He's not goin' to come waltzing in here any minute now, is he?"

The smile on her face slowly slipped away like the night fading into the dawn. There was an air of sadness about it. After a long moment, her nose twitched and she took my coffee cup. "Looks like you could use a refill." She got up and went back into the kitchen.

I wasn't going to let her off that easy. If this thing between us was going to continue, which I hoped it would, I wanted to know the rules going in. I wasn't fond of being involved in a three-party relationship. Things get real ugly real fast. I followed her into the kitchen.

She poured two fresh cups, then turned and handed me one. She held her cup up to her lips but didn't drink. She was searching for words that wouldn't come.

"Look," I said, hoping to help her out a little. "I don't know what kind of relationship you're in. At this stage, it's probably none of my business. But I—"

"It's complicated." She finally took a sip of her coffee.

I slowly nodded. "Aren't they all?"

She smiled softly. "Robbie . . . wants more than I'm willing to give right now."

Robbie. My competition. I could compete with a guy named *Robbie*.

I took a long drink of coffee, buying time while I thought of something to say that didn't make me look like a total asshole. "I'm sorry it's not working out."

Sophia stared at me while a smile slowly crept across her mouth. "No, you're not."

I grinned big and shook my head. "Okay, whatever. I just want to make sure Robbie's not going to come busting through the door and threaten me within an inch of my life. Or your life." I sat my coffee on the counter, then gently stroked her hair.

She sighed. "She's really not the kind to threaten people."

For a fraction of a second, I was certain the world stopped. I knew my heart did.

I spoke very slow, so *I* could understand. "Robbie's a . . ."

"Roberta."

"Whoa!" I threw my hands in the air. I didn't know what I was expecting, but it wasn't that. "But . . . you and me . . ." I wagged my finger between us. "I didn't *dream* it, did I?"

She sighed heavily. "No. You didn't dream it."

"But you're a . . ."

She stared at me, blank-faced, like an innocent little bird waiting to peck the shit out of something. "I'm a what?"

I stared back, completely dumbfounded. There were quite a few words thumping around inside my head but I was scared to use any of them. "Okay . . . forgive me. I'm just a little confused." I finished off the pot of coffee and hurriedly fixed another. I shoved the pot under the brew spout, then spun around to face her. "Me

and you, man and woman. You and Robbie . . ." I didn't know
what to say. I didn't know what to ask without sounding like a
total jerk. "Lesbians? Bisexuals? Homosexuals? Help me out here."

She continued to stare at me, on purpose, knowing I was
drowning in confusion. Then she laughed, almost evil-like. "Does
our sexual preference matter?"

"Well . . . yeah. I mean, no. Not really. Should it?"

"No." She stared down into her coffee for a long moment, like
it held a secret she wasn't ready to divulge. Finally, she looked up
at me. "I enjoy being with Robbie, like I enjoyed being with you
the other night."

"Oh God, the other night. Yeah, look—I'm really sorry about
all that."

She shook her head. "It wasn't *that* bad."

That bad? Although I was pretty certain it wasn't meant as an
insult, I couldn't really take it as a compliment, either.

"That night was not a good night to judge by. I'm a lot better
than . . . that. I'm a . . . I can rock your world, sweet thing. Really.
I can. Let me prove it." I hooked my thumb toward the bedroom.

"What? No. I'm not having sex with you right now. I'm still
on my first pot of coffee."

"Oh, come on. I've got to make that night up to you."

"You don't have to do it right now," she squeaked.

"I just don't want you to think . . . I mean, I don't want you
to . . . have second thoughts about me, because of one bad experience."

She smiled warmly. "Gypsy—relax. It wasn't *that* bad. I was
actually pretty turned on." She gnawed on her bottom lip like a
shy schoolgirl.

"So you might want to . . . again, maybe one day?"

"Possibly."

"I'll probably be free this afternoon."

"Gypsy!"

I threw my hands up in defeat. "Okay. I'm just going to go get my clothes out of the dryer and ah . . . I'm supposed to pick Tatum up at ten, so . . . um . . . I'll go do that." I started down the hallway to retrieve my clothes, then stopped. I turned around and went back into the kitchen. Sophia hadn't moved. "Robbie—what is it she wants that you're not ready to give yet?"

"A commitment."

I nodded slowly. "And how long have y'all . . . *been together*?"

"Ten years."

I nodded again. "After ten years together, it's kind of *assumed,* isn't it?"

She shrugged. "You know what they say about assuming something."

I grinned. "I'm going to go get dressed now."

CHAPTER 27

Jasper the border collie met me in the McCallens' driveway, gnawing at the tires between barks. Tatum burst through the front door and was beside the van before I cut off the engine. His eyes were so wide he looked like one of those baby zoo animals that's all eyes and ears.

"Did you charge your cameras?" he asked, giving me just enough room to get out without stepping on his toes. It was nice to see the kid excited.

"My cameras are always charged." I mussed up his hair. Then made a mental note to take him to get a haircut soon.

"I packed us a couple sandwiches—you like bologna? I didn't know if we were going to be out there at lunchtime or not. I've got a couple bottles of water, too. I was going to go clean out the cooler. Maybe we could stop and get some ice?"

I hoped he didn't talk this damn much at the sinkholes. He followed me through the front door and into the living room, where Burke was parked in his wheelchair near the television.

"Have I got time to clean out the cooler?" There he went with the wide-eyes thing again.

He was killing me. I fought back a laugh. "We've got time."

"Okay. It won't take me long. Need anything, Grandpa?"

Burke slowly shook his head. "Go clean your cooler. I'm good."

Tatum disappeared into the kitchen, then the back screen door popped shut. Burke shook his head again. "Kid's been bouncing off the walls since you called last night. I'm glad *you're* spending the day with him."

I laughed as I sat down on the end of the sofa closest to Burke. He wasted no time while Tatum was outside and out of earshot. "What'd you have on Denny?"

I chose my words carefully, not knowing if Burke was aware of the rumor Rodney had told me concerning Ryce. I decided not to put too much emphasis on Denny's sexual preferences and shrugged. "Same thing that's brought many a man down."

He laughed but there was an air of sadness filtering through it. I didn't know if it was finally knowing the evil that killed his son, or the loss of a former friend.

"Your lady friend still shook up?"

I nodded. "She'll be shook up for a while."

Burke breathed a heavy sigh. "Never an easy thing to witness."

He seemed so tired. I suddenly thought of that twelve-year-old out back hosing down a cooler. "You feeling okay?"

He took a deep breath. "I'm fine. I'm just . . . wondering. You think they'll offer Peterson a deal?"

"I don't know. Seems more likely they'll offer McCoy a deal if he corroborates Denny's evidence. Guess it just depends on the district attorney."

He didn't say anything. He just nodded.

"What's going on, Burke? Something's eating at you and I can't put my finger on it."

He stared at the worn linoleum, then finally took a deep breath and looked at me. "I don't think Tatum understands his dad was just a small part of this whole story. I'm afraid he's going to be pretty disappointed when the only people who care whether Ryce killed himself or was murdered is the insurance company. His dad died a hero and the only thing people are going to remember is Sheriff Denny blew his brains out because one of his deputies was trafficking girls."

"As long as he knows his dad was a hero, does it matter what anyone else thinks?"

"To a twelve-year-old?"

He had a point. The sad fact was he was right—no one was going to remember a good cop was murdered. Tatum, along with Denny's two daughters, would forever be thought of as the children of parents who killed themselves.

"I'm ready!" Tatum yelled as he bounded into the living room. "Can we stop at the store and get a bag of ice?"

I nodded. "Yeah." I don't know how long he thought we were going to be out there. Personally, I was looking forward to a nap sometime this afternoon thanks to Miss Sophia.

"Got your life jacket?" Burke asked Tatum.

"We're not going swimming, Pops. We're just going to take some pictures."

"You can swim in the sinkholes now?" The last I had heard the oil company that owned the land had installed mile after mile of chain-link fence to keep people from being swallowed up by the great holes.

"Not supposed to," Burke said. "But you know teenagers."

"Can we take Jasper?"

I stared at Tatum as if he'd lost his freakin' mind. The sandwiches, the cooler—I was humoring him. A dog in the van? Especially a yapping dog.

"Me and Dad used to take him every Saturday morning out to the T Cross farm and let him run the cattle. He hasn't been anywhere since . . ."

Did he just play the guilt card? Burke was fighting off a grin so hard I thought his face was having some kind of spasm.

"I gave him a bath last week so he doesn't smell bad."

What the hell was I supposed to say? A few minutes later, I tossed the cooler in the back of the van while Tatum buckled up in the passenger seat. Jasper, smelling fresh and clean, had our backs from his perch on the console. Damn dog.

"This is going to be the best science project *ever*."

I cut him a sideways glance and smiled. I picked up Highway 115 about two miles up the road, drove about a mile, then pulled into an old mom-and-pop gas station still offering full service. A man with a belly falling over his jeans started outside but I waved him off. "Just getting ice. But thanks anyway."

He nodded, then went back inside. I could see him through the dust-covered window standing beside the register, waiting to ring up his first sale of the day.

A double-door aluminum ice box sat out front beside a wooden bench that looked as old as the man sitting on it. His skin was tanned and wrinkled as a raisin. He was wearing jeans that could stand a good wash and a short-sleeved plaid western shirt with pearl snaps. He tipped his straw hat and gave a curt nod as I headed into the store.

"Traffic slow today?" I asked the man behind the register.

He shook his head with disgust. "Not much happening on the highway today. You want a large bag or the small?"

"Large." Not that we needed it but I figured, as a small-business owner myself, I'd help the old guy out.

"Two ninety-nine," he said as he punched buttons on the ancient register.

I handed him a five, then dropped the change in the mason jar on the counter collecting funds for a local guy fighting cancer.

I bid the old man on the bench a good day as I grabbed a bag of ice. Tatum already had the cooler on the ground behind the van. Jasper was barking at the wind. I dumped the ice in the cooler, then helped Tatum spread it over a couple bottles of water. Jasper continued to bark. I sighed.

"Your phone was ringing," Tatum said as we climbed back into the van. "I didn't answer it."

I raised my brows over the top of my sunglasses and looked at him. "You have my permission to answer but only if it's your grandfather or my sister. Understood?"

He nodded. "The caller ID said *Claire*. Isn't she the one Rhonda doesn't like?"

I ignored his question and checked my missed calls. Sure enough, Claire had called. She didn't leave a voice mail but she did send a text: *Call me!*

I wondered if Ranger Rick had shown up at her house yet. Or if the husband she didn't love was scrambling now to save his political career.

"Is Claire your girlfriend?" Tatum asked. His curiosity jolted me back to the real world.

"At one time she was." I put the phone in the cup holder, then pulled back out onto Highway 115. I could feel his gaze on me, the questions bouncing around in that preteen head of his.

"Why isn't she your girlfriend now?"

"Sometimes things don't work out the way you want them to. Important life lesson, remember that."

The old man in the store had been right. The highway was deserted. A lone jackrabbit skittered alongside the road, then veered to the left and disappeared behind a cluster of sagebrush. Although it wasn't even lunchtime yet, the heat rose in transparent waves from the worn asphalt and shimmered against the horizon.

"Is Sophia your girlfriend now?"

I glanced over at the pint-sized Romeo and shook my head. "Why are you so interested in my love life? Who says someone *has* to have a girlfriend?"

My phone buzzed and I was glad to answer it. It was Claire and she was upset.

"An agent from the Rangers' office called this morning. What am I supposed to tell him, Gypsy?"

"I guess the truth is out of the question?"

She sniffled. "Gypsy . . . how do I get out of this without involving Steven?"

Was she honestly trying to protect him, or just trying to keep it from him. "I have a tape, Claire. There's a couple conversations between you and Mark on it."

"Gypsy, please. I can explain. How soon can you get here?"

"I don't know. I'm kind of tied up right now." I glanced over at Tatum, thankful for the excuse.

She chuckled sadly. "Tell her to untie you. I need you more."

I couldn't help but smile. "I'm actually out at the sinkholes overseeing a photo shoot for a science project."

"Well, I certainly wouldn't want to keep you from that." She chuckled but I knew she was crying. "Gypsy, I need you."

Damn her! My heart shattered into a million pieces and damn if she wasn't stabbing me with one of the sharp edges. "Claire . . . just answer the questions. Just tell him the truth. Rick seemed to be a good guy."

There was dead silence on the other end. After a long moment, she finally sniffled again. "Okay. Will you call me when you get through?"

I wanted to tell her no. But I couldn't. "Yeah, I'll call you. It's going to be okay, Claire. You'll get through this."

"I love you, Gypsy. I always have and I always will. Just remember that, okay?"

"Claire—everything's going to be okay."

"Tell me that you'll remember how much I love you, Gypsy."

I was starting to get a little worried. Claire had a flare for the dramatic but this wasn't her usual crisis tone. "Let me finish here and I'll swing by, okay? Maybe I can be there when Rick gets there."

She didn't say anything for a moment, then finally agreed. "Okay. I'll see you in a little bit."

I clicked the phone off, then returned it to the cup holder.

Tatum was staring at me. When I glanced at him, he quickly turned and stared out the dusty windshield. A minute or so passed. "Thanks," he said.

"For what?"

"Not dumping me for a girl."

I laughed. "Today's not over yet."

He grinned. He was quiet the rest of the way out to the sinkholes. I wondered what was going through his mind. School, his dad, girls, more girls. I wasn't much older than he is now when Claire and I became an item. Even then when we would talk about the future, she couldn't wait until she would run the ranch, and I couldn't wait to leave.

I pulled off the highway and drove slowly around the perimeter of the great Wink sinkhole number 2. Wink, Texas had a Roy Orbison museum, sidewalks, and two impressive sinkholes. The second, formed twenty-two years to the day after the first one appeared, was much larger than the first one. Aerial photographs resembled one gigantic moon crater filled with water, except no one knew for sure how deep the sinkhole was. Divers had been known to go over a hundred feet down and still not reach the bottom. The hole was several hundred feet wide and equally as long, surrounded by a weathered chain-link fence. Multiple cracks in the dry ground spiderwebbed their way from the hole to the fence and sometimes beyond. The brown earth baked in the oppressive heat.

"You sure this is safe?" I asked. To hell with the life jacket—I wasn't sure it was safe to even *walk* around the hole.

"There's a big section of the fence on that side that's torn away," he said, pointing to the west side.

I glanced at him. "And how do you know this?"

He grinned sheepishly. "Dad brought me out here one time just to tell me not to ever come out here."

I fought back a grin as the van fought the hard ground beneath the wheels. The ground was cracked and parched. I pulled to a stop outside a section of fence that was rolled back like the top of a sardine can. "Close enough?"

He was smiling so I figured that was a yes. After we climbed out of the van, I stood near the back and stretched, raising my arms to the Sun God that saw fit to cool things down for us today with an expected high of only 96 degrees. I yawned. Between the energy-zapping heat and Sophia's snoring, I was more than ready for a nap.

I watched Tatum fill his backpack with a couple bottles of water and two sandwiches. "Got the camera?" he asked like an experienced expedition leader.

"Camera, check."

Jasper was out of the van herding tumbleweeds. I don't know where he was herding them to, but he was intent on getting them there.

Tatum closed the back of the van. "Gonna lock it?"

I looked around at the desolation surrounding us. "Unless the tumbleweeds get fed up with Jasper and decide to drive off, I think we'll be okay."

Tatum wiggled into the backpack, then called for his dog. I tagged along, cussing the sun with each step. The heat was excruciatingly painful and oppressive. My shirt was already wet and clinging to my back. Sweat rolled from my brow, streaking the lenses of my sunglasses. Jasper stopped at the edge of the sinkhole and barked at the water.

"That girl you were talking to earlier . . . was she involved in my dad's murder?"

I felt like I had just taken a punch to the gut. Whatever air I had in my lungs was sealed there, suspended in time for a brief moment. "Not directly."

"But she was involved."

I stopped walking. I didn't like where the conversation was going. And I certainly didn't like being grilled by a twelve-year-old kid. "She didn't kill your father, Tatum."

"Then why is the Rangers' office going to question her?"

"A lot of people are questioned in the process of an investigation. Come on, you know that. What's up?"

He shook his head, then continued on to the hole.

"Tatum—what's going on?" I caught up with him near the edge of the crater.

He shook his head again. "Nothing. Camera ready?"

Damn kid. They could be more tight-lipped than a KGB agent. I handed him the camera and reminded him to remove the lens cap. "Do you know how to set the exposure?"

"It's this button here on the top, right?"

I showed him how, then showed him how to adjust the focus. He snapped off a few, which brought a smile back to his sunburned face.

"You didn't bring a tripod, did you?"

I glared at him, then laughed. "Do I look like I've got a tripod on me?" I showed him to improvise by kneeling on one knee and holding the camera on the other. "Your knee's a little steadier than your hands."

"Cool. Can I take some looking over the edge?"

I hesitated, remembering Burke asking if he had his life jacket. And something Rhonda had said earlier about a pool party and his nonexistent swimming skills. "Um . . . why don't you let me take those. Just in case. If anything happens, my phone's in the cup holder."

We laughed but my heart was steadily increasing its pace as I carefully stepped over cracks in the earth. Jasper was at the edge, barking at the air. I planted my feet at the edge, the toes of my right foot actually over the edge. I held the camera out front and snapped a couple rounds aimed straight into the water. "That's going to be good enough because I'm coming back to safer ground now."

I carefully stepped backward, then handed him the camera. He switched to preview and went crazy over the pictures. "This is like the coolest thing ever! You know what would make it even cooler—a video. If I could set up a DVR player at my exhibit and show a video and—"

"Tatum . . . videos are for when you have action. There is no action here." I swept my arm over the great sinkhole. "Unless the damn thing sinks some more, it's going to be a pretty boring video."

He finally settled down. "You don't think just using pictures is going to be boring?"

"We'll come up with something."

We walked all the way around the perimeter, taking turns shooting at different angles. Jasper ran ahead barking at the dirt. When we got back close to the van, we sat down on the hard dirt and each had a bottle of water.

"Want your sandwich now?" he asked as he rummaged through his backpack for the sandwiches.

"Sure." I wasn't the least bit hungry but didn't want to disappoint him.

We sat there in the baking heat eating warm bologna sandwiches and drinking tepid bottled water.

"So, you going to tell me what was going on a little while ago?" I asked. I remembered when I was his age, I had so many things to say, but no one to say them to.

He tossed a pinch of bread to Jasper. "I was just thinkin' how many people know the truth about my dad but no one ever came forward."

"As long as you know the truth, that's what matters."

He cut his eyes at me, followed by a slight grin. "That's a load of crap."

I sighed. "You're right. It's a load of crap. I used to tell people my old man joined the army and was off fighting a war in some foreign country." I took a long drink of the water.

"You think they knew the truth?"

"I don't know. I really don't even know what the truth was. I don't know if anyone other than him knows why he left."

"Do you still miss him? I mean, I know you're old and all, but—"

"Old? I'm going to let that slide and not throw you over the edge."

He grinned. "You're a *cool* old."

I laughed. "Thanks. I think. And yes, I still miss him. Every day."

He threw the last bite of his sandwich to Jasper. "That girl that called—"

"Her name's Claire. She's Mark Peterson's sister-in-law."

"Do you think she knew?"

"About the girls, possibly. About your dad . . . no." I prayed to God she didn't know.

He slowly sipped his water. "I like Sophia better."

I almost spit my water out. "Sophia . . . Sophia's . . . nice."

"We call it *fine*."

I burst out laughing. "She is that."

Movement coming from the left caught my attention. A car was in the far distance but approaching at a fast speed, leaving plumes of dust in its wake. It was a burgundy Crown Vic. Mark Peterson. Why was he out at . . . the . . . sinkholes? Damn Claire! She sent Peterson out like an attack dog. I was so fucking numb, for a moment I couldn't move.

My chest tightened. I struggled to breathe. I finally shook off the shock. I'd deal with the reality of the true Claire later; protecting Tatum was my first priority. I stood quickly and jerked Tatum up by his arm.

"What's the matt—"

"Get in the van." I handed him the keys. "Get Jasper. Lock the doors and don't unlock them for anything. Understand?"

"What's going on?"

"Just do what I say. My cell phone's in the cup holder. Rodney's number is in my contact list. Call Rodney and tell him where we are and we need help."

"But—"

"Get in the fucking van!"

He fumbled with the back door then ordered Jasper to get in. The panic in his eyes was real and desperate and searching mine for an answer I couldn't give. I heard the door lock just as Peterson wheeled up sideways. The Crown Vic stopped about a foot from the van's front bumper. Peterson was out of the car before I could blink, pressing the barrel end of a shotgun straight into my chest.

"Just couldn't mind your own business, could you?" He pumped the gun; the sound echoed in the sagebrush and lonely tumbleweeds. "You are one cool motherfucker, aren't you?"

If I could have spoken, I would have told him sure, I was a cool motherfucker. But I was too fucking terrified at the moment to speak. If I was going to die right here, chances were Peterson would take Tatum out, too. I wasn't going to let that happen.

In one motion, I dropped and rolled and landed a square kick to his right kneecap. He yelled out in pain as he dropped to his knees. I bounced up and in a roundhouse kicked the shotgun from his grip. It skittered across the ground and landed at the edge of the sinkhole. Peterson grabbed my snake-bitten ankle and brought me down in one swoop. My back slammed against the hard earth with a loud *thud* that reverberated in my ears. Peterson was on top of me, pummeling my face with his monster fists. Blood pooled in my mouth as bright yellow stars flashed before my eyes. Dammit, I hadn't survived a rattler bite to be beat to death by this gorilla. With everything in me, I brought my right leg up and drove my knee so far into his balls, I thought they popped out of his eye sockets. Payback's hell.

He rolled off of me and crumpled to his side, giving me enough time to roll away. I scrambled up then nearly took his head off with a kick under his chin. A stream of blood sprayed the brown dirt around us. I added another kick for good measure, then stood over him gasping for breath. It couldn't be over. For Peterson, this was a fight to the death and I wasn't dead yet. I backed away, moving toward the shotgun. Just as I turned to grab the gun, he fired off a shot from his service weapon that pinged the dirt at my feet. He fired another that blew by my ear. I covered my head with my arms and dropped to the ground just as Tatum and the dog burst from the back of the van.

"Tatum! No!" I screamed. Damn kid! I *told* him to stay the fuck in the van!

Everything happened so fast. Jasper lunged at Peterson but met a hard knee to his chest. Tatum screamed as his dog yelped and fell to the side. The kid attacked Peterson with a blind fury fueled by his murdered father. Peterson tried to knock the kid off but Tatum actually connected with a couple wild swings, sending Peterson staggering toward me. I grabbed up the shotgun and pumped it at the same time Peterson regained his balance. He was holding Tatum to his chest, the kid's feet dangling off the ground, and Peterson's gun digging into the side of Tatum's head.

"You first," Peterson said through bloody teeth.

The anger that flared in Tatum's eyes moments ago was now pure fear.

"He's just a kid, Peterson." I was calculating whether or not I could make a clean shot without catching any part of Tatum. Damn near impossible with a shotgun. "Let him go. This is between me and you."

He cocked the gun. I could feel my heart beating in my toes. I could hear it vibrating in my ears. Tatum clenched his teeth, steeling himself for what he thought was coming. "It's okay, kid. You'll never feel it," Peterson said.

I tossed the shotgun over the edge of the sinkhole. "Do what you're going to do to me, but don't hurt him."

"Gypsy, no!" Tatum screamed.

Peterson whacked the gun against the side of Tatum's head, splitting his ear. Just as he screamed out in pain, Jasper charged at them, snarling like he had rabies. Tatum tried wrestling away from Peterson's clutch but Peterson spun around, fighting to maintain his balance with Jasper biting viciously at his legs. As I reached out for the kid, Peterson scrabbled backward and fell, flinging Tatum over the edge.

"Nooo!" I leapt over Peterson and prayed I jumped out far enough to clear the sides of the sinkhole.

I hit the surface like a bullet, plunging feet first into the dark depths of the murky water. *A hundred feet down and still couldn't find the bottom . . .*

I shot back up as fast as I had sank. I spit and coughed water for a second, then screamed for Tatum. I dove back under but the water was too dark to see anything past my own hand. I came up again and just as I took a deep breath, Tatum bobbed to the surface about a hundred feet away. He was coughing and sputtering, his arms flaying in full panic mode.

I cleared the distance between us in seconds. I rolled him on his back then held him under the arms. He was still fighting for his life, the fear of drowning dominating rational thought. "You're okay, Tatum. You're going to be okay."

A gash above his right eye was gushing blood. He was still sputtering but he had calmed down to only slightly panicked. At least one of us was calming down. I was on the verge of a heart attack.

I swam backward with one arm toward the side of the sinkhole, dragging Tatum with my other arm. How the hell the kid ended up in the middle of the sinkhole is beyond me. My adrenaline rush was slipping, giving way to exhaustion.

With one last rush of strength, I reached a small ledge of rock and earth. I pulled Tatum up to the ledge and planted both his hands firmly on the edge. "Do not let go."

He nodded, slowly regaining his senses. I pushed away enough to tread water but still close enough I could get a hand on him if the dirt ledge gave away. I looked up and down the dirt walls of the sinkhole. Now I knew what a goldfish felt like. The walls were much like a fish bowl—smooth all the way around. There were a few outcrops of rock and earth scattered far enough away from one another to guarantee their uselessness. There was nothing to climb. The situation wasn't looking very good. I turned slowly in the water, scanning all sides of the great hole. The north side was at more of an angle than the others and might be a better climbing option, but it was on the opposite side of where we were. It would be a helluva swim. I couldn't make it towing Tatum. Bile rose in my throat as I realized we were running out of options.

Don't let him see you panic . . .

"Jasper," Tatum whispered in a hoarse voice. "I hear him barking."

Damn dog. The kid was right—Jasper was barking his fool head off. And in between barks, I picked up a siren's wail. It was faint but growing.

"Did you call Rodney?"

Tatum quickly nodded. "And 911."

I smiled.

CHAPTER 28

From my perch in the back of an ambulance, I could see Peterson along with Ranger Rick and several officers. A group of paramedics hovered around Peterson, evaluating several nasty-looking dog bites. One of his hands was handcuffed to the stretcher. I'd rather see it cuffed to an electric chair but the stretcher was a start.

"Jasper got some pretty good bites in," Rodney said in a low voice. According to him, when he arrived on the scene Jasper had Peterson pinned against the Crown Vic. Apparently when Peterson stumbled and fell, he suffered a compound fracture to his leg. He dragged himself to the car with Jasper biting his ass every inch of the way. "I hope he's current on his rabies shot."

"Peterson or the dog? I wouldn't want Jasper to catch anything." I watched a paramedic wrap a bandage around Peterson's nasty-looking calf.

Another set of paramedics were examining the gash over Tatum's eye and debating the use of glue or stitches. Jasper sat at the foot of the stretcher, whining for Tatum's attention.

I had said very little since we were rescued, other than to wave off the ice pack a paramedic kept trying to put on my bruised cheek. The paramedics took my silence as a sign of shock. Maybe they were right. There was no other way for Peterson to have known where I was except through Claire.

"Mr. Moran, we really need to put some ice on your cheek. Your eye's going to swell shut." There she was again, standing in front of me armed with an ice pack.

I shook my head then shook off the blanket they had wrapped around my shoulders. Not that I didn't appreciate it, but it was 115 degrees and steam was literally rising from my wet clothes.

"You really need to keep that on. You could be in shock." She was thick in the middle and wore gold-rimmed glasses.

"I could be, but I'm not."

"He's pretty stubborn." Rodney smiled apologetically. He then nodded toward Tatum. "Why don't you go check on the boy and give us an update in a minute or two." He smiled again and the paramedic took her cue to leave us alone.

She nodded, then headed over to her coworkers. Rodney hiked up his jeans like he did when he was about to get serious.

I saved him the trouble. "Claire sent him here to kill me." The words were fire in my throat, exploding like an inferno off my tongue.

"You're sure?"

I nodded. "She was the only one other than Rhonda and Burke who knew we were coming here."

He hiked his pants up again. He twisted his lips into knots then finally spoke. "Rick and I were on our way to question her when I got Tatum's call."

"I want to talk to her first."

We looked at one another, him not believing what I had just said and me meaning each word to the fullest.

"Gypsy—I don't think I can do that. I mean . . . come on, man. You know I can't allow that. Especially now."

"No, it's *especially now* that I need to talk to her." I pushed my hands through my wet hair, hoping it might clear my head. Maybe it would straighten the thoughts as well as the tangles. "I just want to know why she sent Peterson. I don't care about the case. I just want to know why."

"Gypsy . . ." He shook his head slowly and for a moment I felt sorry for him. I understood the position I was putting him in and my heart was heavy with the burden.

"Ten minutes. That's all I'm asking for. Y'all can come in right behind me and handcuff her right there, I don't care. Just give me ten minutes, Rodney. Please. I'm begging you for this and begging doesn't come easy for me."

He kicked at the dry dirt with the toe of his boot. He shoved his hands deep into his pockets. His face was contorted, bearing a pain I was responsible for. "Dammit, Gypsy."

I took a deep breath and forced a slight smile. "If you're worried about her finishing the job—"

"Oh, I'm not worried about that. It's just I know you're still sweet on her and sometimes that can cloud a man's judgment."

"The woman sent someone to kill me, Rodney. I'm crazy about her but I'm not a fool."

He kicked at more dirt, then sighed heavily. "Go. But when we're finished here, we're coming to arrest her."

I hopped out of the ambulance and headed over to Tatum.

"I don't want to go to the hospital," he said, his puppy-dog eyes turning to me for help.

"You're going. You probably need a few stitches over your eye."

One of the paramedics, a woman with butt-length black hair pulled back in a ponytail, nodded her agreement. "I'd say you don't have a choice."

I combed his wet hair down with my hand. "Look . . . I've got to go take care of something. I'm going to send Rhonda to pick up your grandpa and bring him to the hospital, okay?"

He nodded but I could see the fear in his eyes. I hated leaving him. Damn Claire.

"Mamma wants us to go to the prom. She says you're only seventeen once and she doesn't want me to miss out on anything, I guess," Claire said. She was lying beside me, gently drawing hearts with her finger on my bare chest. We were in the Kinleys' den, naked on a blanket on the floor in front of a crackling fire in the rock fireplace. Her parents were at the Cattleman's Club.

"The prom? Seriously?" I chuckled at the thought of me in a tux.

She giggled and it made me laugh again. "Yes, the prom."

I softly kissed the top of her head. "*Are* you missing out on anything?"

She gazed up, then kissed me. I pulled her on top of me. At the moment I entered her, all my dreams and thoughts of the world outside Wink, Texas, evaporated. Thoughts of anything past the four walls of the Kinleys' den exploded into oblivion. The only thing that mattered at that moment in time was Claire and me.

We moved together slowly, savoring each stroke, our bodies and souls melding together into one. The red-yellow glow of the fire glimmered against her bare skin as shimmering beads of sweat rolled over her breasts. I ran my hands over the small of her back, gripping her ass, directing her movement like a conductor. The moans from both of us became louder as the movements became quicker. With one final thrust, we seemed to each hold our breath, suspending the moment for a while in another universe.

Just as her body went limp and she started to fall forward, she was jerked backward and flung off of me.

"Daddy, no!" She screamed as I felt the pointed toe of a size 12 Justin boot driven deep into my side.

I scrambled up, clutching my side, wondering how many ribs he'd cracked with one kick.

"You sorry-ass sonofabitch," Kinley growled with the ferocity of a grizzly. He connected with an uppercut that lifted me off the ground, sending me backward into the wall. "You're a sorry piece of shit just like your daddy!" He drove his knee into my gut, taking away the breath I was already fighting for.

Claire was hysterical, screaming for her father to stop, desperately trying to pull away from her mother. Her mother had her wrapped in the blanket we had made love on, covering her nakedness and her own shame.

Kinley grabbed the back of my hair, driving my head facefirst into his lifted knee. Blood gushed from my nose and mouth. His massive fist landed hard against my jaw.

"Carroll, stop! You're going to kill him!" Dana Kinley screamed, her voice as full of the fear I felt. She let go of Claire and moved toward her husband.

I grabbed at the wall, clutching at the designer draperies, ready to vomit at the amount of blood, *my blood,* that had sprayed the fabric. I wanted to apologize to her mother and tell her I had money saved and I would buy her new drapes but the ringing in my head overshadowed the guilt. I dropped to the ground in a heap. Blood had begun to seep into the fibers of the carpet. I heard the unmistakable *click-click* of a gun being cocked and braced myself for the bullet.

"Touch him again and I'll shoot."

"Claire, don't be ridiculous," Kinley said. "Put the gun down."

"I swear to God, Daddy . . . move away from him or I'll shoot."

"Claire . . . please," her mother said. She sounded a little shocked and a whole lot confused.

No one dared move for what seemed like an eternity. Claire was naked as the day she was born, standing ten feet away from her father with a gun pointed straight at his head. The look in her eyes was jarring, passion and rage rolled into one. I had no doubt she'd pull the trigger. No matter how much she loved him, at that moment her father was the enemy. She'd kill him in the wink of an eye.

"Claire . . ." He slowly reached his hand toward her. He was filled now with more caution than fury. "Give me the gun."

"Move away from Gypsy. You taught me to shoot and you know I can drop you."

"Claire, sweetie . . ." He took a step toward her. "We can talk about this."

She shook her head. "There's nothing to talk about. Gypsy's a part of my life. You're going to accept that. I'll kill for him, Daddy. Even you."

I thought about the old man as I drove past his house to Claire's. I imagined him feeble and needy as I lightly touched the faded scar permanently engraved on my upper lip. I've often wondered if she was really capable of murder. Now I knew she was. Claire was used to getting what she wanted and back then, at that moment, I was what she wanted.

Her truck was in the driveway. I parked behind it, then took the steps leading to the porch by twos. "Claire!" I yelled as I banged on the door. "Claire, open the door."

A full minute had passed, then the panic set in. What if the tearful "I love you" she had said earlier was a suicide declaration? What if it was her *own* life she wanted to end and not mine?

I kicked the door open and when I saw her, I had my answer. The look on her face was sheer surprise. Not the good "it's just what I wanted for my birthday" surprise, but the "you were supposed to be dead" surprise.

"Gypsy . . ." She recovered quickly and ran to me, wrapping her arms around my neck. "Oh, thank God, you came. I don't know what time he's going to be here and . . . you're wet." She pulled away, then lightly touched my swollen eye. "What happened?"

I grabbed her hands in mine. "What the hell do you *think* happened, Claire?"

"I . . . I don't know what you mean." She pulled away, then turned and quickly went into the family room. "Let me fix you a drink. Black Label, right?"

I caught up to her in front of the wet bar, grabbed her arm, and spun her around to face me. "Claire—your brother-in-law tried to kill me."

She looked at my hand clutching her arm before ever looking directly at me. I didn't turn her loose.

"How'd he know where I was, Claire?"

She shook loose but stood her ground. "I don't like what you're implying, Gypsy."

"I don't like almost being killed!" I was yelling now. "You fucking sent someone to kill me, Claire!"

Her eyes flashed over with rage. She slapped my face with enough force to knock me sideways. She came at me again but I grabbed her wrist. "I was going to help you, Claire! I wasn't going to let you go down for this." I let go of her wrist and pushed her away for her own safety.

"You knew the Ranger was going to question me. Obviously you had already talked to him."

"Of course I talked to him. He was at the sheriff's office last night. Claire—this isn't about you! You fucking tried to have me killed!" I moved toward her but she moved behind the bar. My blood was on fire with a fury I had never known. I swung my arms across the bar, sending bottles and glasses shattering against one another. She screamed and ducked, covering her head with her arms. "You sent your gorilla out there to kill me, Claire! I had a twelve-year-old boy with me—did you ever think what was going to happen to him? And what about those girls? Can you even *fathom* what they're being forced to do?"

"Stop it! Stop it!"

"I can't forgive you this time, Claire."

"Gypsy—please—listen to me." She was stepping over the shards of glass, moving toward me. "I was scared. I didn't know what to do."

"So having me killed was the answer?"

"No, Gypsy—you've got it all wrong." She touched my cheek where the sting from her slap was still fresh. "It was Mark. He was here when we talked on the phone. He overheard me say you were at the sinkholes. He left right after—I had no idea where he was going. You've got to believe me, Gypsy." Tears cascaded down her face. She lightly touched my cheek again, gently touched my swollen eye. "Did he do this? Baby, I'm so sorry."

I held her hand against my face for a long moment, then for the first time since I had laid eyes on her so many years ago, I felt nothing. I felt no pity, no anger, no love. Peterson didn't overhear her say I was at the sinkholes. Because she never said it. I was the one who had said it. I gently brushed her hand down and walked away.

"Gypsy . . ." She followed me into the foyer then stopped, her feet frozen to the slate floor.

Rodney and Ranger Rick were at the door. Rodney had his handcuffs out and opened.

"*Gypsy* . . ." she said again. Her voice grew faint as I went out the door, down the steps, and got into the van.

I turned the van around and never looked back.

CHAPTER 29

I blinked away the sweat rolling in my eyes. I used the tail of my T-shirt to wipe the dampness from my face. The shirt was covered in dirt; I wondered if I looked like I was using one of those mud facials.

"Why the hell am *I* doing this?" I looked at Tatum and tossed him the shovel. "They're your shrubs."

From the back deck, Burke laughed out loud. "Was wondering how long it was going to take you to figure that one out."

I ruffled Tatum's hair as I headed up the deck steps. "Yeah, I noticed he likes to *supervise.*"

I had paid to have the tree taken down where Ryce was killed and threw some cash at the landscape company for some drought-resistant shrubs to plant in its place. Obviously I didn't pay them enough because up until a moment ago when I handed Tatum the shovel, I had done all the planting.

I went inside and grabbed a beer from the fridge, then re-joined Burke on the deck.

It had been a month since Denny killed himself and life went on. Ramirez was heading up a task force charged with finding the missing girls and asked me to help. I hadn't said yes, but I hadn't said no yet, either. Even if I couldn't bring her sister home, I wanted Alvedia Esconderia to be able to grow up unafraid. Claire rolled on Mark Peterson like I knew she would and was awaiting sentencing. Her husband's political clout took a nosedive and couldn't save her from pulling time. Her daddy's money was long gone as the ranch had been in financial trouble for years. It still didn't justify what she did. My stomach churned with disgust knowing she sold those girls like cattle to Mark Peterson. I still didn't know what scared me more—knowing I would have helped her out of the whole mess or knowing she had tried to kill me for a tape she thought I had.

But I was finally beginning to sleep again, unafraid to close my eyes because she no longer haunted my dreams. Whether she drowned in the bottom of the great Wink sinkhole or in the bottom of a bottle of Johnnie Walker, I don't know. All I knew was she was no longer a part of my life, or my memories.

I pulled up one of the deck chairs, then propped my feet up on the railing.

"Are you actually wearing *boots*?" Burke raised a brow as he stared at my feet.

"They're *hiking* boots."

"Uh-huh."

We watched Tatum stomping on the shovel, giving it all he had. "When he gets about twenty more pounds on him, he'll be all right," I said.

Burke shook his head and laughed. "If he gains only twenty pounds, someone's going to have to teach him how to fight." He looked at me.

I took a swig of beer. "He actually did pretty good against Peterson until the gun came out."

"Trumps a fist every time."

I laughed. "You got that right, ol' man."

I watched the kid dig, stomp, dig, stomp, dig, stomp, complaining the whole time about how freakin' hot it was. The smile flittered across my lips so naturally, I was barely aware I was smiling. He reminded me so much of myself at that age. So scrawny a good gust of wind could move you. You made up for it by pretending you were ten feet tall and bulletproof.

I never had anyone teach me how to fight, either. There were days I missed my father probably as much as Tatum missed Ryce. I often wondered if my old man ever loved my mother. If she haunted his dreams, his memories. The flashing pictures in my mind that I could remember told me he did. I remember flowers from the florist, I remember Valentine's candy, Saturday-night dates when Gram would come stay with me and Rhonda.

He used to have this old truck he was restoring that he kept parked behind the house. He'd work on it a little, then we'd take off on a ride. Just me and him. We'd hit every back road in Winkler County, the dirt floating in through the open windows. I can still feel the grit on my face. I can still hear the static coming through the AM radio. When we were far enough away from anything or anyone, he'd pull over and let me drive. I'd scoot to the edge of the seat and stretch my legs out as far as they would go and still struggle to reach the pedals. We'd drive out to the canyons and shoot cacti with the Remington he had given me for no reason at all. He wasn't all bad, my old man.

"Hey . . . I see you two are working hard," Sophia said. She came up the steps and joined us on the deck. She lightly squeezed my shoulder and grinned.

I was jolted back to the present, which wasn't bad, and smiled. She was wearing navy capris and a white vest as a top. If I'd been a stick of butter, I'd have melted. "Five minutes earlier and you would have caught me working."

"We can't have that."

We all laughed and it felt good. I got up and offered her my chair, then pulled another out for myself.

"Whatcha got there?" Burke asked, peering at the two envelopes Sophia was holding.

She smiled as she sat down. "This is a little something for Tatum." From the larger, padded envelope, she pulled out a framed copy of the *Odessa Record*, front page above the fold. She handed it to Burke.

It was an exposé of our investigation, emphasizing a twelve-year-old's tenacity and his father's bravery. It may never win her that Pulitzer, but it won my heart. Ryce was a hero and Tatum now had the proof framed and ready to hang on the living room wall.

Burke sniffled as he read the article. He turned away, embarrassed at the tears spilling from his eyes. "You did good," he said, brushing his hands across his face. "Real good. He's going to like this."

Sophia smiled tenderly. "I'm glad you're pleased. And this is for you," she said, handing me the other envelope.

I opened it and laughed. "Office spaces for lease," I said, reading the local real estate printout.

"In case you ever get licensed in Texas," she said, smiling.

I peeked in the envelope, then pulled out the brochures that were still in it. There were several for apartment complexes in Odessa, and even a few in Kermit.

"In case you want to stick close to home," she said softly.

I looked up at Tatum, still digging his way to China, and smiled. He brushed his bangs to the side, then wiped sweat from his brow. He really did need a haircut. Maybe I could take him tomorrow.